Author introduction:

H. G. Shuler was born the summer of 1959 in Douglasville, Georgia, spent a few years in Augusta, Georgia before growing up in Cobb County Georgia where he attended South Cobb High School. Harold was the last of nine children; because of that his mother claims she ran out of names, and he was not honored with a given middle name. He has chosen a middle initial 'G' which stands for Gil a shortened form of his mother's maiden name, Gilstrap. Thus 'H. G. Shuler' is his pen name since the story-tellers were on his mother's side of the family.

He now resides in a small town in North Georgia called Ellijay. This town reminds him of the small town where he grew up, but which has lost that small town feel as it was engulfed by Metro-Atlanta. Harold has told stories his entire life, as a youth to entertain family and as an adult to practice for the moment he was published. He has yet to run out of material and plans to be busy for years to come.

The Fifth Pinnacle is the first book in a series of three Earth Chronicles' stories by H. G. Shuler and his second novel published. This second novel is much different from the first. It falls into the category of Science Fiction Thriller whereas the first was a Psychological Thriller.

The Fifth Pinnacle copyright registration 2019.

Look for *The Reconstruction of Mary* also by H.G. Shuler, completed in 2016 and finally published in late October of 2019. This novel explores the brain's ability to repress memories from trauma and portrays how the process of memory recovery affects relationships. It's set in the small town of Ellijay, Georgia. The characters are total fiction, but the story is very real to some.

Follow the author here: https://www.amazon.com/author/hgshuler
Look for new releases as they become available.
    The Blue Woman/Earth Chronicles, Book 2, relea℥
Traces of Caledonia/Earth Chronicles, Book 3, releas

Acknowledgements:

I want to thank a few dear friends who worked as readers for me. Their thoughts and expressions were of great help, and they are among some of the most discerning people I have the privilege to know. Many thanks to John and Janette Innes and Jessica Gilleland. You each were key in boosting me and my editing 'team' along this long, hard and arduous road to publishing. Without your encouragement, I may have never ventured into the Sci-Fi genre where this story finds itself. It is my hope that this story will only 'wet' your appetite for the stories that follow in the Earth Chronicles' series.

I would also like to give a special thank you to my beautiful wife, Becky. Without her hard work, turning my words into print would have never happened. "Thank you, my dearest, for the many hours you have given to make this happen."

H. G. Shuler

EARTH CHRONICLES

Book I: The Fifth Pinnacle

A Novel by: H.G. Shuler

Chapter 1

What if the aging process that we have been groomed to accept, and doomed to live, turned out to be a previously undetected virus? A super virus so intelligent that it hides by wrapping itself with other molecules. A virus emitting its antigens so methodically, so gradually, and in such small numbers that it mimics complete silence, producing invisibility. What if what we think we know turned out to be an illusion? And what if one day the illusion started to crumble?

When 75-year old Harlan Landcaster wakes to a loud knock at his door, he was unprepared for what would happen next. He has no clue that his whole uneventful life is about to change. He slides out of bed, hurries with an unusual quickness in his steps, and begins a confusing, antagonistic conversation.

"That's nonsense!" His grandson Carter shouted. He was amid one of those shocking, all-embracing looks, the kind that stops a person dead still. The eyes of a man he didn't recognize were looking back at him, hanging innocent and free from the other side of the door. "Who on earth are you anyway? Tell the truth! Where's Gramps? And what are you doing here in his house?"

"For God's sake, son! You don't have to get all authoritative on me. It's me, Harlan. And stop looking at me like that. I just got out of bed that's all. I never met anyone who looked the same in the morning as they did the night before. For a moment there you had me doubting my own existence. Besides, doesn't that creamy baby face of yours look a little paler when you first crawl out of the sack? You want some coffee? Because apparently, *I* need some to come back from the land of the living dead!"

Carter tilts his head a little to the right, which he has a habit of doing when he's confused. He leans in closer making eye contact, the look of astonishment still clearly visible on his face. Blinking hard a couple of times, he sighs as he calms down a little. "No. Sorry... I um... just left Starbucks."

"Starbucks? I've never understood how the blazes someone could get hooked on a four-dollar cup of coffee. Whether it's blended with flavors or not for cryin-out-loud, it's just a cup of coffee. Well, don't just stand there looking all discombobulated, come on in the house. I suppose you have a reason for being here. I mean *other* than to infer that I look like I just walked off the set of one of those god-awful zombie movies everybody's all crazy about." Harlan reaches his hand out placing it on Carter's shoulder. "For a minute there you looked like an animal about to run, like if you did no one would ever catch you."

"You looked in the mirror today, Gramps?" His voice faded somewhat behind a more subdued face while his eyes continue to stare at his grandfather.

"No, Carter. I haven't looked in the mirror today! You gonna start that up again? Like I said I just got out of bed, and not a soft-pillowed bed either. And anyway, I told you at the hospital yesterday that the mirror I hung in my bathroom fell and shattered into about a million pieces. Took me over an hour to clean up the mess."

"Next time use contact glue or silicone caulk. Those plastic clips don't always hold."

"Maybe you could re-teach me the Alphabet while you're here. No, really, tell me something else I don't *already* know!"

Carter has a fleeting sensation as if he's floating in a void between two worlds. *If* this man was his grandfather, and he now believes that it is, then the symptoms of regeneration had developed much faster than expected. He looks straight down, like he's inspecting his shoes, sighs deeply, then looks up and cracks a small smile. "Sorry... I just... Do you still have that mirror hanging in the living room? The one with the fancy antique frame?"

Harlan turns looking through the foyer all the way to the far end of it, then to the left where it enters the living room. "Your grandmother had me hang that up over ten years ago, not too long before she died." He looks back at Carter with a more subdued, solemn face. I guess cancer is going to get me the same way it got her. That is unless you and your fancy equipment at the hospital can cure me. I feel good this morning though." He moves his arm in a circular motion. "No pain at all today."

"You mind if we take a look at the mirror?"

Harlan looks at his grandson with a sort of long disgust on his face. "No, Carter, I don't mind! But I swear, me and you getting along this morning seems about as unattainable as finding water in the desert."

"It's not morning. Its four o'clock in the afternoon." Carter said this as the two men went walking into the living room.

"Really, four o'clock?

"Really. And the hospital treatments were three days ago."

"What?"

"Just look in the mirror, Gramps. See what I mean? I'm not so sure I'm comfortable calling you Gramps anymore."

Harlan is nearly overcome with shock at what he sees staring back at him. Instead of the wrinkles and dullness of a 75-year old man, there is the appearance of himself at a much earlier period in his life. Lightly touching one hand with the other, he slowly glides several fingers over his wrist and forearm tracing the smoothness all the way up to his shoulder, then up his neck and onto his cheeks. While still looking in the mirror, his fingers are pressing up and down like he doesn't believe he's real. He sees a freshness, a vigor, and a beautifully smooth-contoured face. His hair is thick and full, completely covering his head with an almost forgotten glossy brown pigment. His muscles are tight and toned again. Put together collectively, he sees himself in the condition of being young again.

"Is this some kind of dirty trick? You know, like I'm really knocked out in a hospital bed under heavy medication, dreaming all of this just before I die." After saying this he moves his eyes horizontally toward Carter with his face quickly following. "Or is this gonna be one of those end-of-life stories where I wake up, and you tell me I died on the operating table, stayed dead for like three minutes, then suddenly burst back to life. Because if this is one of those stories, I don't see no bright lights."

"It's not a trick, Gramps. What you're seeing is real."

"Okay... then I take back the whole pissed off conversation about you not recognizing me. Of course, I do want to know how on God's green earth this could possibly happen? I'm guessing those cancer treatments were a little out of the ordinary. Am I right?"

"You want to sit down for this, or are you going to just keep staring at yourself?"

Harlan doesn't move or even flinch from looking into the mirror. "Can't blame a man for being curious after he's just been handed the fountain of youth."

"We don't know if it's the fountain of youth, but I see what you're saying. You might still age though. Truth is, we don't really know at this point."

"You gonna start telling me how this all came about? Cause I gotta say, I'm just dying to find out. Or maybe that term doesn't apply anymore. Maybe we need to invent a new one."

"I think I'll take that cup of coffee now. And after three days of sleep, you, young man, need to eat something."

"How young you think I look?"

"I don't know, Gramps. I think you look a little younger than me though. Maybe late-twenties. You know, twenty-seven, twenty-eight."

"More like mid-twenties I'd say."

"Just remember, the evidence may say one thing, but the reality is you're still seventy-five."

Twenty minutes later the exhilaration ran like NASCAR through the clock-work of Harlan's veins. He was having the kind of moment most people could only dream of or read about in books. But even in the absence of old age, there was an air of occupancy, of familiarity hanging out inside him. He was the same person he had always been, only now with an energetic figure to lift him and propel him into the future.

Carter sat across the kitchen table from him, sipping coffee and watching him demolish a huge ham and cheese sandwich. He felt an amazing, almost god-like feeling, realizing what he has accomplished. For the past ten years, he had been working on the cell-regeneration project. The branch of government where he worked came under the authority of the C.I.A. Even then the project was under 'need-to-know-only' restrictions. Very few people knew about it, and the ones who did were powerful, and sometimes dangerous men and women. He could see something in Harlan's eyes, a sort of sensation one might see in an athlete after a surprising triumph. Proof, he thought, of a new power lurking inside him. He was hoping this power would continue to regenerate his cells. But without further testing, he couldn't be sure. And even if it did, how long would it do so? How often would treatments be needed, and what kind of side effects would there be? There were so many variables. It was too early to know exactly how this thing was going to play out.

Then seemingly out of nowhere, he pictures Harlan's face starting to regress. His eyes move forward, extending until they're bulging from their sockets, like at any moment they will pop out and roll down his cheeks. He pictures wrinkles forming, turning to deep crevices, his nose sagging at its tip, then drooping, pulling from its base and falling off right into his plate of potato chips. He watches in his imagination as Harlan's whole face slides off his head, covering his plate of food in a mortifying scene. He pictures this because he really has no idea what the future holds for him.

Harlan grabs a toothpick from a dispenser in the middle of the table. "You gonna tell me what's happening to me or you gonna keep me in the dark?" He starts digging at his teeth.

"Have you ever heard anything about cell regeneration?"

"Course not. Sounds like something out of a science fiction movie."

"In a way, you're not too far off. The human body seems to have been designed with an innate healing ability which allows it to heal *all* disease. I'm talking about everything from a cut on the hand to cancer in the colon, and everything in between. That is, if there is no interference. All of us have witnessed this amazing healing in action. Think about a paper cut. Once you've stopped the bleeding what do you do to cause the cut to heal? You may cover it with a bandage. But does the bandage heal the cut? No, the cut will heal with or without the bandage. Maybe you use some antibiotic cream to kill germs, which is good. But does the cream heal the cut? No, the cut will heal with or without the cream. In fact, that little paper cut set into motion over twenty microscopic biochemical reactions. Those biochemical reactions cause the blood to coagulate, form a clot, and prepare the injured area for the rest of the healing process. That automatic process is so complex that if only one step is absent, even one little enzyme, your blood will not clot. Then there's cancer.

Cancer cells are produced and killed in the body every day and you don't even realize it. It's part of the normal process of cell replication. However, if something goes wrong in that process, a mutated cell may develop and form a tumor. Your body doesn't need any help to heal you of these cancer cells. It just needs no interference. Approximately every seven years our bodies have fully replaced each cell. In a way we are a completely different person, physically speaking. As long as there is no interference the body keeps up the process and everything functions smoothly."

"You make it all sound so reasonable, like what's happening to me is normal when any ten-year old could tell you it's not. Breaking news, Carter! I'm young again! And not that shabby looking plastic surgery young either. No this is certainly not normal so don't *even* try to... Frankly, I think its some discovery that the government will suppress for the next twenty years while they build up an army with the technology."

"What! Build an army. The army doesn't even know about this."

"You grew up in this country. You know what they're capable of."

"Look, we're getting way off track here. There's no government conspiracy taking place, and there's no plan to use it for the military. I've been at the center of this for the past ten years. I think I would know. And to be clear about this, cell replication, although similar, is not the same as cell regeneration. The human body naturally replaces or replicates dead cells. But we *can't* replace whole body parts, and we still grow old and die. We've known for hundreds of years that certain animals *can* replace body parts. For some time now we've been trying to duplicate what these animals can do. We've been growing certain body parts in labs, but with mixed results. However, during the countless experiments, we fell upon the process of cell regeneration. We've thought for decades that a virus, somehow able to hide itself, has been interfering and malfunctioning the process. We've been experimenting with mice and guinea pigs for the past five years with success. But I've never seen the results I see in you. Normally it takes months, even a year or more for the patient to return to a state of youth, and they never get to the point you have. You regenerated all the way back in just three days."

"You really call the pigs and mice patients?"

"This isn't a joking matter Gramps. This project is eventually going to be judged by what happens to you."

"But I'm young again. Judgment rendered. Case closed."

"How can you stand there making a mockery out of this. If you would just listen to me. I wish it were that simple, but good God!"

"Okay, Carter. You got my attention. Just how serious is this?"

"Only I and two other employees even know about you. And none of us even remotely expected these results. We weren't even sure it would work at all."

"You telling me, you three went rogue on this one?"

"It's just that with your cancer prognosis you would've been dead in three months, six at the most. I figured why not give it a shot, what could it hurt?"

"If they find out about me, this thing's going to go sideways isn't it?"

"You don't want to know what happens if they find out. It wasn't supposed to be used on humans for another five years."

"What were you thinking, Carter?"

"I don't know. But I know I wasn't expecting a young man to answer your door today."

"What do we do now?"

"I don't know that either."

"You'd better get a plan quick. Won't be long before that daughter of mine comes snooping around. Once Emma puts her nose to the ground all of Clint county will know what's happened, if not the whole state of Kentucky. Since I got the cancer, she comes by two, sometimes three, times a week. You saw her lately?"

"No. But you're right, she won't be easy to fool. Aunt Emma always did like a good investigation. Right now, I'm more concerned about your neighbors though. They're going to take notice of an unfamiliar man coming and going. So, stay inside as much as you can. If you must go out, try to make it after dark. That should help. And if anyone does ask, tell them you're Harlan's great-grandson from just south of Macon, Georgia, down where the peaches grow. Tell them you came up to help out while he's sick."

"Great-grandson?

"Yes."

"What about Emma?"

"I don't know Gramps... tell her you're a nurse with the hospice program. Do you still have that cell phone I gave you?"

"In the nightstand by my bed, been there since the day you saddled me with it."

"Anytime you leave the house take it with you."

"You mean like everywhere?"

"I mean like even to the mailbox. If I need to talk to you, I don't want to have to hunt you down."

Harlan scratches his head just above his ear. "I guess I can do that."

The afternoon light was sifting through a double-sized

window into the kitchen. It was causing sort of a white illumination like the air had been cleaned with bleach. When Harlan suddenly pushes himself back from the table and stands up, the strange light forms an outline around his body. To Carter, it looks like an apparition of a spirit creature is standing in front of him. This is when it hits him just how young and fresh his grandfather had become. Harlan yawns and stretches his arms straight up with a movement that shows he hasn't moved much for the last three days. When he does this, the white air seems to open around him, moving back and forming an outer ring of air. There is a visible aura emanating from Harlan's body which is forcing the white air away from him. It looks like a kind of steam that would come off hot coils or pipes. He slightly lowers his arms and watches as the strange white sphere moves out and away from him, widening and filtering farther into the room.

"Okay... this is weirding me out. What's going on Carter? Just what have you and your friends done to me?"

Carter stands up, tilting his head to one side. "I'm not sure. This kind of thing has never happened before. How do you feel? Does it hurt?"

"There's a little discomfort, but no, I feel fine."

The unusual light seems to be closing in around him like earlier. But just when the room appears to return to normal the process starts up all over again. The white light quickly forming an outer ring of air as the visible aura radiates from him even more than the first time. He moves his arms straight out beside him like he's in a flying position. Both men are watching the curious white aura when something even more unfathomable starts to happen. The aura which now appears trapped inside the outer ring of air is changing colors. There is a pinkish-purple sphere growing larger around Harlan, pressing against and pushing at the outer ring. His face now looks rounder, almost swollen but with a naturalness or normalcy about it. The tone of his skin is in a constant state of flux, mixing blues with pinks and greens with a sort of fluorescent illumination. After about two minutes of this, the colored aura fades back to white. And now even the outer ring

13

of air starts wrapping itself back around Him as both rings quickly dissipate. The illumination of colors is now completely gone, and the white air seems a little paler, giving the room an almost dreary look. Harlan is left with an even fresher, more youthful-looking face.

"You've changed Gramps. You look even younger, like twenty or twenty-one." Carter's head is bent a little downward, his eyes looking up slyly at his grandfather. He lowers his head farther, closes his eyes and sighs. "I wish I could tell you what's happening, but I've never seen anything like this before. I need to get you back to the lab for more tests... but I need approval for that. It may take some time before I can work it out. I'm sorry about this. It's not going anything like I expected."

"Harlan allows his arms to relax and fall down to his sides. He gives a nod with his head and a patient expression with his face. "Don't sweat it, son, not for a second. The cancer, what it did to me, destroying my resolve. My thoughts were all sluggish. I probably didn't tell you that. I was tired, nervous, in a state of dying. I was being reminded, painfully I might add, of the limits of my own shrinking existence. Heaven's sake, I couldn't even walk up and down my own street without giving out. And I was drinking those awful herbal teas, too. You know how I hate those. Your grandmother tried forcing those on me for years, but I never took to them. I've always been a coffee drinker. The only tea I ever liked is iced tea. What I'm trying to say is... I don't blame you for any of this. The way I look at it is you've brought me some relief. I feel good now, really, I mean unbelievably good. I'm not sure how this thing's going to end up, maybe I'll live another lifetime, maybe not. Heck, I'm not even sure I care. But I do know, I don't blame you."

"We need to keep close watch of the symptoms, any more physical changes or..."

"Or what?

"It's just that... well, your voice has changed, too. You sound much younger now, more in line with how you look. It was different when I first saw you earlier, but not like this.

Even your accent has changed. There could be other changes coming, possibly with the brain. Do you still have your complete memory?"

Harlan looks unutterably confused. He scratches the side of his head again. "How would I know that?"

"I see your point."

"I know who you are, and I still remember Emma, and, of course, your mother. I think my memories fine."

"Be sure to let me know if there are any more changes. And I mean physical, mental, or emotional. I hope your male dignity hasn't taken too hard a blow being so incredibly young again."

"Are you kidding? I'm younger and prettier than my grandson, who's only thirty-two. And I'm still smarter."

"You still joke like Gramps even if you don't look or sound like him."

"There is something I should probably tell you, but I'm not so sure it's connected or even matters."

"Everything about you matters right now. Just tell me what it is."

"While that strange light was coming out of me... I saw... It's sort of hard to explain."

"There's no rush. Take your time, concentrate."

"It was all in my mind of course. I mean, I wasn't seeing it with my literal eyes. There were images. You know, streaming images of sleep, I mean of dreaming. The kind of images that run through your mind when your dreaming."

"What kind of images?"

"Of animals, and scenes of the forest mostly."

"You said they were *streaming* images?"

"Yes. It was like I was walking, sometimes running through the forest. Or maybe I wasn't walking, maybe everything was moving past me. I'm just not sure. I was noticing all the foliage, the ferns, tiny red and blue flowers, scrub pines, and huge beautiful white oaks. And the animals. There were lots of them, a gray fox, wild turkeys, bears, squirrels, deer, all sorts of birds, even wolves. All of them streaming passed me slowly at times, and really fast at other times. I really don't know what to make of it. But I was comfortable with it, like I was meant to be there, like I was part of it, if that makes any sense."

"I get the picture. Anything else?"

"Kind of..."

"Are you going to tell me?"

"I could smell *everything*."

"Do you mean you could smell whatever that was coming out of you? Because from where I was sitting I couldn't smell anything."

"No. I mean the forest. While the images were streaming passed me, or I was streaming passed them, I don't know which. While this was taking place my sense of smell was heightened. I mean really heightened, like to some ridiculous degree. I could smell everything, the pine needles, limbs, and debris lying on the forest floor, even the tiny particles of leaves. And the animals, their smell was almost overwhelming. It was like the smell of a zoo."

"I see. Strange, anything else?"

"A few more images, mostly of houses. It was like a neighborhood, but an unfamiliar one. It was nothing like mine. My subdivision's been here for like sixty years. Your daddy grew up here." Harlan lifts his arm pointing out the kitchen window. "And you used to play horseshoes in that backyard. No, the subdivision in the images was newer, much newer. It's funny though because I could see the people. It was like I was looking through their windows right into their homes. But still, it all felt comfortable, like what I was doing was normal. Anyway, when the strange lights went away, so did the images and the sense of smell."

"Do you mind if I take a sample of your blood."

"You think it will help?"

"I'm not sure. I'm not sure about anything anymore. I was planning on taking a sample of your blood today anyway, even *before* I saw what's happened to you. But I gotta say, I'm a lot more curious about what I'm going to find then I was this morning."

"You and me both. I wanna know if I'm turning into some

kind of mutated animal!"

"Animal! Seriously? That's what you think?"

"Well it's not like any of this has ever happened before. I don't know what to think."

"Let's not jump to conclusions, okay?"

"Fine by me. But what do you make of all the images?"

Before he could find a fitting response he had cut him short with a question. "My phones vibrating. You mind if I take the call?"

Harlan points to a door at the back of the kitchen. "Go on, you can take it on the back patio if you need some privacy."

"Thanks." Carter opens the door. "I won't be long." He swipes the front of his phone. "Ansel, what can I do for you?"

"We got a problem. In-fact we got two problems."

"Okay, and you wanna tell me what they are, preferably one at a time."

"I was looking over some paperwork on Dillon's desk. I was curious because... well it looked like he was taking extra precautions to hide them. Anyway, as soon as we left work today I doubled back and managed to use a safety pin to open his desk drawer. They know Carter, they've known all along!"

"You mean they know about Harlan. How's that possible?"

"We thought we knew Dillon. Turns out we didn't. According to the paperwork I'm reading right now, it seems he's an operative for the C.I.A. And there's a file here on your grandfather, too, Harlan. G. Landcaster. They know everything about him. Looks like this file was started about the time he was diagnosed with cancer."

"It's starting to make sense now."

"What do you mean?"

"I don't think I ever told you, but it was Dillon's idea. He's the one who first suggested I use the treatments on Harlan."

"It gets worse, Carter."

"Worse. How?"

"The formula we used, or maybe I should say, the formula we thought we were using..."

"What! God, Ansel, what did we use on my grandfather?"

"I don't know. I mean it's similar, but different and way

17

stronger, like twenty times more concentrated. It must have come from a different lab. There must be a second lab operating with C.I.A. authority that we don't know about. How's he doing anyway? He okay?"

Carter turns towards the house looking through the kitchen window. He sees Harlan eating from a package of chocolate chip cookies and swaying his body back and forth like a teenager at a school dance. "Funny you should ask. I'm looking at him right now."

"I know it's way too early, but does he look okay?"

"Better than okay, really, he looks fine." His first impulse was to hide the truth about Harlan. But he knew that sooner or later Ansel would find out. Worse still, he knew that sooner or later *everyone* would. When he hears music coming from the kitchen he turns again and looks through the window. Harlan is dancing by himself like he hasn't a care in the world. "We'll talk later Ansel, but right now you need to get out of the office. If they catch you... Just get out of there, okay?"

"Roger that, Carter. On my way out now."

Carter punches his phone, then turns and looks beyond a huge crape myrtle at a set of horseshoe pins. They are half covered in fallen leaves like they haven't been used in years. When he looks back to the kitchen he sees Harlan still dancing. While watching he is surprised to feel a summer breeze blow across his face. Simultaneously, a sensation is tingling underneath his skin. When it subsides, he realizes that he's finally accepting the scene of Harlan's sudden transformation. What has seemed like an unreality is now trying to settle in. He slips his phone into his pocket, lifts his face upward while closing his eyes. There's still an excitable, lingering sense of panic tunneling through him. He tries a deep breathing technique. Then suddenly it hits him that he needs to take the blood sample. Walking around the outside of the house, a cool anticipation in his eyes is taking away what is left of his near panic attack. Talking to Ansel was disturbing but seeing his grandfather in a state of youth was overriding any possible consequences that were likely to occur.

Oddly, while walking he hears an argument. Looking up he

18

sees three figures step behind a van. Crossing the street to his car he notices them again on the other side of the van. They've huddled together about three cars down from his. One was a girl with her head shaven clean and wearing a fleece jacket. He slows down wondering if they're part of a gang. But he's never heard anything about gangs in this area. As soon as the girl notices Carter she lifts a brown hood up over her bald head, turns her back to him and continues the dispute with the other two. She is obviously agitated about something. "It's the pinnacle, we all agreed!" the girl wearing the jacket shouts. While she chastises them, Carter makes out the words: *dimwits* and *screw-ups,* which makes a brief smile spread over his face. The three were quite young-looking, probably neighborhood kids in their late teens, so he brushes it off as the usual immaturity of that age.

It only took a half-minute to secure his medical briefcase from his car. In two more minutes, he was back in the kitchen turning down the radio, then flipping on a wall switch for more light. After giving several firm taps to the inside crease of Harlan's left arm, he inserts a 3mm, 18-gauge needle and pulls back on the syringe. While taking the blood, Carter notices that the overhead light sheds brightness upon Harlan's hair. There were moments when he would move his head and the light seemed to strike sparks that looked like jewels hanging from his head. The contrast from earlier in the day was amazing. Harlan had grown even younger right before his eyes. His youthfulness and beauty were uppermost in Carter's mind as he stared on in admiration. Not that he had the patience for it, but if Harlan were back in college he would dazzle the young women. And he always did have the looks for that. Carter had heard the numerous stories long ago from his grandmother. Simplicity had always been at the core of his personality, but his good looks and charm drew the women in like metal to a magnet. "His good looks could not be ignored," his grandmother had said. "That face was like an echo that kept coming back to me no matter where I was. I couldn't get him out of my head." That face was back, only more vibrant and prettier than it had ever been before.

After securing the sample of blood, Carter squeezes a rubber cap onto the vile and places it back into the briefcase. Then he leans back against a seat cushion and smiles.

"What are *you* thinking?" Harlan asked with a smirk on his face. "You're up to something. I can tell."

"Can't someone smile without being up to something?"

"Yes, but there's a difference with you."

"What... or how do you mean?"

"You have different smiles. And *that* smile says you're up to something. I dare say it's true and not just my imagination. So out with it, you got a plan don't you?"

It struck Carter as almost being providential that Harlan could read his face. And it struck him too that Harlan was acting like the two of them were about to embark on a journey together. He knew that no matter how much he might try to overemphasize Harlan's reasoning as mere guesswork, he couldn't fool him. Not this simple, common sense, intuitive countryman. His face had already given him away. He didn't want to tell him straight up what he was considering and was trying to devise some means of an approach that would keep Harlan's curiosity at bay. But now he just couldn't come up with much. "Plan? Yes. I admit I have a plan."

"When were you going to tell me?"

"I don't know. Not at this point though. At least not until I've worked out the details, which I haven't yet. There's been a development and I'm just waiting on an opportunity to..."

"To what?"

"Look, Gramps, could you just be prepared to leave at a moment's notice? Like if I show up at your door no matter when... you'd be ready to leave straight away."

"That must have been some phone call you got a while ago."

"You could say that."

"I'll pack an overnight bag."

"You might want to make it a suitcase with two sets of clothes, and..."

"And..."

"Keep a phone close by."

20

Chapter 2

Carter Timothy Landcaster had a history of turning in the wrong direction. It was a history he wasn't proud of; one he had worked on in recent years to correct. He was hoping in this instance with his grandfather that he would perceive the right road before it was too late to take it.

Six years ago, he had become severely disturbed by his own self-complacency. It had cost him his new wife and nearly cost him his job. He had always thought that a lack of motivation was harmless enough until it became the source of some extremely harmful complications. After losing his wife and going through what he viewed as ill-luck in a rebound relationship, he tried one night to logically trace the causes of his troubles back to his father's death. Carter was only seven when a drunk driver veered into a crowd of people exiting a movie theater. Eleven were injured, and one was killed. That *one* was his father. The terrifying screams at times still ring in his head like the constant, piercing fizz of static. Even after all these years he still re-lives the scene at least once a week in his mind. His father had saved his life shoving him clear of the car a split second before he himself was hit by it, breaking his back, severing and crushing his spinal cord. Everyone felt a deep sorrow for Carter, which had led to years of him being spoiled. His whole life became an experiment in sentimentality. He grew up never having to lift a finger for himself. The cause of all his troubles he realized that night, could not be placed on his father. It wasn't a sudden epiphany that would immediately change his life for the good. Rather, it was more the discovery that he needed to take ownership of his life, to sign the paperwork with his own hands. For awhile he had over-swung taking too critical of an approach, becoming his own antagonist. When the smoke finally cleared he was twenty-eight years old, had been divorced for nearly five years, and had been the victim *and* instigator of several broken relationships.

He had grown up a little since then, and recently he had adopted a whole new approach to dating: no more fast girls. The whole idea of dating just to hook-up had become offensive to him.

He went to work for Futurelab Pharmaceuticals straight out of college. They courted him for months prior to his graduation and paid him a salary much greater than expected. They were looking for the brightest young minds to help get a new research program launched. His highest honors degree in chemical engineering from Bucknell University was exactly what they were after. The new research lab was stationed on the outskirts of Lexington, Kentucky, not far from Carter's hometown. Ansel had graduated from Bucknell at the same time and was also scooped up by Futurelab Pharmaceuticals. There were ten other chemists, including Dillon, whom recently graduated from Auburn University, so they were told. It was a whole year before Futurelab Pharmaceuticals divulged that they were owned and operated by the U.S. Government.

These were just some of the things sweeping through Carter's mind as he walked around his grandfather's house, wondering where in the world he had disappeared to. He called his cell phone for the fifth time in the last hour. When he hears it ringing, he twists his head toward the bedroom, the phone was still inside the drawer of the end table by his bed. "Trouble," he whispered to himself. "I've got some serious trouble on my hands."

Harlan couldn't ever remember seeing a more radiant girl. Maybe it was because he hadn't been around many girls, or truth be told, he simply *couldn't* remember. The more he concentrated, meditated and strained his mind, he still couldn't see any further into the past than three months. That's about the time he had shown up in this busy, heavily touristed beach-front town in South Carolina. He had an impulse to ask her out directly, but instead he just watched as she strolls passed. When she suddenly stops, turns and catches him in the act of staring, he is caught completely off guard.

"Your momma ever tell you it's rude to stare?" She said this while slightly bending one knee and cocking her hourglass hips to the side like she was sitting on them.

He didn't respond quickly.

"Cat gotcha tongue, country boy?"

Still, he doesn't answer.

She cocks her head matching her hips and smiles for the first time. "Hey, you worked here long?"

"If it really matters... bout three months." He said this while staring at a girlish smoothness in her face and a purity of tint running like milk down her arms.

"You like giving me the eye-over, don't you?" She cracks another small, curious smile. "Should I just call you country or you gotta name?"

"I gotta name like everybody else."

"Okay... you gonna tell me?"

"It's Harlan, best I can remember anyway. But..."

She tilts her head back straight. "But what?"

"But my boss, he owns this food stand." He pauses looking over the stand. "He calls me H."

"Why? I think Harlan's nice. It reminds me of back home in West Virginia."

"My boss-man, he's one of those people that thinks using single letters and acronyms makes you look smart. He's a good guy though, I must admit. Hired me right off, and without a background check. He even gave me a place to stay. It's just a little shed that he calls a shack, but it serves the purpose. Anyways, what's your story. Are you visiting here from West Virginia?"

"No. I just... well my family... we just moved here about a week ago. Can I get a hot dog and diet Coke? You know what, make it a regular Coke."

Harlan scoops up the hot dog, lays it in a bun, then lowers his forehead in a motion pointing beyond her. "The

24

condiments are on that table behind you, next to the jet ski rental." He reaches out the hot dog and Coke. "That's $2.25 for the hot dog and $2.00 for the Coke. The total's $4.25."

Her hand slides smoothly into the tight pocket of her cut-off shorts. "I hope it's good. This is my last money." She hands him a five. "You mind if I call you Harlan? If that's really your name."

"That's my name."

"A minute ago, you weren't too sure."

"I've had some trouble with my memory lately, but it's all good. I'm fine, really, I feel great."

"I wouldn't argue with that. I mean you *look* great." She gushes a little. "What I really mean is... you look like you feel great." Her face is now brimming with pink. She shoves the hot dog into one side of her mouth and starts talking out the other. "So, is it always this hot around here, Harlan?"

"I guess. I mean it *is* summer." He squints his face pulling back from her a little. "You always eat hot dogs plain?"

"Sometimes."

"Careful not to choke."

She jams the rest of the hot dog into her mouth. "My momma always said I was a 'disgusting' eater."

"I'm gonna have to agree with her on that one."

"Besides, I'm starving."

"How old are you? You mind me asking?"

She swallows hard. "I don't mind..."

"You gonna tell me then?"

"Eighteen, and you?"

Most people can answer the question of age immediately. But not Harlan, not now anyway, and he doesn't know why. He hesitates, looking up into the blue Carolina sky. His head slowly moves in a crisscross motion like he expects the answer to be hanging there written out for him, so he can just read it. He stares so long she too looks up hoping to see what he sees. When they drop their heads, she now sees what was there all along, uncertainty in his eyes. "About the same, I mean eighteen, same as you."

"You act as though you don't even know your own age."

"Like I said, I'm having some problems with my memory."

Her head moves back a little. "It's mysterious, like a book I once read where people who didn't know their own age were actually immortal. They had lived for so long their age no longer mattered."

"You don't believe everything you read in books do you? Immortality is just an illusion dreamed up in writers' imaginations. You know that, right?"

"Course. And I'm not so sure I'd want to be immortal anyways. It's like... well don't you wish you could eliminate just one day from your life?"

"I guess everybody has those moments they would like to forget, to just be able to put out of their minds. But a whole day. How could you distinguish the exact day? Which day would you consider less or more valuable than another?"

"I was only being half-serious. I didn't expect the conversation to go this deep. It's cool to think about though, at least the part about being young and immortal."

"I'm not so sure."

"Why? Wouldn't you choose to be immortal if you could?"

"Living forever in a world where everyone else dies. Can you imagine the enormous responsibility?"

"I hadn't thought of that."

"After hundreds of years, everything you said would have to have some kind of profound influence on the world."

"I hadn't thought of that either. But all that aside, you do look about my age."

"Like I said. I am."

"What luck. Maybe we can hang out some?"

"If you're good with it, I'm good with it."

"What time you off today?"

"I got a couple more hours to go."

"Then I'll see you in two hours. Oh, but wait. Are you a gun person or knife?"

"What?"

"Just answer the question."

"Gun, I guess."

"Good, that means you're not a serial killer. They never use guns, just knives or blunt objects."

"I could be lying."

"Your eyes would've flinched."

Harlan sways his head at her, smiles while scooping up another hot dog and handing it to her. "This one's on me."

"Oh god, yes. Thank you." She smashes it into her mouth.

"You gonna tell me your name before you go, or should I just call *you* country?"

"It's Daniela, but I mostly go by Danny." She was talking out of one side of her mouth again while turning to leave."

As Harlan watched her walk away he thought how delightful she was to the eyes. She had a certain charm, geniality, even humor. Her looks and personality had cast a spell on him, and although now he didn't realize it, his had cast a spell on her.

It was well over two hours when Danny came sprinting up to the food stand. She was gasping, nearly out of breath and pouring with sweat.

"What's your pleasure?" another man attending the food stand asked. Then due to her condition, he quickly reverted. "Are you alright?"

"Where's Harlan... or H... or whatever you call him?" As soon as she got the words out she leans forward resting her hands on her knees, breathing hard and deep.

"His shift ended a half-hour ago."

Twice her head springs back and forth looking over her shoulder. "I know that, *Einstein!* Where's he gone, or where does he live?"

"It's on the beach-front, about three... no four lights down if you take the road. Wait just a second." He motions quickly with his head. "There he is talking to Edwin at the jet-ski rental."

When she turns, she sees Harlan waving a hand at her while still in the middle of a conversation. Running up to him she immediately interrupts. "Can we go? I thought you had left." She looks around in a panic. "I have to go now! Can you come with me?"

"Sure, just a sec..." Before he can finish his thought she

27

snatches his hand and rushes him off.

"Sorry I was late."

"Slow down! I almost fell on my face. Where are we going anyway?"

"Underneath the pier, it's safe there."

"Safe!"

"Yes." She turns looking all the way back to where they had just come from. Her face has changed from one of panic to one of concern.

"What are you running from, and what have you got *me* running from?"

"Two men."

"Okay, could you please tell me *why* we're running from two men?"

"I stole a backpack from them, and they saw me. When one of them shouted I dropped it, but they came after me anyway."

Once they reach the pier, their pace slows to a crawl. They walk underneath it between the support pillars. "What's going on Danny. I mean why steal a backpack?"

"I had to."

"You don't really expect me to accept that answer do you?"

"Well, it's true. I need money. How else am I gonna support myself?"

"How bout like every other person walking round' this beach. You're able to work, aren't you? And you do live with your parents, don't you?"

"I might not have been completely upfront with you earlier."

"Can you be upfront with me now?"

"I already told you, I've had some really bad days I would like to wipe from my life. Can we just leave it at that?"

He shakes his head while carefully leading them between the pillars. "You sure do like being economical with the truth." Suddenly he turns his head concentrating his eyes between several creaking, dank crossbeams under the pier. "You hear that?" He cups his hand around his ear and leans his head in the direction of the beach.

"Hear what?"

He doesn't answer.

"How can you hear anything with the waves crashing in?"

"I think your two men have found you."

She looks toward the beach but sees nothing. "What makes you say that?"

"Because I just heard them talking."

"What! But how?"

"I don't really have an answer for that. Just tell me what you want to do."

"Hide!"

"I think it's too late for that. Here they come." As soon as the words leave his mouth, a long, dark shadow shoots out from a series of giant creosote covered support pillars. The shadows narrow, separate, then shrink and disappear as the two men come walking into view.

Both men stand about six-feet tall. They're overweight, around the 240- or 250-pound range, not muscular, but strong looking. Spewing out a rough, jagged edge from his voice, one of them shouts out ahead of them. "You wanna give it up now, Missy!"

"I don't know what you're talking about," Danny shouts back in a firm, confident tone. She grabs Harlan's arm and looks him straight in the eyes. "I think we should make a run for it."

"Are you serious? No! You need to face this down right here. This ends now!"

The two men continue walking straight on until they are standing directly in front of them. "You'd be the thievin' girl that took the ten twenties out of my backpack. We want them back. Now!"

"You're joking, right? You saw me drop it."

"That was *after* you took the $200 in green. If you know what's good for you." The man turns to Harlan. "And what's good for your pretty boyfriend, then you'll cough it up. And I mean now, Missy! You already wasted enough of our time. Anymore, and somebody's gonna get hurt. So, hand over the freaking money! Now!"

29

Danny looks at Harlan again, her faceless, confident guilt, glares at him. Sweat beads up and runs down her cheeks.

He forces a small smile. "Look, Danny, I understand when we're desperate we do crazy things. But this situation just got serious, and I mean in a weighty, 'there are consequences' kind of way. Your past isn't anything that you can control, but your future is. Give them the money and be done with this."

She gives a quick nod, squeezes her hand into the pockets of her shorts and pulls out a wadded-up roll of money. Before she can reach to hand it to them the alpha man with the jagged voice snatches her by the wrist with one hand, tearing the money from her with his other. "You're coming with us to the beach patrol, you thievin', good for nothin'..."

Harlan quips back while throwing up a hand in a sort of 'hold on there' position. "What you fellas gonna do with her? It's that tough love thing isn't it? Like you would do with a family member. You gonna make her *get right*. That's it isn't it? Boy, I don't envy her, I tell you right now. Even though she's a thief, in your hands she's gonna *get right*. Gonna put her thievin' ways behind her and *get right!*" He wipes at sweat running down his face. "But you got your money. No harm done. Now why not just let her go."

The alpha man jerks his head around to Harlan, his eyes squinting, his face wrinkled up in a fit of rage. "You value your life, sonny? You'd be like swatting a fly. Hell, even easier, like stepping on a cockroach or kicking a three-legged dog."

"Probably. But in the scuffle, she'd get away and you'd get those nice khaki shorts a little dirty." He allows his head to tilt down a little and starts smiling. "Okay, I realize my trying to stop you would have as little permanent effect as the passing breeze. But look, nobody's day's been ruined here, mister. Could you let her go this one time? Tell you what." He slides his hand behind him, then draws it back exposing his wallet. "Here's an extra twenty for your trouble." The twenty flutters in the breeze as he stretches out his arm. "What a ya say? Deal?" In such an intense moment Harlan's demeanor remains calm.

The two men look at each other with an uneasiness showing on their faces.

"Deal?" Harlan repeats. "It's the easy way out for everyone."

"How much is in the wallet?" the alpha shouts.

Harlan smiles again. "I work at a hot dog stand. Be nice mister, take the twenty, and let's call it a day."

"Empty the wallet... no, on second thought hand it over."

"Do the right thing. What I'm offering is fair."

The alpha looks at the other man. "Bobby, take his wallet. If he resists... you know what to do. Pretty-boy is involved anyways. She probably was just doing his dirty work for him."

"It'll be more difficult than you think, Bobby. You got what... 60, maybe 70-pounds on me? But I wrestled in high school if that means anything to you."

It was in the framework of Bobby's nature to do anything his older brother told him. It had been this way his whole life, and he didn't see Harlan as a difficult task.

When he makes his move forward Harlan quickly steps back, and in the process jams his wallet back into his pants. Bobby's massive hands went for his throat, and as soon as they make contact something violent stirs inside of Harlan. It was characterized by an unsettled activity; an involuntary impulse was set into motion. He could feel it taking control, could feel flashes of energy surging in his muscles, his blood blazing like electricity, like 10,000 unmanageable volts ripping through his veins. This powerful, quickening sensation was roused inside of him; it was not going to allow him to give out or fail. He is aware that Bobby is choking him but feels no pain or fits of suffocation. All at once there is a tingling in the tips of his fingers and the light glow of a white illumination emanating from his skin. It moves outward like a fast-rolling fog and forms a ring around Bobby and himself. In nothing flat the white illumination is being pushed farther outward by a brighter, reddish-blue illumination, creating an outer and inner ring. The outer ring continues what is now a dull, almost muted glow of white, while the inner ring radiates dramatic varying colors, mixing blues, reds, and now greens in a

31

constant state of flux.

In what appears an automatic, involuntary motion, Harlan seizes Bobby under the armpits and lifts the large man up as if he were weightless. He raises him up so high that his head jams into the bottom of the pier. Like the shifting of a train from one track to another, the tingling sensation in Harlan's hands transfers into Bobby causing an immediate vibrating, shaking, even burning in all of Bobby's outer extremities. It begins penetrating deep into his arms, legs, and finally progressing throughout his whole body. A forceful, out of control reckoning is consuming the bully, and just when it looks like the man will be consumed by the energy, Harlan tosses him into a patch of seaweed next to one of the many support pillars.

For a while there is silence, the eerie kind that lingers and can overtake a situation like some quiet invisible force. Everyone looks around at each other, but no one speaks. After a minute that seems much longer the alpha of the two bullies shouts out. "Okay! Okay! Now it's obvious you're a whole lot more to handle than I gave you credit for, sonny boy. For that I sincerely apologize. Fact is I'm about as confused as a fart in a fan factory right now. And I *don't* mean this to be offensive because you have some sort of stupid superpower and all. But in case you haven't noticed, I still have the girl, so *back* away from my brother. Go on, back away. If you don't want her pretty, little neck snapped, you'll do as I say."

Harlan takes a half-step back with one leg and puts up his fist in a defensive posture. "Mister, I just gotta say, and this *is* meant to be offensive, you got the brains of a jellyfish."

"Jellyfish?" The man holds one hand out in the stop position. "You're choosing now to make silly jokes?"

Harlan raises his shoulders and tilts his head giving a small smile. "Point being, jellyfish don't have brains. But hey, don't feel bad, I wouldn't expect you to understand that. What I do expect, about now I might add, is for you to finally get a clue. So, don't make some brainless mistake and try to hurt the girl. I can do the same to you as I did to your brother."

The alpha looks over to his brother, sees him holding his

head between his hands and rocking on his butt in the sand.

"And anyway, the girl won't get hurt no matter what you try I can promise you that. You got what you came for, so just release her before this thing goes *really* bad."

"Okay, sonny." He lets go of Danny, and she immediately runs to Harlan, latching onto him like a child. "We have decided to forgive the girl for her temporary... misguided... thievin' ways."

"Good. Now you can go back to where you came from."

The man pulls four fingers slowly down one side of his face, then repeats the process. "For now, sonny... for now."

Once the two men had scurried off another brief silence sets in. Danny releases her grip on Harlan and steps back putting her hands over the bridge of her nose like she's praying. "I never experienced anything like that before. And I've seen some twisted... She lets her hands fall. I don't mean you're... What I mean is... It's like... you were a volcano hidden by snow. You just suddenly woke up, or... you know, erupted. I don't know what that colorful thing coming out of you was, but it was like... not real, like I was seeing a vision, like some dreamy, half imaginary, half.... Are you from another planet? Tell me the truth. I've seen things. I can take it."

Harlan's eyes were somewhat surprised. "I guess I can see why you would think that. But what you've just witnessed? I don't understand it any more than you."

"Okay, well when did this all start?"

He rubs his hand across the back of his neck. "The colorful thing, it's happened twice, now three times since... like I said, I can't remember much lately. But since I've been working at the food stand, three times.

"God, Harlan, maybe you *are* from another planet. Or maybe worse."

"Worse?"

She smiles, takes him by the hand with a sort of insistent tug and begins walking him towards the beach. "Maybe you're immortal after-all."

"You'd think immortals would have better memories, aliens too."

As the two new friends cleared the underneath of the pier, Harlan notices his vision is unusually sharp. He can see faces some fifty yards down the beach with perfect clarity. He can even see nuances in their facial features, distinctions like imperfections in skin tone, scars, darkness under eyes, moles, and freckles. He can see any uncovered tattoos, can even make out the colors and designs. On one attractive petite girl, he makes out a dragon tattoo on her arm just below the elbow. The

man attached to her shoulder has a lion roaring and raising its legs into the air in the middle of his chest. Harlan now has the vision of a sculptor, and far better. As they continue walking he decides to keep his discovery to himself. As one arm hangs helplessly by his side, he cups the other softly around Danny's shoulders and whispers mischievously in her ear. "Maybe I was a marble statue for the past 800 years and I've suddenly come to life."

She leans her face into his arm and kisses it. "No. I don't think you could've ever been made of something so hard as marble, or brick and stone for that matter. I do think you have the form for it though. And I don't think your history goes back such a long way. No, you're eighteen same as me. Anyone looking at you could see that. You're just a little confused due to the memory loss, sorta like a flower that just sprouted in the crack of a sidewalk. Suddenly it finds itself in the middle of all the decay and change of a modern city. Who wouldn't be confused? I've heard of people losing their memory after a blow to the head or a dramatic event. Maybe you had an accident or maybe you witnessed something horrible. Whatever happened, you can't rush it. Your memory will come back when it's good and ready."

Chapter 3

The day was warm and slow-moving, like a train that eases along in a steady, drowsy rhythm. Harlan and Danny are alternating sipping from a Coke and rubbing suntan lotion on each other at a poolside. They cannot tell at first if the voice they suddenly hear is watching them or not. "Fit made in heaven, that's what you two are."

When Harland turns to look, the warm, bright sunshine catches him in the eyes. He throws up a hand squinting and makes out an old man leaning against an aqua colored block wall. With one hand pushed behind his back, the man appears to be hiding something. In the other hand is a half-smoked cigarette. He takes a strong puff, rounds out his mouth, blows two quick bursts and watches his chemical breath ascend like an Indian smoke signal.

"Is he talking to us?" Danny asked.

"I don't know." Harlan lifts his hand higher into the sun. "You talking to us, Mister?"

The old man pulls his hand free revealing a bottle of beer. He takes a quick sip, then moves it back to its former hiding place. "They don't like it when I drink at the pool. And yes, I was talkin' to you."

"Why?"

"Because I don't usually talk to myself. My kids would love it though. If I started doin' that it would give them a reason to put me in a nursing home and take control of my money. I meant what I said though. You two youngins' sure-nough' a fit made in heaven."

Danny leans sideways in the hard-plastic pool chair she's

sitting in. Her shoulder touches Harlan's. "I think he means match... match made in heaven." She leans forward like she's about to stand up. "I think you meant to say *match*. Right, Mister?"

"Being I'm a might older than you, Mister would seem to do just fine. However, my name's Gabriel. Course you can call me Gabe if you like, that's what most folks do. Anyways, I didn't mean match. I know precisely what match means, and it's different than fit." He turns up the beer, guzzles down what's left of it, wipes a few drops of the golden liquid from his face and tosses the bottle into a nearby trash can. Then he lifts his hands motioning with his eyes to look at them. His thumbs are tucked flat against his palms. With his fingers pressed against each other he reaches his hands about chest high, twists them in the opposite direction so that one palm is facing the other, slides them horizontally and cups both hands together at the fingers. His face starts straining red as a tug-of-war ensues. "You can't pull apart something that fits this good. Just because two people are a match don't mean they'll last. You have to be a good fit for that." He lets his hands fall back to his side. "Match... good lord. If two things are the same color, they're a match. But fit. Sometimes even opposites fit. I been watching you two the past couple days here at the pool. You're a *fit* alright. After seventy-four years I know it when I see it."

Danny leans forward again, this time standing all the way up. While speaking she rubs at some suntan lotion showing on her leg. "You a retired football coach or something like that? Maybe a corrections officer or policeman? Or..." Finished with the lotion, she lifts her hand up from her leg. "You know... one of those professions that after you spend a lifetime in, leave you wise and all-knowing. Is that what you are, Gabe?"

"Since we done found ourselves in the middle of a conversation, before I answer that, you mind if I ask your names?"

"I'm Daniela, but I go by Danny." She motions with her hand. "And this here's Harlan."

"Now that we got the formalities out of the way, me being a policeman would never work. Although as a kid I must admit I gave it some serious thought. Use to think police work was a noble profession. That's before I was harassed out of my mind one night by one of Columbia's finest. That's where I grew up. The incident was just after I started driving. Soon after my family moved to Myrtle Beach and started buying up properties. Since then, me and law enforcement never really got along. I do like the retired football coach insinuation though or is it interpretation? Wish I could say yes, but I never coached anything in my life."

"What *do* you do, Gabe?" Harlan interjects.

"Nothing. Never had to. Oh, I used to fake helping run some of the properties. But mostly I just tried to stay out of the way." He looks up scanning the high-rise hotel. When things got too crazy, I slipped away to this place. It's a little quieter, and the last... or at least I think it's the last, of the properties my family purchased. I own them all now since my parents passed. You two don't have a room here. You know how I know?"

Harland stands up next to Danny. "Sorry, Gabe. You're right. We have no business..."

"Its the colored bans. We have all the guest wear them." he motions with his hand. "See."

"Is that why you started talking to us?" Danny asked. "Are you trying to tell us to move on?"

"If I wanted to do that I would've done it yesterday. You're free to stay as the personal guest of the owner."

"If you're the owner then why were you hiding the beer?"

"Well, now I'm glad you asked that, Danny, because I see what you're saying, and because it's a pet-peeve of mine. Doesn't make any sense, does it? But it's company policy, of which I didn't have anything to do with. Never was interested in all that lawyer jargon. No alcoholic beverages allowed at the pool. And even though I own the place... Well, let's just say there are employees that know my fully grown and pain-in-the-ass kids. The more I try to disconnect from them the more they... It's classic; kids born with money. Grandchildren, great-grandchildren, all with overripe minds, living in high-rise buildings, full of imaginary importance. I never knew a hoity-toity generation would be my legacy. The money has gone to their heads. They think they live in the garden-of-God. These days, I'm more comfortable around poor people. You two are poor. I can tell because you been sharing the same drink. Nobody does that anymore, not anybody with two pennies to rub together anyways. I guess I'm just an old dude that misses the olden days, or is it by-gone days, or back-in-the-day? I swear, the English language is in such a constant state of change I can hardly keep up. Things were different though, you know, way back when."

While Gabe spoke, Harlan was looking passed him across the pool at a strange-looking group of people. "You know those people, Gabe?" They are filtering out the back door of the hotel lobby, gradually dispensing themselves around the pool. There were three men with spiked hair intermixed with a lot of women. Some of the women were wearing brown hoods, the others were bareheaded and completely bald.

"I know, right? They look like they just waltzed out of prison. They arrived last night from Tallahassee I think. Anyways, from one of those Floridian cities."

"Danny eases over next to Gabe. "What're the black flowers for?" All the girls are carrying a single black rose, holding them with both hands in the middle of their chest.

"Not sure, maybe... some cult thing. You two stay clear of 'em. They might be here to recruit. You don't *even* want to be a part of that."

In a sudden turn, one of the hooded girls walks up to Danny, reaching the rose up to her nose. "If you sniff the rose, it means friendship."

Danny's head jerks back. "And if I don't?"

The girl releases one hand from the rose, moves it upwards and flips back her hood revealing her bald head. "Don't be afraid. It just means the mystery will go on."

"What mystery?"

"We are either a mystery to each other or we are friends. The rose symbolizes the unknown. If you choose to sniff it I will tell you my name, and you will tell me yours, no more mystery."

"I was taught to choose my friends more carefully than that."

The girl doesn't flinch. She moves the rose to the point of barely touching Danny's nose. "If you sniff the rose it means friendship."

Danny closes her eyes, sniffs lightly, then opens her eyes with a surprised look. "That smells nice. I never saw a black rose before."

"There's no such thing as a true black rose. This one's dark purple. We darken it more with heat, then dip it in scented oil. My name's Angela. What's yours?"

"I'm Daniela, but I go by Danny."

"We are friends now, Danny." Angela turns toward Harlan and reaches out the rose. "If you sniff the rose, it means friendship."

Looking beyond her at the other numerous bald girls he wonders what their game is, then decides he doesn't want to find out right now. Leaning forward he takes a quick sniff. "I'm Harlan."

"My name's Angela. We are friends now, Harlan." She immediately turns to Gabe. "If you sniff the rose it means friendship."

He pushes the rose back. "It's customary to say excuse me."

She doesn't flinch, just moves the rose around his hand. "If you sniff the rose, it means friendship."

He pinches two fingers over his nostrils.

She turns back to Harlan, stepping closer. "What precipitated the change?"

Harlan's eyes move toward Danny, then back to Angela. "What do you mean?"

"There are two answers to that question. One, I read eyes, and I'm good at it. Yours are a nice green, but they have a darker ring surrounding the green. We call it an age ring. We've never been able to eliminate it. And two, you don't remember me do you?"

40

"I've never seen you before in my life."

"It happens a lot. It's a side effect. We've never been able to eliminate that either."

"You do understand that I don't have a clue as to what you're talking about?"

"You will."

His head springs backward, his face squinting. "When?"

"Hours, weeks, it's hard to say. But in the meantime, there's something you need to understand."

"Okay, I'll play along. What is it?"

Angela turns back to Gabe. She compares his older, slighter frame to Harlan's. Then she glances a moment at Danny, smiling. "You need to understand... that you are no longer tethered to human frailty."

Gabe reaches his arm in between Angela and Harlan. "You a witch or psychic? Because if you're a witch..."

She places the rose in his hand and squeezes it shut.

"What the... Why did you do that?"

"Your memory will come back soon Harlan. When it does, your story begins its course. You will walk the streets as brave as ever. But because there are no laws to govern you, you will be driven like a shadow in a forest. People will not understand you, even those who helped to create you. Some will hunt you." She glances back to Danny. "Some will love you. You will feel like the most peculiar face in a crowd, that is until you've found your identical." Angela backs up slowly, makes a dip with her face while placing the hood over her head, then turns as if to leave.

Harlan grabs her by the shoulder. "Okay. I admit for a minute there you had me going." Her eyes are penetrating his. He can feel something out of the ordinary, a power coming from her shoulder into his hand, something exquisitely sensitive. "What you're saying, it doesn't make sense. I can't believe it." The power coming from her is getting stronger. He feels it fantastically radiating from her whole body now, enclosing him in a sphere. It was familiar to him, like the same all-encompassing power he had experienced coming out of himself. They are both continuing to stare into the face of each

41

other. "I can't believe you."

"She flips the hood back off her head. "You will soon."

"Why should I?"

"Because you feel it, and I know you feel it. Because *not* believing me would be like throwing your heart out in the street to be trampled on. You are so full of life, Harlan, so handsome, so physically well-developed. I did some of my best work on you. You have indefinable characteristics that will soon come to light. When they do, embrace them, explore them and learn to control them. Stay close to Danny, you're going to need her. And find out what it is she needs to tell you. Don't make her endure it by herself."

Harlan watches with a sort of gloss in his eyes as Angela walks away from the pool into the hotel. When he turns to Danny there is an appeal in his face, as if he is soliciting support. Tears are building in his eyes. He looks helpless, mute, almost pathetic like he is somehow at fault.

"What's wrong? I've never seen you look like this."

"Nothing."

"I think its *something*. I think you know what she's been talking about."

"It's just that, as she talked... I started to remember things."

"That's good, your memories coming back."

"Yes, but you don't understand. The memories are of a past life."

She could see something conspicuous in his eyes. The tears had dried up and they were moving rapidly side to side. "Everybody's got a past, Harlan. You're just a little confused. It can happen when one's memory suddenly comes back. Don't worry, you're going to be fine."

"There are intervals of pictures. A gray brick house, and a half-obliterated retaining wall. The house is old and in a state of decay. I see images of children, varying in age and... one of them... a boy... is mine."

"You have a baby?"

"No. I mean, yes, but the child is like eleven or twelve."

"But that's impossible."

"That's not all. There are other images where the boy is

42

grown. I'm talking about like 30 years old. And when I say the boy is mine... what I mean is... he's my grandson."

"But it makes no sense."

"There's more, so much more. His father, my son was run over and killed by a drunk driver. I can remember it, and I can feel it, the emotions I had when it happened."

Gabe strikes a match, cups his hand covering it while he lights up another cigarette. Then he tilts his head back avoiding Danny and Harlan and blows a stream of smoke straight up. "You can calm down, son. It's the girl, Angela. Everything that came out of that girl's mouth was malarkey. She's a witch, or wiccan, or maybe one of those devil worshipers. They seem to be increasing these days. That weird group probably came here to practice their magic on the innocent. Don't you worry. More than likely it'll wear off in a day or two. I'm goin' inside the lobby to see what they're up to. I'm calling the police if they keep harassing the guests."

As Gabe walks away, Harlan's mind, and especially his memory, spins with unusual activity and keeps bringing up other scenes. The scenes were of rows of brick houses, of a quaint little town, and an old decaying house. Scenes of his mother and father with anxious, loving, needful faces. Both young and supremely beautiful. Then there were other scenes that made no sense at all. Scenes of a medical room complete with doctors and their assistants with surgical masks on, all wearing green scrubs. All eyes concentrating on him as he lay on a gurney. It was all mixed with spectral images of animals streaming passed him and of oddly shaped trees in a vast forest. These images are intermingled with recollections of a whole life already lived. Passages of schooldays, childish quarrels, all the little domestic traits of an old man, and everything in between. One picture precisely as vivid as another, as if all were of similar importance, all swarming back like they were trying to find their place.

Danny leans into him. "I'm not sure what's happening to you Harlan." She reaches her arms around him pressing her face into his chest. "But there's something I haven't told you. Something I've been afraid to talk about. Something that's

43

been happening to me, too."

He softly moves her head back away from his chest, tilts his head down and kisses her on the lips. "You wanna tell me? It can't be as weird as what I'm going through."

"I'm afraid it is. And I'm still not so sure I wanna talk about it."

"You're gonna have to get it out in the open sooner or later. So just talk. What else we got to do?"

"Okay then, if you're sure. I've been here two weeks now. One week before I met you, and one week since. I told you that I came from West Virginia. Truth is I don't really know. For some reason, it's stuck in my mind. I also told you I moved here with my family. You might have guessed by now that was a lie. How I got here? It's a mystery. And like you, I can't remember anything either. I only remember the past two weeks. None of that really bothers me, I mean, not that much anyway. What bothers me, really scares me I mean, is what has happened to me every night since I woke up here. I'm still having trouble saying it. It just seems so unreal, so completely impossible..."

Harlan kisses her again on the lips, then on the forehead. "Take your time and breathe. I'm not going anywhere."

"Thanks. I needed to hear that." She tilts her head downward, breathes in heavily and sighs as she releases it. "The first week I lived here, before meeting you, I always slept on the beach. You know the sand dunes just south of town. It's safe there. I never had any trouble. I would wait until late, then go to the public restroom just up from there. I would go to wash up and clean my teeth before going to sleep. The mirror there was dusky with a sort of glaze over it. I guess it doesn't get washed much. What I'm trying to tell you is that... when looking into the mirror, I saw something. Something overlapping my face, like two faces staring back at me. I know that must sound crazy...I just..."

"It's okay, Danny. You already started telling me, don't stop now."

"Right. So, one was my own face, which of course I recognized, and one was a face pale and thin with eyes dim, almost colorless, and a face wrinkled, slightly deformed, and …how do I say this? It was an old person's face. I mean like very old. Even though the mirror was dirty and glazed over, still, there was the lucid image of an old, wore out face overlapping my own youthful face. Since the first time I saw it, the old face seems to have a strange, penetrating power, like it has ownership over me, like it can read me, like it knows everything about me."

"Okay, maybe you…I mean maybe the mirror… Do you think you were just feeding on your imagination?"

"What!"

"You couldn't remember anything. You were all alone, out late in a dank, under-lighted bathroom, not even knowing how you came to be here."

"Right, but since I moved into your little shack it keeps happening. Every night when I look into the mirror it's the same thing, the same exact old face, overlapping and intertwined with mine. But it's more than another face, it's…another…another human soul…another…person. I believe it's me in the future, I'm convinced of it." She turns her eyes downward and touches her face with her fingers to assure herself she is real. "It's me in the future trying to… I don't know…tell me something or make me aware of something."

"Do you hear yourself? Seriously, do you hear what you're saying?"

"I didn't want to tell you. I didn't even believe it myself until now. You must believe me. If it's not me then there is another person, another consciousness. And I am the object of its observation. And there's more…'

"Danny, you need to get a handle!"

"Why won't you believe me? Didn't you hear what Angela said."

"Angela?"

"Yes. She said don't make her endure it by herself. You were listening."

"Okay, so let's just try to reason on this. First off, it makes no sense. How could she know things about you?"

"She knows things about you, too. Doesn't she? You might

as well go ahead and say it. I think we both know the answer."

Harlan looks across the pool and sees an Indian dressed in his native garb. He is standing next to a short white man who is also dressed in Indian garb. Next to the two men is another man. He's dressed in a sharp-looking three-piece suit. It's a strange array or disarray of modern and vintage costumes. He turns back to Danny. "So, you really think you're being observed?"

"Yes, and there's more."

"I'm listening."

"I think it's trying to communicate something about me. No, wait. I think it's trying to communicate something about *me and you together*. I think it knew we were going to meet, and it wants us to stay together. If that makes any sense."

"It makes sense...just doesn't seem real."

"No, it doesn't. We finally agree."

He glances back across the pool to the Indian and the two other oddly dressed men. "Strange things are happening."

"Yes. Strange happenings seem to be the order of the day for both of us."

"They flew the coop," a voice shouted from behind them. When they turn to look Gabe is staring at them. With a sudden wave of his hand, he slowly bows his head courteously. "No need to thank me, they knew I had my eye on them. Nobody wants to deal with an ornery old man. When Angela seen me following her around, she knew I was about to jerk a knot in her tail. I would've, too. But they checked out faster than a one-legged man in a butt-kicking competition. Good riddance to that odd-ball group. I'm still not sure what their game was, but they were lower than a snake's belly in a wagon rut." He glances beyond them. "Now we got a native Indian convention arriving. They're infrequent visitors." Pointing across the pool he continues. "They might have attracted your notice already. There's a little hoopla with their visit but I like 'em. They're peaceful, and most of 'em have remarkable intelligence in their features. Seem's kinda strange though doesn't it, them standing in their native garb on such a hot day? And who's the dude in the three-piece suit? Strange!"

Harlan turns to Danny. Her eyebrows raise slowly as they speak simultaneously, "Strange!"

Chapter 4

He lay there on a hospital operating gurney, his body chilled by the cold and impersonal nature of the room. The wearer of the brown hood hovered above him. With his eyesight blurred from clinical injections designed, he thought, to possibly chase the cancer away from his rapidly failing body, the strange hooded person appeared translucent, like an apparition, but with a perceptible consciousness. The wearer of the brown hood had her eyes bent on him, perceiving that he was awake. He felt a convulsion internally, a strong force that caused him to utter a cry of pain. But the stranger did not at first seem to hear, or possibly even care, because her face had not even the slightest change in it. He reckoned her to be a girl due to the roundness of her face, and its smoothness was like silk fabric pulled taut and perfectly placed over her facial structure. The femaleness spread across her face like no other he had ever seen. She seemed like perfection.

And then she spoke. "There's a little discomfort, Harlan, I know. Sorry, it can't be helped. But hang in there, you're doing well."

As soon as he heard her voice, it only added to her aura. She had a distinctive quality or atmosphere, and he instantly knew there was some remarkable intelligence inside her features. Her physical and mental harmony was unmistakable to the point of peculiarity, way beyond anything he had ever seen. For a second he wonders if she was not human. And then he wonders if he was dreaming.

"There are things I need to tell you, Harlan. But you won't remember, so I'll just wait on most of it. I probably shouldn't tell you anything, but I feel compelled because it's going to be difficult for you, at least for a while. What is happening to you goes far beyond cancer treatments. In a way you've been tricked, but for your own benefit. Right now, you cannot conceive of how this will affect you. You're going to have dreams and visions of animals in the forest, you're going to feel them, connect to their senses. You may even think you were once one of them, some mythic four-legged creature turned into a human. Don't worry, you're not. It's just the natural connection all humans had with animals when life began on earth. You're going to have other dreams, too; some familiar, just things pertaining to your life up until now, and some a little disturbing because they are so completely unfamiliar. The reason for this is that you are being reconnected to the earth, not just the animals, but everything. You are being brought back into harmony with it. You will have abilities you have never experienced before. These abilities may scare you, and they are incredible, but they are less powerful than they will seem. In effect they are just your senses being exacerbated by the injections. Man's senses were once far more than they are now. All of this is part of what we're doing to you for your own good, otherwise you were simply going to die from cancer. We are regenerating you all the way back to your youth. Yes, Harlan, you will wake up young again, only better, so much better. I'll apologize for the memory loss now because it will make things a lot more difficult for you in the beginning. When your memory does come back, you will at least understand that which I'm telling you now. It will be of great help. I wish I could tell you more, but there's no more time, and there's no sense to it right now anyway. We were careless at first. We did something that caused side-effects, and we've never been able to discover the change in the formula that causes it. Eventually, one day, we will."

Her look into his face and over his body became keen and penetrative. Her eyes were like a snake gliding swiftly over him, making one little pause at a specific point, assessing and continuing. She was so precise that what she was doing seemed to be controlled by a tremendous effort of her will, other than a single moment when she paused, where a look of concern came over her face. The expression of concern subsided and turned to one of calmness, then she began again. Another convulsion hit him, and he gave out a grunt of pain. "Are you alright, Harlan? Can you endure the pain? I couldn't put you to sleep because it works so much better when I hold off. Let me know if you are okay?"

He calmly raises his hand. With it hanging in the air he gives a thumbs-up gesture, then he lowers it to his lips and motions for a drink of water.

"I'm sorry again. I can't risk diluting the formula. The thirst will pass soon, and you will naturally fall into a nice relaxing sleep." She touches his shoulder and a sudden penetrating warmness causes his convulsion to grow almost imperceptible. He slowly and calmly raises his hand again, this time all the way up to her face and touches it. She smiles, then squeezes it with her own hand into her face even more. "You are going to be so unbelievably surprised the next time you see yourself." Finally, after about a minute, he lowers his hand down beside him, giving in to the depths of sleep. She checks his pulse, touching his forehead with the backside of her hand as she sits down in a chair beside him. "We will talk again, Harlan. I need to tell you that you are different. Different from all other regenerated ones that we've found up until now. I need to talk with you about your amazing brain."

She turns to a man clad in all-white standing by the entrance to the room. "Go tell Carter that his grandfather has been put to sleep. He and Ansel can do their procedure now. That's all I want you to say. Say it and then leave. If he asks any questions don't respond, just leave. Do you understand?"

He nods without speaking, turns and exits the room.

Miss Emma had been treading the floor for about half an hour when Carter arrived. When he looked at her, he knew she had something devious in store for him. No one was more aware of this fact than she was. "You're late like always," she said with her arms crossed while tapping her shoe on the floor.

She releases her arms pointing a finger. "And wipe that darn fatalistic look off your face. Even if you are, you don't have to appear so confounded by me. You've been lying to me, and I know it, so don't try any of your doctor lingo or mumbo jumbo, or what the heck ever else you've got up your sleeve to try and put me off any longer. I want to know where Harlan's at and I want to know now. So, use that pretty, little logical mind of yours. I'll even accept that severely logical thing you like to do sometimes to show off your smarts, but I want the truth. So, give it to me straight, Carter. Where's Harlan?"

He tilts his head downward and rubs his chin with his index finger. "You're the prettiest mean person I ever met. You know that?"

She starts tapping her shoe again. "It's just a coincidence, prettiness runs in the family. And your lucky it does because if it didn't, with your smarts, you'd have a brain-shaped head. As for me I'd be as ugly as ten miles of bad road if it meant getting the truth out of you right now."

"It's complicated."

"No! Don't tell me that. I *knew* you were going to start that crap up again."

"Well, it is."

"That's not justification. Tell me where he is."

"I don't know where he is. I've told you that before."

"Yes, you do. The complications you're talking about are just harnessing your friendliness to tell me. But I'm not leaving you alone until you do, so just spit it out."

"Funny you should mention friendliness."

"You think you've seen mean? Because I can show you meanness, just keep giving me the run-around."

"No. I didn't mean to. I think he's… what I mean to say is he might have taken a bus to who-knows-where. The cancer injections, I think they confused him, like really messed with his memory. He's out there somewhere, probably another city, and doesn't know how to get back or even who he is."

"But you've reported him missing. He would've been found by now."

"I didn't really report him missing. Besides, it doesn't

work like that. Databases don't always connect, especially when it's another state. And even if someone brought him to the police, if they have no name or address it's nearly impossible to connect the dots."

"Those treatments probably killed him."

"They were experimental injections that have had good success, and they probably *saved* his life."

"So, you think he's okay?"

"I think he's a survivor. And people just love him, they always have. He's the best I ever saw at giving compliments, especially when it means getting something in return. Someone's probably taking good care of him right now. I doubt he's anywhere near as worried as we are. And I suspect that your instincts, civilized or otherwise, are telling you the same thing." Carter dips his head again and smiles. "You just love playing the role of the antagonist, don't you?" He lifts his head up and raises his eyebrows. "Tell the truth."

"I won't deny it, it makes me feel useful."

"And you love it."

"I admit I get a *subtle* pleasure from it."

"Subtle?"

"Maybe a little more than that, but it's sort of how I work with others. You go at things logically, whereas I pound them with questions until the answers start appearing. With both of us working together to find Harlan, imagine what we could accomplish."

"While I appreciate the sentiments, wait, I'm not even sure about that. I love you, Aunt Emma, really, but you are way too self-engrossed to...what I mean is, it would be a little too weird, distracting is a better word, to partner up with you."

"All I'm saying is the difficulty of this situation calls for more than one brain. However, due to your unflattering belief in me, I'm not requiring for us to tag-team this thing together, whether it be socially, professionally, or whatever-ly. You know he never seemed like a father to me. We never had that kind of relationship. When I was younger, I used to admire that about him. He was like a playmate, a friend who spent a lot of time with me. Then I grew up and started resenting him.

He was older too and started hanging on mother's arm a lot more. The older he got the more he seemed to need her. Anyway, he had a gift when it came to children, not so much with grownups. It was hard on him when mother died. Truth be told, it's a miracle he survived it. Those two were attached at the hips."

Even though Carter's conversation with Aunt Emma hadn't exactly been a walk in the park, he understood her. Her impulses and her ability to express them were like no other he had ever known. Being in her presence and listening to her was like an echo going all the way back to his childhood, some of it wonderful, some of it unsettling. But he knew that, somewhere beneath the thin, pink layers of her heart, she meant well.

The fact-of-the-matter was that people were beginning to talk, and being that Danville was such a small town, that talk would soon find its way to Futurelab Pharmaceuticals. This fact alarmed him more than Harlan's disappearance. He was at first irritated, then puzzled, to find him missing. He hated gradually losing control of the situation. Despite his not understanding what had happened to Harlan, he had not told Ansel or anyone else at Futurelab Pharmaceuticals. Aunt Emma was still roaming the town searching for Harlan, keeping everyone informed of his disappearance. After their conversation she would no doubt extend the bounds of her search. She was sensitive and confident in her powers to find him. It was her relentless involvement that seemed most likely to attract the attention of Carter's working peers.

He decided on a bold move. He said his goodbyes to Aunt Emma, walked out of her house to his car, pulled out his cell phone and started punching in Ansel's number. He had decided to spill the beans on everything. When there was no answer he drove back to his house. Ansel was sitting on the front porch, waiting. It was obvious that he was keenly conscious of something as Carter walked up to him. "How long you been here, I tried to call you?"

Ansel starts patting his pockets. "I'm a little nervous. I must have left my phone in the car."

Carter inserts the key in the door, turns it until he hears the latch click. "Come on inside. You want a Coke, or I could get us a beer?"

"No, Coke's fine or just water."

In the kitchen, Carter presses the aluminum tab on two Cokes. "Have a seat here at the table, and why are you nervous?" He reaches the Coke out to him.

"That looks good, thanks. They searched my house today."

"What are you talking about? Who searched your house?"

"Our awesome employer the U.S. government. They were amicable about it though, didn't cause too much damage."

"Did they tell you *why?*"

"No. I was hoping you might know something."

"Ansel, I hate to have to tell you this, but you're about to have a strong reason for disliking me."

"I don't think I like the sound of that, go on."

"Harlan's missing, and I've been keeping it a secret from you."

"Missing? What the heck, Carter! That's why you've been deflecting my inquiries. How long? I mean when did he disappear?"

"Personal feelings aside, and I know you're bothered by this, it's been a while now, over two months, probably closer to three. I'm sorry, but it's probably why they searched your house. More than likely they know something's up. They might even know he's missing. For all I know they're the reason he's missing."

"They'll search your house, too."

"They already have. I noticed some things out of whack when we came in."

"So, what now?"

"Now I tell you the rest of what I've been keeping from you."

"There's more? I think I don't like you already."

"The last time I saw Harlan he looked to be about twenty-one years old."

"You're kidding. But that's not possible. Is it?"

"No. At least not with the technology we were using. I've

been thinking a lot about it. Even with the formula change, it doesn't make sense. Whatever happened to him we didn't do it. What I saw is the equivalent to being immortal on earth. It made a deep impression on my senses, seeing my grandfather so much younger than me, so incredibly good looking. It was amazing. I came to check on him only three days after the injections, and he was already young. And he grew even younger right before my eyes. I wish you could have seen the transformation. By now he could be even younger. I think whoever did this had something to do with his disappearance. I saw some people hanging around outside his house but just didn't put it together because they were so young. I just thought they were neighborhood teenagers. One of them spoke of a pinnacle. Maybe that's a mountain or another location where they've brought him to observe him."

"Then why would they need to search our homes?"

"I see what you're saying. That's a good question. Maybe they're just trying to find out what we know." Carter takes a sticky note pad from the counter next to the refrigerator. He pulls an ink pen from his shirt pocket and starts scribbling. When he's finished, he holds the pad in front of Ansel. It reads; *"if that's the case they've already bugged our homes. They could be listening right now."* Carter continues. "For now, we'll just hold put, keep the doors open in case he comes back. If someone has taken him at least he's alive and well. Better than well, he's young again. If he's lost his memory, that will eventually come back, and we'll hear from him at some point." He scribbles on another sticky note and lifts it for Ansel to read. *"We're not staying put. We'll do some digging around at work and see what we can find out. We can't let anyone know what we're up to. Agree?"*

Ansel nods his head yes. "My own feelings on the matter are to wait this thing out. We are chemist for a pretty important branch of the government. Whatever they're up to, they'll probably make us a part of it soon. It's exciting to be involved with technology that will change the world." This time Ansel scribbles on the sticky note. *"I'm not excited, I'm scared. The people above us will never let us know what they're up to."*

56

"I agree, Ansel, completely."

Later, as Carter walked the streets of Danville, he tries hard to banish the troublesome thoughts of Harlan and Futurelab Pharmaceuticals. His employer lay only twenty minutes up Highway 27 between Danville and Lexington. He wonders if his rash tactic with Ansel will work. Rash tactics sometimes lead to brilliant victories. Maybe he could find out what happened to his grandfather, or maybe the whole scheme would simply cave in on them. For the moment he was trying to put it out of his mind, to return to a preoccupation with another matter.

He steps from West Main to 3rd Street, turns left and enters The Hub Coffee House. He immediately spots the man he's looking for, a surly man with a bit of a grunge look about him and clinging to a leather briefcase. He is the owner of a local pawn shop and the recent recipient of a cease and desist order from the Danville police dept. Carter stops at his table, hesitates, then looks over to a girl working the register. He waves. "Jen, could I get my regular?"

She waves back. "Sure, Carter. Would you like a shot of espresso in that?"

He nods his head yes, then sits down. "You got what I asked for?"

The surly man taps the leather case. "A Glock G19. It's a 15-shot, polymer-framed, striker-fired pistol. It's considered to be one of the best guns Glock has ever produced. It's reliable under all conditions and is an excellent choice for personal defense."

"Plenty of ammo?"

"Everything we talked about is in the briefcase. Mind if I ask why you need this because if you need a little help with something, I know people. I can get you help with just about any situation. Just say the word. All you need is money."

"No. I'm fine, but thanks. I'll keep that in mind."

Jen interrupts. "One large, caramel, iced-coffee with a shot of espresso. That's $3.78, Carter."

He reaches behind him, pulls back his wallet, and hands her a five. "Keep the change."

"Thanks." She carefully places her hand on his shoulder, presses down and gives a light massage. "I get off at six today, could be ready by seven if you wanna do something."

"Anything, in particular, you had in mind?"

"A movie, or we could just hang out at my apartment, maybe order some Chinese." She pushes down harder on his shoulder. "Or we could do whatever you like."

"Not sure about the Chinese. The movie sounds good though. I could use a diversion about right now."

"It's a date then?"

"It's a date."

She turns to the surly man. "Jimmy, I'm feeling good and generous right now. Carter hasn't dated me in near three months. You want a refill of coffee? It's on me."

He looks at his cup. "No, Jen, one's enough, but thanks."

"Okay, suit yourself. See you, boys." She lifts her hand off Carter's shoulder and raises her index finger, brushing the hair away from his eyes. "I'll see you at seven?"

"You gonna leave the door unlocked?"

"If you want me, too."

"You're never ready on time. I haven't forgotten, so yes."

She glides her hand to the back of his head and gives him the lightest caress. It was somewhere between a pat and tap of her finger like one would do to pet a dog. Then she turns and walks back behind the register.

Jimmy turns up his cup, swallows down the last of his black coffee, sets the cup down and picks up his phone. "I see the deposit's already been made to my account." He slides the briefcase across the table. "This would be all yours now. You do know how to use it?"

"I'm almost teared up by your concern, Jimmy. Yes, I know-how. But I do plan on a little target practice outside of town, just to get the feel of it. And just to let you know, I don't plan on using it on another person. It's more a *just in case* kind of situation."

"Don't get caught with that thing. If you do, it can't be traced back to me, just saying. And I've heard all about those *just in case* situations where doing it legally with a permit is undesirable. But hey, good luck with whatever it is you need it for."

"Good luck to you too, Jimmy, on getting your store re-opened."

"My lawyers got that under control as we speak. Remember what I said. If you need any more help just say the word."

Carter nods, puts his lips over the straw and sips his blended coffee.

When he opened the door to Jen's apartment, he wasn't thinking about any fleeting moments he had had with her the last three months, which only amounted to a few customary 'hellos' and 'how are you doing,' and so on. After the disappearance of his grandfather, his responsibility in their relationship had taken a nosedive. He wasn't thinking about how he had mistreated her, of how terribly hurt she must have been. There had been intervals between the two of them, intervals where their relationship had clicked to near perfection. These beautiful intervals had vanished when his grandfather went missing. He wasn't thinking about any of that until she enters the room. Suddenly, he remembers how their two breaths had been inseparable only a short time ago. That is until he had gone and blown it all to smithereens.

After she walks into the room, he raises his arm making a motion with his hand that tells her how hot she is. "You're still the prettiest girl in Danville."

"Yes, and you don't deserve me."

"I know. Why do you put up with me? Why haven't you..."

"Found someone else? I have thought about it."

"Then why?"

"Several reasons. My father likes you and I admire him a great deal. He's the kindest person I've ever known, and he's a good judge of character. And your morals, you've never chased me... like... like every other man. I never liked being looked at like I was just some sex object. When I'm with you I know it's not just to hook up, I know it's real. You're smart too, and you don't have a clue as to how attractive that makes you. And then there's the thing about how handsome you are."

59

He smiles, leans against a wall and crosses his arms. "My Aunt Emma says it runs in the family."

Jen shakes her head, smiles and the smile quickly blossoms into laughing. "I've noticed that." Suddenly a mischievous look comes over her, and she inhales deeply, sighing as she lets it out. "Are you ready to get your act together now?"

He makes a little gesture of impatience with his face. "I've been distracted with some...truth is I..."

"Wow, you're really *not* ready to get your act together, are you?"

He uncrosses his arms, lets them fall to his sides and places the palms of his hands against the wall, tilting his head toward the floor. "Probably not." Suddenly his head jerks back up. "I want to make one thing clear. I know you're the girl for me. I've known it for a long time. It's just that right now there are things going on. Things that..."

"Have you ever once thought that I might could help?"

He shakes his head. "Not with this."

"How do you know unless you try me?"

"Fine then. My grandfather's missing. How are you gonna help with that?"

"You mean like Alzheimer missing or missing, missing?"

"I mean like missing, missing. And it's been a while now, like three months."

"That explains a lot. Have the authorities been looking for him?"

"Not exactly."

"Is that a yes or a no?"

"It's definitely a no."

"Then he's gotten himself in some serious trouble."

"You could say that."

"But he's like really old. What kind of trouble could he possibly have gotten into?"

"It's the kind of trouble that's not his fault. It's the kind of trouble that's more like... my fault."

"Okay, that really explains a lot, too. I guess you are distracted. Care to let me know *why* it's your fault?"

"That's not going to be easy to explain."

"You said I'm the girl for you. If you meant that then sooner or later you'll tell me. Why not make it now?"

Carter couldn't hold back any longer. He winced, turned and leaned his back against the wall while clenching his fist. "You know the work I do?"

"I know you work for Futurelab Pharmaceuticals, and I know you're a chemist."

"Have I ever told you the kind of work I do there?"

"Some kind of DNA research? You work with animals. You're trying to find a way to grow body parts. Right?"

"Yes, to regenerate body parts. We've had only limited success with that. However, there's another area in the field of regeneration that has seen a recent breakthrough. What I mean is a huge breakthrough, as in a groundbreaking, life-altering breakthrough. It's going to be stunning for you to hear."

"This is when you tell me you brought a dead guinea pig back to life."

"Not exactly. I'm not sure how to tell you this, so I'm just going to say it. We have made guinea pigs young again."

"What!"

"Are you sure you're ready for what I'm about to tell you, that you even want to know? Because it's going to change everything you know about life. And by life, I mean our physical bodies."

"I'm all in. I want to help you with this. And if it changes my perception of things then so be it."

"Consider your perception about to change. We have made a *man* young again, and that man is my grandfather."

"What! How is that possible?"

"I can't really claim to know all of the technology behind it, so I'll just tell you the basics. From the single-celled product of conception, humans grow into a uniquely cognitive being. The human brain far exceeds those of animals. Sometimes we use the term plastic brain because it appears to be primed from an extremely young age to learn and change. It can mold itself to whatever its current environment happens to be. We now understand that the brain is like having a universe inside your head. There's nothing it can't do to adapt to anything in life, and that includes regenerating the body, keeping it young. For a long time now, we've wondered why the human body ages, because according to our research it shouldn't. Something is interfering. I'm not going to bother you with the chemical and electrical makeup that fuels and energizes the body, or the fact that we are 78% water. All you really need to know is that through years of testing liquid formulas that mimic the brain's makeup with varying degrees of chemicals along with experimenting with electrical charges, we've had a major, breakthrough. The results are amazing. I can say that because I'm one of the few who have seen it with my own eyes."

"This is just... well, it's fascinating! I can only imagine what you've been going through. So, what do you suspect has happened to your grandfather? Do you think the Russians or Chinese found out and kidnapped him to do their own research?"

"That thought had completely gone over the top of my head. No, I don't think in any way, shape, or form that that's what happened to him. Actually, it might be more complicated than that."

"How could it get any more complicated than the Russians or Chinese?

"Have I told you that I actually work for the US Government, that Futurelab Pharmaceuticals is really just a cover?"

"You're joking, right?"

Chapter 5

Jen watched through the car window as billboards, peaches, and pecans came shooting by at a harrowing pace. It was practically all that existed along the I-75 corridor between Macon and Valdosta, Georgia. Carter was driving, and they were making haste to Seminole country, aka: Tallahassee, Florida.

Hours later they were cruising through the genteel southern town known for its good manners, rolling hills, oak canopied roads, and plantation homes. After crossing through the historic district, they pass a bar, a couple of restaurants and an art gallery, and then turned down a tree-lined street that looks more like a canopy of green and white flowers. When emerging from the canopy, Carter lifts his foot off the accelerator, conceding to the car as it slowly rolls itself to a stop, barely touching the curb. They are parked just across the way from a series of office buildings. He swipes his hand over the windshield smearing a little moisture buildup from the air conditioner. "Jen, can you read the number on that building?"

"I think so." Sitting up in her seat, she presses a small knob and the electric motor can be heard lowering the window. "It's 2442. It's called the Tallahassee Government Building."

"One would never know the CIA has their southeastern headquarters here."

"You can't be serious?"

"I am absolutely serious."

"But you told me we were just visiting one of your coworkers who was transferred to Tallahassee."

"We are. Dillon works here."

"Dillon, the chemist?"

"The chemist, the CIA operative, the Futurelab Pharmaceuticals *spy*."

"What! Are you certain?"

"Is the air humid in Florida?"

She sinks back into the seat. "I guess you're certain."

"Dillon and the CIA pulled a fast one on us. He knows all about my Gramps. They used technology on him that Ansel and I weren't aware of. We were kept in the dark for who knows how long on that one. He knows about his transformation, and I'm pretty sure he knows where he's at right now. I suspect they may even be keeping him at this location."

"You had to come then; I get that. It is safe though, right?" She's looking into his eyes for confirmation. "I mean, this is not something you're accustomed to."

Carter lifts his arm moving it across the seat behind her head. "I always did love the tint of your hair." He brushes it back and starts massaging her neck. "What color is that anyway? It's not brown, or red, or..."

She moves his hand around to her face and kisses it. "Sugar, it's from a bottle. It's called Intense Auburn."

"I thought it was natural."

"A girl's hair, natural, in today's world? Not likely." She kisses his hand again. "But thanks for the thought. Sorry if my confession disappoints you."

"I still like the tint."

"So, when are we going inside?"

"You, Darling, and your beautiful hair are staying in the car."

"No, I'm not. I didn't come with you all the way from Kentucky to sit in the car and fiddle my thumbs. I'd go crazy."

"You asked if it was safe. The thing is, I don't really know." I'm thinking probably, but..." Carter pats his side under his arm. "I'm packing just in case."

"What! Do you even know how to use a gun?"

"Why does everybody assume I'm clueless when it comes to guns?"

"Because, Carter! Hello, you're a chemist, which is almost like being a professor. You're not exactly the gun handling kind. You got it from Jimmy, didn't you? No wonder they shut him down."

"I've been practicing out by the old, closed down, coat factory. It's a Glock, and it's easy to use. I only have it just in case. So, don't worry. I'm not going in there waving the thing."

"Oh, I'll worry alright." She reaches out and places the back of her fingers softly on his face. "Do you remember a few years ago when we first met. We hit it off from the start but never really got to the next level. I couldn't stop thinking about how handsome and smart you were, although maybe a little spoiled. I used to chase you around the coffee shop like you were a butterfly, like I was trying to see your colors, and in a way I was. I wanted to know everything about you, but you just kept palpitating out of my reach every time I thought it was going to get serious." She can sense something in Carter. His eyes are widening. "Your wings still flutter in my heart."

He chuckles loudly, not even trying to hold it back.

She slaps at his arm. "Stop that. I'm being serious."

"You've been reading in that book of poems again, haven't you?"

"Okay, so I overshot a little…maybe a lot, but I think you know how I feel. I don't want you to do anything that might put you in danger." She slowly moves her fingers to his lips, slightly presses down, hesitates a few seconds, then moves them to the other side of his face. From there she glides them down to his shoulder, then farther down until her hand rests atop the Glock pistol. "If you leave it in the car, I'll stay put. Otherwise... Besides, it's a government building. You'll have to pass through security, and there will be cameras everywhere. You'll just end up in jail."

He puts his hand over hers and the pistol. "I *had* thought of the security. This building's a little bit different than other government buildings. There are certain rooms you can't get into without authorization. Those rooms are heavily guarded. Otherwise you can maneuver around like any other building. I did some poking around at work the other day. Dillon's office isn't guarded. I've been working out the details for months, ever since Gramps disappeared. I've covered every possible scenario. So, if you feel like you must come, then come. Truth be told, I kinda expected it. But, I'm not leaving the gun. Like I said, it's for just in case."

Her eyes have a heaviness to them. She squints at him, then relaxes and starts smiling. "Who are you? I mean I've never seen you act... It's like you've reinvented yourself or changed to another person. I'm not sure if it's for the better or the worse."

"I feel the same way. But my Gramps is in danger, and I think I'm responsible. I have to do something."

She removes her hand from the pistol, moves it across her body and opens the passenger side door. "Then we'll do it together."

While they both make their way through the crowded lobby, Carter suddenly stops, fixing his gaze on an information board with directions. He is keenly conscious that he is breaking the law by carrying a concealed gun into a government building. He presses his finger on the board and starts scrolling it down until he reaches Dillon Hatcheck. He chuckles at the caption: 'Chemical Engineer' and turns taking Jen by the arm. "We need to go to the third floor." After exiting the elevator Carter and Jen immediately notice two armed guards standing outside of room 301. Dillon's office is the adjacent room, 302. Carter tries not to squirm, nodding politely and calmly at the guards as he and Jen walk by. When he stops and turns the nob to Dillon's office, he finds it locked.

One of the guards shouts, "You need something from Mr. Hatcheck?"

Carter's stomach is cringing intensely now, but his expression remains calm. He smiles in an act of acknowledgment. "We're old workmates, and I was just..."

"Carter?"

When he turns, he sees Dillon holding a cup of coffee. His stomach is now officially in knots. "Dillon. I bet you're surprised to see me."

"That would appear to be the understatement of the day. Tallahassee's a long way from Lexington." He swipes the key-card, opens the door then turns around. "You two coming in?" As soon as they walk in, he shuts the door behind them and gives Carter a hard look. "Why are you here? Don't tell me you're on vacation and just thought you'd drop by. We've never been close, not by a long shot."

"Okay, all animal crap aside, I think you know why I'm here. Where's Harlan?"

"I don't know what you're talking about. Are you going to just stand, or do you want to sit down?"

"Right now, standing seems the prudent thing. Are you going to keep denying, or you gonna play it straight with me? I already know you're an agent for the CIA."

"An agent for the CIA." He starts laughing. "Who told you that?"

"Nobody. Nobody was ever going to tell me that. It took a little snooping around to find *that* out."

"Carter, I'll tell you the same thing I already told you. I don't know what you're talking about."

"Yes, I think you do. It was you who encouraged me to use Harlan for the injections and this is all I get, a denial. The least you can do is tell me if he's okay."

"I have no idea where Harlan is. I didn't even know he was missing."

"Even though I know you're lying, that's your story and your sticking to it. Someone's controlling you, someone higher up the ladder."

"You need to stop pushing this."

"Just give me a name or point me in the right direction. I'll take it from there."

"I could open that door right now and have you arrested."

"Why would you do that unless you were guilty of something?"

"You have the opportunity right now to just leave. I

strongly suggest you walk out and then keep walking. Go back to Lexington, Carter. You don't belong in Tallahassee."

"So that's it? That's all I get for my trouble?"

"Trouble is exactly what you'll get if you keep digging around Tallahassee. I promise you; you don't want the kind of trouble you're about to step into. Go home, go home now!"

Carter turns to Jen hoping to see support in her face. She grins with concern and takes his hand. She can see a fierceness in him like something has hit him hard in the face, like he's so bothered he's about to lose it. When he turns back to Dillon he sees him looking into his phone. He tries to choose his words cautiously this time. "I see they take good care of you here, much better than Lexington."

"I can't complain." Dillon is now punching his phone and fidgeting like he's in a hurry to go somewhere.

"I notice you have two-toned dress shoes and straight creases in your slacks, but in Lexington you always wore jeans. Their dress code must be pretty strict around here." Dillon seems to be in his own thoughts. What Carter was saying was going in one ear and out the other.

He keeps punching his phone. "Right, right, and the traffic is much worse here. They got us in the city so..."

"Traffic? I suppose that can be dangerous."

"What more do you want, Carter?" He says this without looking up from his phone.

Carter reaches into a round container sitting on the desk, pulls out a yellow pencil, holds it up into the air, and snaps it in half, causing Dillon to look up surprised. "You must be out of your mind if you think I'm leaving without any kind of an answer."

"It's too bad you can't let this drop. But I'm not your nursemaid, and I don't owe you anything." He turns his gaze on Jen. "You got a pretty woman with you. Why don't you show some responsibility toward her, wait to settle this another time? Your negligence in this matter could cost her, too."

"Negligence! There was a time when you weren't such a fart. It's been awhile, when we were straight out of college. I don't know what infected you, maybe it was the CIA, or maybe you think you got some *great* road lying in front of you. Whatever it is, it's sure turned you into an ass!"

What happens next is over in about a minute. Dillon lunges from his seat shooting halfway across his desk and flinging a fist wildly. Carter meets him with two hands snatching at his throat. The two men fall across the desk, twisting their bodies trying to seize the first thing they get their hands on to strike the other with. While straining to hold onto each other, the container of pens and pencils along with a writing pad and Dillon's coffee go flying, crashing into a wall. They roll one way then the other re-positioning themselves. Their heads are bent down, their foreheads touching, their arms and hands clasping onto the chest of the other. They are so enraged they cannot even utter a word. Suddenly, the door bursts open and the two guards separate them.

"I ought to have your head smashed in!" Dillon shouts. His shirt is ripped at the chest and he has a red mark on his chin. With a superhuman effort, Carter shakes off the guard clinging to him. Breaking loose he backs against the door, pulls the Glock pistol from its holster and aims it at Dillon. All the struggles Carter had dealt with the last few months were now at a crossroads. One of the guards started after him but seeing him point the gun his way he changes his mind. Seeing the guard stop Carter hurried the gun, pointing it back at Dillon.

"I should shoot you right now for what you've done." He was so worked up that it looked like he was going to pull the trigger. Dillon backs up covering his face with his hands. Carter grabs Jen by the hand. "Consider yourself lucky this time." The two back out the door, slamming it shut behind them, and go running down the hall. As soon as they turned into another hallway they are instantly stopped by several security guards and the *wearer of the brown hood.* The guards quickly seize him and get control of the pistol.

When Jen tries to turn around and run she bumps right into the arms of two more guards coming from the other direction, the same guards they had just run away from. Dillon was closely following. "Angela!" he shouts. "You need to put these two in lock up. They're the ones I've been texting you about."

She walks up to Carter and leans in close to him. "You poor man, there is so much mystery in your eyes. If I have them release you, you won't try to run will you?"

"Do I have a choice?"

"Of course not. I need to talk with you. I was hoping you would relax though." She turns, throws up a hand motioning for them to release him. "If you try running we'll just catch you again."

"Where's my grandfather?"

"If I tell you that you'll go and try to bring him back."

"You bet your life I would."

"She shrugs her shoulders. "See what I mean? You're not thinking rationally. If you have questions about Harlan, go ahead, ask."

"Is he safe?"

"Perfectly. You don't have to worry about him. It's not like he's sleeping in a dirty gutter reeking of cats and spoiled food."

"Where *is* he sleeping?"

"It's a small place but it's comfortable and safe. And he's not alone. He has a female companion."

"What!"

"Neither of them knows it just yet, but they're just alike."

"You mean regenerated to youth?"

"That's exactly what I mean."

"Was there a reason you chose them or was it just their age?"

"We quarreled about the selection process for a long time. In the end, we decided they had to be clever people with an unusual sense of observation. If you could have known your grandfather when he was young… his brain is amazing. He has the natural gift of decision making, of always turning in the right direction, of avoiding conflicts that hurt. Did you know he's never been injured in his life, and that includes four years of heavy action in the jungles of Vietnam."

"No, like you said, I never knew him when he was young. How could I?"

"There's a lot of things you don't know about your

grandfather. Having a sense of humor was considered a plus, too. All these senses would be heightened after the regeneration process was complete, and it would help them in coping and seeking out their identical. In time you'll learn more about him, but that should suffice for now. We've been keeping watch over him, but not the girl. They just found each other. It happens."

"You're saying there are others?"

"Yes, we've been successfully regenerating individuals with failing health for several years now."

"What kind of scale are we talking about? The U.S., North America, or is this thing global?"

"I'm not at liberty to answer that."

"Well, I'm sure there's some comprehensive plan involved, a purpose behind this whole project. I'm not looking for an argument, but the implications... surely you can tell me something?"

"I would think the purpose would be obvious."

"Now you're just being condescending."

"Isn't it enough to know that people can be made young again and can live indefinitely?"

"I worry about the ones calling the shots."

"What of it?"

"For starters, who are they? And how many regenerated people are we talking about? Is there some sort of selection lottery involved? I mean, there's a lot of clever, old sick people."

"Are you listening to yourself? You're overthinking this."

"I'm pretty sure it's not possible to overthink something of this magnitude. And what's the Pinnacle? Is that the location where you're keeping him?

"I'm not at liberty to tell you that either." She starts smiling. "They told me you were smart."

"Apparently not smart enough, because I'm getting nothing out of you. Maybe I should go about this from a different angle. What *can* you tell me?"

"I can tell you that I received a message from our leaders yesterday. In it they said, 'They sympathize with those like yourself.' There are other relatives of those whom we have regenerated. They have similar questions to your own. In the future, everything will come out but there is nothing to be said now."

"So that's it then?"

"Yes, Carter, that's it, at least for now." Angela makes a motion with her arm, pointing it behind her. "Do you see those double doors?"

He looks passed her to the far end of the hallway. "Yes."

"Beyond them, you'll find a circular stairwell. At the bottom are doors leading to the outside. You are free to go."

"You're not worried about me going to the police?"

"It wouldn't do you any good. You know very well how this story would sound. You haven't gone to the police yet and you're not going to. You've tried what you thought to do, now your free to go."

Dillon watches as Carter and Jen walk passed Angela. He is still enraged about the altercation and without thinking walks in front of them, blocking their exit. "You owe me an apology."

Carter's head tilts downward slightly. "I already told you once, you should count yourself lucky this time. You got a nice set up here. Maybe you should be satisfied with your 3-story corner room with a view and leave this one alone."

"I don't think so." Dillon starts to make a move when a swiftness from Carter catches him off guard. He takes a fist to the stomach buckling him at the waist and emptying all the breath in his lungs. Before he can respond, Carter smashes him with a right cross to the jaw, splitting the air with the sound of breakage and pummeling him backwards to the floor. He lies there holding his gut, gasping for air.

"You always were a half-wit. You never listen to anyone but yourself." Carter turns back to Angela. "You mind if I have my gun back? I didn't attain it legally, so it cost me triple the money. I won't try anything."

"I'm not worried about that." She turns to the guards. "Give it back."

"Thanks." He places the pistol back in its holster, takes Jen by the hand and glances down as they step over Dillon. "You'd better get up soon dude, I see the graveyard and the pallbearers coming to get you. I think this funeral's over." They now had a clear path leading them to the outside. They walked away with resolute steps, calmly though, as if they were already home.

In the wee hours of the morning, Carter's house sits dark and empty. Only in the small foyer did a tall floor lamp cast its dim light down a long hall, barely touching the other rooms. He was beside himself, wondering if his position at Futurelab Pharmaceuticals would be threatened or if his reputation would suffer from the incident in Tallahassee.

He and Jen plopped down on the sofa, tired from the long drive.

Jen leans her head on Carter's shoulder. "Do you think the news has already spread? I mean..." She yawns. "Do you think they'll fire you?"

"I wish I knew. It doesn't matter though, whatever the cost I've got to find Harlan. I won't stop until I know for certain he's okay."

Another reason for his agitation was that he had once again fallen for Jen. There was something unique about her. Something that made his attraction irreparable. He had no time for romance and yet he found her irresistible in a crazy, desperate kinda way. He could feel her hair against the cheek of his face, could smell her femaleness, could almost taste it. He lay his hand atop her head and started lightly pulling her hair through his fingers. "Intense Auburn?"

"Yes, that's the color."

"I really like the tint, and..." He moves his head downward, kissing her on the lips. Even though she worked at a coffee shop, Carter realized that she was a woman entirely unprejudiced, a woman with views like his own, a woman that would support him no matter how deep he decided to go to find his grandfather, Harlan.

He often thought of the night the two of them met. His car had broken down and he decided to take a cab from Lexington to Danville. When he put his hand on the cab door, her hand fell atop his. When they realized they were going to the same town, they decided to share the ride. There were instant sparks and they started dating. Thinking back on it now caused him to calm down in his mind. The trip to Tallahassee was over. They were both back home and safe.

"You want to get together right now?" she asked. "Don't you?"

"Yes."

She pulls him so close their noses touch. "Me, too."

Chapter 6

Her name was Grace. She had made her appearance without introduction, just sort of took up with Harlan and Danny like a stray dog would have. As a painter of faces she displayed considerable artistic talent and had set up an easel only twenty feet from the hot dog stand. Her production drew in a regular stream of tourists. They seemed to enjoy her warmth and passion, and the odd sense of comedy in her drawings. She had a great deal of softness and color in her personality, and she managed to reflect it in her paintings. For Harlan and Danny, it had seemed easy to become acquainted with her. Soon their relationship had developed into a friendship. She was so easy to be around, so when she had invited them to move into her newly rented beach house they readily accepted. Although it was a fairly expensive house to rent, she could easily afford it with her considerable earnings from her art set up. They had already moved in with her before they noticed her other subtle qualities. Even though she was over-the-top friendly, she had the ability to keep people at a certain distance, like there was another inner world to her life that she wanted kept secret.

One night they noticed an intense light radiating from around the door of her room. When they cracked the door to look, the light was streaming out of her body causing her to shine brightly. She was wearing a two-piece bathing suit, her figure, although glowing, had all the usual human markings. This is when they discovered that she was completely bald. She had been covering her baldness with an expensive, perfectly crafted wig.

Suddenly she turned and took several steps towards them.

She is now only an arms-length out of their reach. There was an observable power coming from her that made it impossible for her to get any closer to them. "Don't be afraid, it's not an illusion. This sometimes happens to me. If I stay this distance, you won't be harmed. We three are friends in the truer and closer sense of the word. All of us are more favored individuals. Tonight is the start of this becoming obvious to you." Her heart and mind flowed out towards them in a way that they could lightly feel physically. As this was taking place the bright light dimmed considerably, and she no longer had to use her vocal cords to speak. Her voice, although different in pitch and power, was emanating from her body more clearly than before.

"I don't mean to scare either of you. What you are experiencing is much more natural than it looks. The vocal box in humans was only meant to be used as a back-up communicator. There are certain areas on earth where the magnetic pull is so great that it interferes with our original means of communication. We have the ability to transmit frequencies much like a short-wave radio, and, of course, to receive them as well. Our brains, although far more advanced than computers, can in a similar way communicate. However, we are chemical in makeup. So instead of needing the use of hardware and software such as computers, everyone is a walking, liquid communication center. This has nothing to do with conjurers or spirit forces. It's simply the original, natural abilities of man.

We have discovered a liquid formula that regenerates humans back to their youth. You, Harlan, a few short months ago, were 75-years old. I hope that explains the dreams and out of ordinary memories you've been having. Danny, you were harder to do background on, but it appears you had great longevity. It is believed that you were 98-years old when we regenerated you back to youth. Sorry about the face in the mirror, it's another side effect that happens to about 15% of the recipients. You both might be surprised to know that Angela, whom you both have met, is 237-years old. She was born on May 1, 1786. In 1863, during the Civil War, she was regenerated. She was already 77-years old at the time. A chemist named James Jenkins happened upon the formula during a research session at Oxford University. He found the formula and a brief explanation along with it inside an old chemistry book. Today, it might even be considered ancient. It dated back to the year 1016, over 1100 years ago. The note was dated only one year later. That was shortly after Mr. Jenkins moved from England to the United States, New York to be exact. That was in 1822. Five years later, he used the formula to regenerate his first human. You both know her. It's me, Grace. I was 72 when I was regenerated making me 263-years of age today.

In recent years, we noticed that we were starting to age, although at a much slower rate than other humans. Something is interfering, we just don't know what. By some experimentation, we discovered that by shaving our heads the aging was slowed down drastically. Apparently our hair takes in the decaying effects of an atmosphere depleted of ozone. But that's only a theory.

I hope some of the things that have been happening to you will now start to make sense. I suppose I should ask if you have any questions for me? Don't hold back. I'll tell you what I can."

"Will the face in the mirror stop tormenting me now?"

"Danny… how can I say this? It's not tormenting you. The face in the mirror is you but at 98-years of age. It's what you looked like before regeneration."

"Wow. I thought it was me in the future. I thought I was somehow looking through time."

"Could I ask a question now?"

"Yes, Harlan. What do you want to know?"

"If you can keep regenerating yourself, why do you need to shave your head?"

"That's a great question. We've found that if one tries to regenerate too quickly, there are serious complications. Deformities can occur and some have died. Regenerating intervals need to be a minimum of fifty-years apart. It works better if it's a longer interval. Anything less than fifty-years starts to get dangerous. If we shave our heads, the aging process is only about one-tenth the rate of other humans. Actually, it's a little less. Otherwise, it's closer to a fifth or 20-percent. What that means is all regenerated ones remain extremely young-looking."

Danny moves her hand toward Grace. "Can I touch you? You're not glowing as much as you were earlier."

"You may. You can't be harmed now."

"It's much dimmer now, but I can still see it. How can skin give off light?"

"Its sort of like the science behind effervescence or the bubbles coming from sparkling wine. There is an enormous amount of electricity in our bodies. This electricity is in a constant state of growth because it feeds on the earth's natural electrical properties. When it reaches certain levels, a chemical reaction takes place between our bodies and the atmosphere. This reaction releases excess electricity in the form of white light. Sometimes it is accompanied by other lights, varied in color. This especially happens when the regenerating process is active or when we release adrenaline. This also tends to make the skin glow. The regenerating process is like a vegetable plant bursting out of the ground. At first, it is nicely formed but with much growth and many changes to take place. In a few months, it's all complete, so too with regeneration."

"I have another question."

"Sure, Harlan."

"A little over two weeks ago, we met Angela at the pool of a high-rise hotel. She was wearing a brown hood and there were others like her. Were they all regenerated?"

"Yes. I was one of them."

"What about the men with them? They had hair; it was spiked."

"The hair was fake."

"How many more are there like you, and..." He glances at Danny. "And like us?"

"We are alike. Let me be clear about that. The sudden emergence of youth is just new to you two, that's all. You'll get used to it soon. I promise. As to how many? I can't be sure.

I'm not privy to that kind of information. I do know that for many years the numbers were purposely kept low. Until a few years ago there were only twenty-five per year regenerated. The total count across the whole earth was still well under three thousand when we consider the ones who died from early regeneration. Harlan, Danny, you two are part of a project designed to eventually populate the earth with our kind. As to the numbers involved, I'm sure there must be a goal to fill. I was told it was a ten-year plan, but I think recently that has changed. Sorry, I wish I could tell you more about that. I'm doing the best I can to answer your questions."

Again, Harlan glances at Danny. "It's okay. We understand. I would like to know 'why now?' I mean if you don't mind, why after all these years do you suddenly wanna fill the earth with... *our kind*? If that's the right way to say it."

"*Our kind* is a good way to say it. We took a vote, Harlan, all regenerated ones. It had to do with wanting more friendship with our own kind, to reduce loneliness for our kind and the subsequent lack of intimacy with our kind."

"Why couldn't other humans fill the same needs?"

"To a degree, they can. However,..." She reaches out touching Harlan on the face with the palm of her hand. She gives a small amount of pressure, and he can feel a tingling sensation. All at once he can see not only her but also what she sees. He sees his face as she sees it alongside her own face. "We are much more than other humans, Harlan. Our brains are closer to perfection. As you said, we are our own kind."

"That's amazing."

"Yes, and there's much more for you to experience. Can you see why we want to regenerate more of our own kind? Why we desire that kind of companionship."

"I do now."

"We also want to curb or stop death one day. Have you noticed your vision improving, your strength increasing, your touch, sense of smell and hearing all have been heightened?"

Danny wraps her hands around Harlan's arm. "He picked up a man twice his size to protect me. Is that what you mean?"

"You probably don't realize it yet, Danny, but you have

the same powers. All regenerated ones can lift five-times their weight. They can see with clarity ten-times farther, can smell many times better than a bear, hear better than dogs, can feel the miniscule imperfections in a flat sheet of paper. Man was originally much more than he is today."

Harlan moves his hand atop Danny's. "Incredible. What happened? How did man lose these abilities?"

"He still has them. They're just not as pronounced. We're not sure, but we think it has to do with the reason man ages. Something happened a long time ago that started that horrible process. We still haven't completely solved it. We can regenerate and drastically slow the aging, but we're not very close to eliminating it. Truth be told, we don't have a clue as to how to stop it."

"Can you regenerate someone from the dead?"

"No, Danny. We can only make someone who is old, young again."

"Could you tell us more about our capabilities?"

"Yes. Did you have anything specific in mind?"

"Can we pick things up with our brain, without using our hands?"

Harlan shakes his head simultaneously giving her a slight shove. "Be serious."

"It's okay, Harlan. I don't mind. Not usually, Danny. However, if we are threatened and our adrenaline spikes very high, then all bets are off as to what we can do. The energy being released at that point is so high that we can do a lot of impressive things. It's not levitating. It's just the release of a superabundance of energy. Under normal circumstances, when we are calm, our brains need a connection, and that comes through touch. Generally, we pick things up the way everyone does, but we can handle much heavier weights with ease. However, if we experience an adrenaline rise while touching an object or something connected to the object, the subsequent energy being released will easily move it. If our mind is focused, we can maneuver the object in the direction we desire. So, if we are being assaulted by an animal or person and our adrenaline kicks in, we can safely defend ourselves even if we are not able to physically move them. It may appear that we are levitating something, but like I said it's only the energy being released.

Something to keep in mind is this: anything that is a conductor of electricity tends to increase our energy. For example, if you're leaning against a metal object you will be able to lift even more weight or see even greater distances. All your senses will be heightened beyond their normal functions. You'll have to learn to be careful because compared to others you are super-human. People will learn about you soon enough, don't give yourself away by letting them see your capabilities. Do you have any more questions?"

"I have one more at least for now."

"What is it, Harlan?"

"Our families, where are they? Are they close by? Are they concerned about our disappearance?"

"The safest way to answer that is your memories are telling you the truth. I will try to elaborate. You first, Harlan. Your wife died nearly ten-years ago, and you have been living alone in the same house ever since. I'm not at liberty to tell you where right now. You may try to go back home and for obvious reasons that could cause problems. Your memories in time will answer all your questions. You also have two daughters, one who still lives in your hometown, and one who lives in Canada. You had a son too, but he was tragically killed by a drunk driver twenty-five years ago. You have a grandson by him who also lives in your hometown. Your daughters know nothing about your regeneration. Your grandson, on the other hand, knows a great deal about it. He even saw you afterwards, before you lost your memory and we ended up bringing you here. That's about the extent of my knowledge when it comes to your history.

Danny, I'm sorry to have to tell you this, but our records of your regeneration were not handled properly, which is not like us. It appears we took you from a nursing home. The only records we could gain access to showed that you hadn't had a visitor in over seven-years. That was from a great-granddaughter who, as far as we know, is still alive. Don't blame her though. During the last eight years of your life, you couldn't communicate with anyone. You were bed-ridden and had to be taken care of head-to-toe.

So, you see, what you two are experiencing is what everyone who grows old wants: a second chance at life."

Early the next day, about eleven o'clock Harlan and Danny barely hear a voice calling to them from behind. They are walking pass several of the beach-front shops while the voice repeats their names more than once. When they turn to look they notice a gentleman advanced in years, walking with a cane. His face has that hard, grizzled look of experience. Due to his age, they feel sympathy for him and stop.

He quickly motions for them to enter one of the beach-front shops, which, upon seeing no danger in him, they do. He pulls them to a corner where racks that spin are covered in trinkets for tourists. Leaning close to them he rests his hands on the ebony top of his walking cane. His eyes have a startled, half-frightened gleam to them as he starts to speak. "You two have the responsibility to speak out!"

Both Harlan and Danny are surprised by the authority in his voice.

"You absolutely have to confess your situation. By God if you don't, a lot of people are going to suffer… are going to die!"

Harlan places his hand on the man's shoulder. "What are you talking about old-timer?"

The old man looks nervously around the shop, then out the window to the street and back. "You mean you haven't figured it out yet." Raising one of his hand's palm up he begins gesturing emphatically. "Listen closely. The responsibility of man lies greatly with you two. We are at a crossroads in human existence. They have us on a pathway." Next he bends his head down, almost as if in silent prayer. "My time is almost over." He holds his hands farther out away from his body looking them over. "Do you see what they've done to me." Tilting his head up again he continues. "Notwithstanding how I am now, how god-awful I must look to you. I am a man who you *must* take seriously. Only one week ago, I was every bit as young as you." He slowly buckles forward holding his stomach and coughing. "I'm sure I was seen... They must have slipped something in my drink or maybe my food." He goes down to his knees, wheezing, straining to breathe, but continues talking. "All regenerated ones were at a meeting... deciding our future. Specifically, whether to increase the number of those we regenerate each year. There were also other things on the agenda, but not as important. I was one of twelve on a panel of oversight. Because of that I had information that others didn't. There were other things they were planning that I was completely against." The old man grunts with pain then falls over on his side.

Harlan and Danny immediately kneel next to him.

Even though he is weak he continues in a whisper forcing out the words. "Can you hear me? Do you...understand?"

Harlan gently guides him from his side to his back. "You're sick. Let us get you some help?"

"No. It's too late." He grabs Harlan by the t-shirt. "Listen to me. The eliminating and repopulating humans on the earth I fought them on it. They're going to allow humans that are eighty and above to gradually die off. However, unless you're chosen, if you are under eighty they are going to infect you with a formula that will age you dramatically within a week's time. It's what they did to me." He coughs hard, shakes violently and then lies silent and motionless.

Harlan takes him by the wrist, checking his pulse. He shakes his head to Danny. "He's gone. We better not hang around here. Neither of us has I.D."

She turns Harlan's face with her hand, looking him straight in the eyes. "What do you make of him? Do you believe his story?"

"I don't know, Danny. I do think there's more to this regeneration thing than we've been told."

Chapter 7

(The Year of 1827)

When Grace Mitchel woke it took a moment for her to adjust to the brightness of the room. She lay quietly in a large, unfamiliar bed watching particles of dust hang almost motionless in the iridescent atmosphere of her small accommodations. She pushed herself up slowly and carefully, bewildered by the strangeness of her surroundings. It was cold in the room, and a ray of light reflected off the wall beside her. It was bouncing off the backside of a neighboring building and shooting through the window. She thrust her hand up out of irritation and to soften the effect the sharp light was having on her eyes. When she did this she could sense a vigor that had not been with her in many years. Her mind felt sharp, and her body no longer ached with fatigue or constriction in her chest. For longer than she could remember there had been physical discomfort after awakening from sleep, but this time there was absolutely none.

Even though she felt a freshness, a comfort penned somehow within the confines of her body, still, she wondered about the situation she had stumbled into. There was corresponding mental anguish because she hadn't a clue where she was or how she came to be here.

As the worry was beginning to build in her, she noticed that there was the smell of cooking penetrating the bottom of the door. While sniffing and looking in that direction, the door opened and a man wearing a hat and tie, carrying a tray, came walking in. His hair was a milky gray and matched almost imperceptibly with the tones of his skin. His face looked a little swollen, and his eyes cradled a good bit of tension and worry in them.

He glances at Grace. "How do you feel?" His tone was one of seriousness.

"I feel fine. Who are you?"

"We'll get to that soon. I promise. Would you like some tea, and I have sandwiches? You need to eat. It's been days. I think you'll like them. I cooked the chicken myself."

She raises her hand up to take the tea. "What did you mean by days?"

"I'll just come out and tell you. You've been sleeping for three days."

"I know I've been over-tired, but I can hardly sleep through the night without waking up five or six times."

"All the same, you did sleep for three days."

"I remember now. You brought me here didn't you, in a carriage? Did I have a nervous attack?"

"You were not well, but it wasn't a nervous attack."

"Well then, I'm glad you brought me here." She reaches for a sandwich and starts eating. It was a relief to her when she saw him walk over to the fireplace. She wanted the room to be warm.

After kneeling in front of the logs, he turns to her. "I hope this doesn't alarm you." Suddenly there is a spark, and he holds a small fire in his hand. "It's called a wooden match. A chemist friend of mine, John Walker, invented them." He places the match at the base of the logs where a small grouping of kindling is piled

"That's amazing. How does it work?"

"It's fairly simple really. When the match is dragged along a striking surface, the mixture of sand and powdered glass causes friction and heat, which is enough to convert some of the red phosphorus to white phosphorus, a chemical so volatile that it ignites in the air." He stands up and walks to the side of the bed next to her. "It's good to see you eating. I was afraid you would wake up weak and lethargic."

"Just the opposite really, I feel better than I have since… since I can remember is all. I should have tried sleeping for three days straight a long time ago. I'm done eating now. I would like to get cleaned up and dressed."

"Of course." He turns to leave, then turns back around. "I'll be just outside the door."

"Are you going to tell me who you are before you leave?"

"If you like, yes. My name is James Jenkins. I'm a chemist residing here in New York. There might be a couple of other things I should tell you before you get out of that bed and see yourself in the mirror."

"Well, what are you waiting for James Jenkins?"

He hesitates to answer, and she can see him peering deep into her face. "I'm waiting for the right words, I suppose. Let me start by saying, you were ill when I brought you here."

"Yes, well you've already told me that now haven't you?"

"You're not going to make this easy, are you? Yes, anyway like I said you were ill but not ill in the usual way. You were simply over-worked. I was surprised to find out that you were working for a colleague of mine and at seventy-two years of age. Housework and cooking, sometimes even helping with the yard-work. You blacked out one day, working over a hot stove. Later, you told me that you had no choice. You had to keep working to take care of yourself. You have no relatives other than a niece in New Orleans who never corresponds. That's when I decided on you. I had been looking for a subject for an experiment. The experiment would not cause any harm, at least not to my knowledge, but could help the subject in a considerable way. By considerable, I mean... life-altering. Miss Grace, I brought you here under the pretense that I was going to inject you with an herb-infused revitalizing formula. What I didn't tell you was the formula had other chemical properties, and that it would do much more than give you energy and a more youthful appearance. I think this is the point where I ask you to stand up and take a look in the mirror."

"Are you serious?"

"I am. Please, look in the mirror."

Grace plants her feet on the floor, stands and walks to a large mirror attached to a dresser. Just before she reaches it she glances mysteriously at James, then sways her body slowly, moving it in a circular motion towards the mirror. Traumatized by what she sees, she jumps back as if she is in shock. "How can this be? You're a spook. You're a spook that's done killed me and brought me back to life!"

"No, Miss Grace, please, you must not use words like that. Quite to the contrary, I've saved your life by regenerating you back to your youth."

Stepping forward and leaning in towards the mirror she pulls her once gray but now shiny long blonde hair back away from her face. "But that's not possible."

"Until five years ago, I would have been in complete agreement with you. But you can see it clearly for yourself."

She starts a careful examination of her face by rubbing her hands over her cheeks and pulling at the skin. "By God, I'm young again. It's really me, only fifty years younger. Only the hand of God could do this."

"I'm not God, Miss Grace, neither am I a spook. I'm just a chemist and… well come to think of it, I guess there is more to it than that."

Grace turns from the mirror, gazing at him. "Would you care to elaborate on that?"

"Are you sure you want to do this now? You said you wanted to get cleaned up and dressed."

"You're not leaving this room until you've given me an explanation."

"Right. I'll get to it then. Maybe you should sit down first. Would you like some more tea?" He reaches for the tray, re-fills her cup and walks it over to her.

She dips her head in thanks. "Go on. I'm waiting."

"Let me make something clear to start with. At first, all we thought we were looking for was a panacea for all physical disorders. Doctors and chemists have been searching for that since… since forever I suppose. I didn't realize I was about to stumble onto the actual elixir of life. Something of this magnitude…something that…" He turns his hand over, palm up, and moves it toward her as if pointing. "Something that could do this. Although there had been some speculation, and some talk based on some old documentation, none of us knew it existed. I say none of us but there is a little more to this part of the story that I'll get around to telling you later.

When I first came upon the formula as part of my investigation, it was scribbled into the pages of an old chemistry book. The book itself was covered by stacks of others at Oxford University. Afterward, in the solitude of my own room I did some serious contemplation of what I had just discovered. A note scribbled with the formula told specifically what it could do. I knew I had found what I was looking for because it bore the initials SRL, which stood for Solomon Ray Lett. It also bore his formula marking LLF, which stood for Lett's Life Formula. And, of course, the formula itself which is quite long. This was exactly what our documentation told us to look for.

Very soon I realized that keeping hidden what I had just discovered was of utmost importance. The implications of the discovery could not begin to be calculated. I moved away from England on the flimsy pretext that I needed a change. Soon after I began experimenting with the formula. My first test subject was an old orange cat. At first, I thought it was going to die because it wouldn't wake up. After my second experiment on another cat, I realized that being asleep for three days was just part of the process. My first two experiments were a complete success. From the beginning, I've never had a failure, which includes dozens of animals, mostly cats and dogs. Now I'm thrilled to say that success includes a human subject. You, Grace, are the first human to be regenerated back to youth. I hope you understand the significance of what's happened to you, and that it needs to be kept a secret. You can't even entertain the thought of... well you can't talk about this to anyone other than me."

"Why did you wait so long?"

"I'm not sure I understand your question?"

"To try it on a person, why so long? You waited for five years."

"I had worries. I've had them all along. Still do."

"I should think you would be over those by now." Grace

sets her cup on the dresser, spins in a complete circle, smiles, and curtsies. "Can't you see how I've turned out? Stop the worryin. I'm nearly perfect."

"Yes, you are beautiful. Truth is though, it's not you that I'm worried about."

"Then what?"

Turning around, James leans his back against the dresser, moves one shoe so close to the other that they touch, and crosses his arms. "This is the part of the story I was hoping I would never actually have to tell you about."

"And yet here we are."

"Here we are. Grace, I hope you won't think the worst of me, but when I was much younger I made some decisions without giving them much thought beforehand. When I was about thirty years old I was approached by a couple of mates from my university days. What I'm trying to say is… I used to be a member of a secret society. They recruited me for a few weeks, using my educational background as their reason for interest in me. To be specific, my doctorate in chemical engineering and biomolecular engineering. Soon after I was a member of a team searching for a link to some documents we had in our possession. According to these ancient documents there was a powerful formula stashed in the pages of a book. After working with this group for a little over two years, my disdain for them grew and we eventually went our separate ways without ever unearthing the book.

The reason for my growing disdain was that gradually I began to understand the ulterior motive of this society. As is often the case, money was at the center of their push to find the formula. As I mentioned earlier I think, we thought the formula would be a cure for all types of medical problems, a true panacea for physical ailments. Proceeds made from the sale of products, the ensuing windfall of money would inevitably be used to finance other priorities, many of them political in nature.

It was many years later and I had all but forgotten about the book and hidden formula when I bumped into one of my mates from the research team. We were at a pub, and he was a little wasted; one thing led to another and he started talking. They had as much given up on finding the book, and due to a lack of funding, their numbers had dwindled severely. Later that week I decided to pick up where I left off all those years ago.

After searching in my spare time for nine months, I was looking down into the pages of a book containing the formula. Until now, here seeing you, it was the best moment of my life.

Grace, I don't want you to think that you must stay here, but I was hoping you would. I need help, someone to watch over me while I regenerate myself. Then there's the question of regenerating others, which I fully intend to do. How many? How often? Where would they be housed? All of these are just some of the questions we would need to work out. That is if you're willing to stay. You don't have to decide now. A decision like this needs time to think about. Would you do that, Grace?"

"It's the least I can do, James, for the absolute wonder of what you've done for me. How soon were you thinking?"

"How soon?"

"Yes, how soon before you regenerate yourself?"

"That depends on you. If you're willing to stay then I'll make the needed arrangements within a day or two."

"Then make them."

"Are you sure?"

"I have virtually no family, and even if I did they wouldn't recognize me. Make the arrangements. I'm not going anywhere. Besides, you've been most generous to me. Perhaps you don't realize how I feel about that. My memory is coming back more and more so I know you've incurred expenses on my behalf. You brought me here after my collapse from exhaustion. Took care of me head-to-toe until I had recovered. And now this? Allowing me to stay, to have a part in this astonishing... what's it called? Transformation? The regeneration of people? I will never forget your kindness. Thank you for making me young again."

"If you're going to stay here there are some things I need to discuss with you. But there's plenty of time for that. Right

92

now, you need to get cleaned up and dressed. I took the liberty of buying a few new things for you. There are clothes and shoes more attune to your age bracket in the closet, and... a few other things in the dresser drawer. Then I would like you to spend some time outside in the sun. The weather's good so at least an hour. It will be good for you. We can talk more about this in the evening."

Words refused to shape themselves, so Grace stood silent. She nods in agreement and can scarcely suppress the smile his seeming devotion has provoked. The smile grows so emphatically that she looks like a spray of sunshine hovering there in the natural light of the room.

He tips his hat, turns and walks out, closing the door behind him.

Emerging later in the day from the dimming sunshine outside, Grace walks inside the house. She had leisurely enjoyed a nearby park for the better part of the afternoon staying outdoors for nearly three hours. Although at present she did not see James, she soon heard sounds coming from the kitchen. She was happy, and so sprung the door open to see what he was up to. To her surprise, it was not James, but another man older in years fumbling with the icebox. "Who are you, sir?"

Upon his immediate turning around he snatches an ivory topped walking cane propped against the icebox. "Never mind that," he grumbles loudly. "Who the devil are you? And where's Mr. Jenkins?"

"Why does it matter to you who I am?"

He beats his cane three times on the floor. "Consider this an emergency that could do you harm, Miss." His hand swings back and along with it the flap of his overcoat revealing a .50 caliber flintlock musket pistol. "I'll ask you again, Miss. Who are you and where is Mr. Jenkins?"

"Do you plan to do me harm?"

"If you don't answer my questions, yes."

"The only reason I'm going to answer questions from a stranger is that you're threatening me."

His hand slides back again, this time coming to rest atop

the musket. "You darn fool. You'll have me kill you won't you?"

"That's not necessary, sir. My name is Grace Mitchel. I only just came from walking in the park, so I'm not sure where Mr. Jenkins is off to. I *can* tell you he was here earlier, but that's been near three hours now."

"You're a young one. What would you be doing here? You his kin or something?"

Grace quickly dips her head. "Why yes, sir, how clever of you to guess. You are looking at his great-grandniece. My mother insisted I stay here while she travels to England on business."

"Shouldn't your father be doing that?"

"No sir, not since he died in the war of 1812. I was only seven at the time. My mother has handled our affairs quite admirably ever since."

The cane sends a whizzing sound through the air as he whips it up, pointing it at her face. "Tell James old Jack was here. Tell him I'll be back tomorrow at this same time. Tell him that he darned well better be here."

"Don't you worry, sir, I'll be giving him the message as soon as he returns home."

In a move that startles her, old Jack cracks the floor with the cane so hard that an echo shoots through the room. "I'm not worried, Miss Grace. If he decides to run, my men will catch him soon enough. And I'm going to do some digging about. I suspect you've been lying to me about your relationship with him. I don't recall James ever had the first brother or sister, which would make you a deceiver or an apparition. One of those I can't stand, the other I don't believe in. But maybe it's just my memory going bad on me. I'm getting pretty darn old. If you do happen to be lying to me," he taps his side. "I wouldn't be here tomorrow when I show back up. I might be tempted to use this musket."

Not twenty minutes after old Jack had left, Grace hears footsteps in the Hall outside her room. She holds her breath, listening intently to the steps coming closer to her door and then the subsequent knocking.

"Grace, are you there?"

The voice brought her instant relief. It was James. After sighing, her breathing started up normal again. She stands up from a make-up desk where she had been gazing at her new face and applying minimal amounts of makeup. "You may enter." Her voice was soft but loud enough to be heard without effort.

When the door swung open his appearance gave her a subtle encouragement. His elegant familiarity even building in her a small amount of confidence.

"I'm glad your back." Although she was trying to smile, her face gave evidence that something had upset her. It was reflecting the harrowing experience old Jack had put upon her.

James rubs his chin while staring at her. "Is everything okay? Do you feel alright?"

"I'm fine. You had a visitor is all."

"Visitor? But I never have visitors."

"You did today, and not a nice one either."

"Did he leave a name?"

"He said to tell you old Jack was here."

Paleness along with confusion instantly creeps over James' face. He walks straight to the bed and sits on the edge of it peering downward. "Grace I hate to have to tell you this...the situation, it's... we should pack some things and leave here tonight." When he looks up he sees her shaking her head no.

"He said if you run his men would catch you."

"At some point, yes, but what else can I do? He's after the formula, and if he thinks I've got, it he'll stop at nothing to get it."

"If you run he'll know for sure you have it. I've known men like him before. He's vulgar and makes claim to anything he pleases. When he tracks you down he'll be your judge and executioner. That walking stick will be his judge's gavel."

"Walking stick?"

"He walks with a cane. You didn't know?"

"I haven't seen him in years."

"Well, he does."

"I've got a good deal of money. Maybe I could just buy him off."

"He'll just take your money *and* the formula. You must lie, and you must do a darn good job of it. Haven't you ever made up a story to... I don't know... keep yourself from embarrassment?"

"I can't say that I have."

"Well, I have, more times than I can count. He needs to see that you have absolutely nothing to hide. Have refreshments waiting when he arrives. Act surprised and happy to see him. Shake his hand hardily, like you would after seeing a friend after many years. When he brings up the formula, start brooding over your failure. Tell him you've thought about giving it another try. You have to be all in, or he'll know."

"So, you think it will work?"

"You know him better than I do, but as I've tried to make clear, the alternative is not good. Yes, I think we have a chance to pull it off."

"That's it then. We'll use the trick of deception on old Jack." He slips off the bed. "You understand what could happen if we fail?"

She places her hand over the top of his. Her emphatic nod is all the response needed.

"Then we had better prepare our stories. If we're to make this work they have to match in every tiny detail."

Again, she nods without speaking.

It was already a full hour later than when Jack showed the day before. The waiting is nerve racking. James and Grace hear the door to the house fling open, and the sound of a cane progressively taps nearer to them on the floor.

Grace's eyes lock onto James. "When he enters the room, stand up quickly, and for God's sake smile. You look as though you've seen a ghost, James. This is the moment of truth."

"You are quite right, Grace. Yes, don't worry. I'm prepared."

When old Jack enters the room there are two rather large Italians with him. One with a face pushed in as if it has been smashed by a boxer's glove, and one with a scar running from his left eye down to his cheek.

James springs to his feet smiling and making a gesture with his arms like he can't believe his eyes and wants to give old Jack a hug.

"We'll dispense with all the showy display, James. Sit your butt down right now before I have my men do it for you. We never were that close, so stop acting like your happy to see me."

"But I always thought we..." James sits back down. "At least we parted ways amicably enough."

"That's your opinion. If I had a do-over on the whole thing again, I might not let you off so easily."

James points to a small service table that sits between the two men. "I took the liberty of having vodka and tonic ready. If my memory serves me I believe it's your favorite. And I have cheese and crackers, and..."

"Pour me two fingers, no, make it four and skip the tonic."

After James hands him the drink he immediately downs it, shoving the glass back at him.

"One more, four fingers again." He downs the second as quick as the first and his eyes suddenly turn bloodshot. The vodka was having the effect of giving old Jack an even stronger will. "I'll come right to it, I want the formula and any other research you've done along with it."

James had been pouring himself a drink. He takes a sip then holds the glass up staring into it. "After all these years I still feel bad about that. My failing the whole group, and then I just couldn't do it anymore. Lately, I've been thinking about giving it another try." He swishes his glass and takes another sip.

"While I appreciate your seeming misery over it, I think you should know something before you carry on with the lies. I've had you watched the past year. You've been doing experimentation with animals, injecting them with a greenish-blue liquid."

"But that's just a potion of mine to immune them from fleas."

97

"The reports I've received tell a different story. Old cats suddenly full of vigor, acting young again. Seems impossible I know, but that's what's been happening inside the walls of this house, your house. How long have you had the formula?"

"You really think I have the formula?" He points to a sofa next to Grace. "Why don't you and your men have a seat."

Old Jack turns looking at Grace. "You know I wouldn't mind that, wouldn't mind that one bit. Not my men though. You understand don't you Jack. They need to keep an eye on things in case you got something up your sleeve. You're not going to try anything, are you, James?"

"Why would I do that?"

"Good. We understand each other." Old Jack walks over to the sofa, sitting on the side of it nearest Grace. "I've not been married in years, but if I ever did do it again, I'd want my wife to make other women feel small. I'd want her to make a plain white dress look as if she were wearing a crown. You, my dear, are of that sort." He reaches his hand out placing it atop her knee. "I know I must look vulgar to you, but if I ever did marry again, my wife would want for nothing." He pauses a moment, then removes his hand and turns his eyes back to James. "For the past few weeks you've had an older woman staying here. She has not been seen in four days now." He glances at Grace a split second, then back to James. "Her name coincidentally is Grace Mitchel. You care to elaborate?"

"I would think it would be obvious." James holds his hand out pointing at Grace. "They are the same person." He starts laughing, then turns up his drink finishing it off. "Grace is my niece. The woman you saw is her mother. She has gone abroad for a few months."

"No, James. I think your first explanation is the truer one. Years ago, there was speculation about what the formula could really do. You remember don't you, James? We discussed it at length one day. Some of our documentation hinted that the formula could restore a person's youth again. It used the word regeneration. Of course, at the time we concluded that it could only mean a person's physical appearance." He looks back at Grace. "How does it feel to be young again?"

She stands up straightening her dress at the knees. "It feels great. Then again I haven't a clue what it feels like to be old."

"You're a smooth one. I'll give you that. You can cut the bull now, both of you. The evidence speaks for itself. You and the old woman are indeed the same. And you, James, have done a lot of work for me. I want to thank you for that. Really, I mean it from the depths of my heart. Now give me the formula or this thing gets ugly starting now!"

"I don't have what you're asking for."

"I could have my men tear this place apart, but I have a feeling it would get us nowhere. So instead, I'll just take Grace with me. If you don't present me with the formula by this time tomorrow, she dies. Grace needn't worry right, James? You wouldn't let that happen, surely." Old Jack motions with his head and one of his men snatches her by the wrist. His grip is so hard that her wrist starts turning purple.

She jerks her arm trying to break free. "You're hurting me. Let me go!"

Old Jack makes another motion, and the man squeezes even harder. "See what you've done, James? The poor girl, or should I say, old woman."

Grace jerks her arm again but to no avail. However, this time a strange thing starts to happen. There is an energy propelling her other hand through the air, palm open into the man's chest. When she makes contact there is an immediate flash of white that bursts out from her body, like illuminated grains of sugar swirling and encompassing all the space around the man. The white energy is swirling, moving her hand upwards, and the man lifts off the floor powerless to resist. Grace's eyes widen and faintly glow as massive amounts of energy come streaming out of her. The energy is characterized by a quickly developing white ring broadening and encircling the two of them. She is experiencing a powerful quickening sensation and so easily brings back her wrist that the man had previously been squeezing. She recoils the hand back to her side. However, her other hand is involuntarily attached to the man's chest. Although she supports well over two hundred pounds with one hand, there is absolutely no strain anywhere in her body. The white ring now becomes an outer ring as a second more colorful ring develops. The first white illumination is now suddenly being pushed outward, forming a giant white sphere. The newer ring is growing brighter with green and reddish-blue illumination. While the outer ring begins to soften, becoming a duller almost muted glow of white, still, this outer ring is now encompassing everyone in the room. At the same time the inner, colorful ring radiates dramatic energy, its colors varying, mixing blues, reds, greens in a constant state of flux. At this point the man Grace is holding into the air is starting to shake violently.

Old Jack pulls his musket and without hesitation aims it at Grace and lets it fire. The musket ball blasts unabated through the outer white ring. When it penetrates the second inner colorful ring it instantly stops and hovers like a firefly hanging solitaire in the dead of night. The room falls silent as everyone watches the musket ball floating and glowing inside the translucent energy. After a moment it falls straight down bouncing off the wooden floor, rolling and coming to rest at the feet of old Jack. When it contacts his shoe he is startled, swings his arm back and throws his musket at Grace. When the pistol hits the inner ring, a burst of energy sends it flying backward's in the direction it came from.

The musket catches old Jack in the head, opening a huge gash, knocking him out, and sending him spiraling downward to the hard, wooden floor.

Chapter 8

(19th-Century Tallahassee)

The moonlight touched them across their shoulders as they stepped up to the carriage. They hesitated before climbing aboard turning instead towards a streetlamp, where a man stood twirling a walking stick in one hand. Upon seeing Grace and James staring at him, he bends his head down a little, touching the top of his hat with the ivory head of his stick in a gesture of goodbye. When he did this his face came out of a shadow into the light, identifying him as a much younger version of old Jack. Beneath the streetlamp he pulls at a chain attached to his trousers, looks at his watch, which says ten o'clock, then turns, slowly disappearing into the dark.

After his departure the regenerated couple step up into the carriage, carrying with them abilities and youthfulness that are astounding.

"How long do you think, before he figures it out?" Grace asked while taking James' hand into her own. She was looking up at the stars, a group of them shone brightly while taking possession of the night sky.

"I've given him steps that are time-consuming and ...confusing. He's so full of himself that he'll keep trying. He's not thinking at all or suspecting anything. He thinks the world revolves only around him. Probably after a few months he'll realize he's been tricked, but it doesn't matter. The formula's safe, and so are we.

No one will ever think to look for us in Tallahassee. Ralph Waldo Emerson recently called it a grotesque piece of land. It's just that it's still a little wild is all. Reports are that it's full of beautiful rolling hills and has ample sources of water. Because of these attractions, it's become the destination for several. Northern planters from the areas of Virginia, Georgia, North and South Carolina have arrived in considerable numbers. Some of these have already started up cotton and sugar plantations, and it's only going to continue. There's still a large Native American population, but it's been near ten years since General Andrew Jackson fought those two skirmishes against the Seminoles. It's known to harbor runaway slaves, but I think it's ready to grow into a real town. I like the thought of growing up with the frontier capital of Florida. It's not a state but that's only a matter of time. They've had territorial status for six years now. They're entering a new period, a new beginning, and, Grace, so are we."

James' voice fell silent as the horse-drawn carriage moved briskly over the brick streets of a city just starting to slumber. The young couple sat quietly, watching the tranquil splendor of the moon. The carriage crept closer to the bustling and famous New York harbor, where they had booked passage to the city of Saint Augustine. From there they would travel by coach to Tallahassee. The things in their possession were not many. They brought only their clothes, a few toiletries, the formula, and themselves. Everything else could be replaced upon arrival.

They could not have been more pleased or displeased six weeks later after getting situated. The stories about the beauty of the surrounding areas were true. The land was softly rolling, the vegetation colorful, lush and bright, and the soil was next to perfect for growing. Farm animals were easily available, in good health, and affordable. However, the town itself was nothing more than a heap of unfinished boards and Georgia red clay bricks. Newer, more polished buildings were just starting to pop up, but it was obvious that it would take another ten years before this town would look like a real city.

The boarding house where they settled didn't give a good first impression either. Its walls needed whitewashing, and the living room and front porch were still littered with dishes from a sizable, enthusiastic gathering of people. From the ceilings hung red glitter and green illuminated masks leftover from the new celebration called Mardi Gras. A good deal of the house showed signs of the party, pointing out that efforts to clean it had been neglected. There was a rather large contingent living here from New Orleans and they had rented the place for the event a week earlier.

At night there were snatches of band music that would float through the streets, creeping into any open windows. Unfortunately keeping windows shut at night was not an option due to the heat, so Grace quickly learned to hang cheesecloth over the openings to keep the immense number of bugs out. Behind the boarding house were two unkempt dusky gardens. In between them was a pretty stream good for sitting, listening and meditating, or for reading.

The area hadn't progressed as far into peace and solitude as they had expected. But this was the world, the time and place. This was 1827, take it or leave it, Tallahassee. James and Grace decided to take it and to make the best of it.

In no time, James had met a man through the Mercantile Association and contracted him to build a two-story, six-bedroom house on a five-thousand-acre tract of property he had purchased. The land was part of the fields the Seminole Indians had abandoned years before after their battle with General Andrew Jackson. Plans for a capitol building and other government buildings were already on the drawing boards at an adjacent location. James and Grace would soon have plenty of space for a new facility to regenerate and temporarily house more people.

For a year Grace watched James almost unbearable gaze. He was overseeing the construction, fumbling around, and walking back and forth with such determination that at times he appeared to be fleeing. After leaving New York what remained of his pride was solely focused on his justification for his work. The workers began to regard him as someone who knew the construction trade well. Part of this was his attire which usually consisted of suit and tie, making him appear several years older. Another reason was his demeanor.

'Come here' was a regular phrase of his, as he pointed out changes or intricate details he wanted to be done to the house. He fired more men than he allowed to stay and work. When it was all done he had exactly what he had envisioned, a place to live that would double as a facility to work in.

Afterward, he was overseeing the construction of a barn and lean-to when Grace shouted from the steps of their new house. "James come over here." She had purchased several rocking chairs and wanted help lining them up on the porch. When he moved in her direction his approach was slow like a man brooding or possibly in the middle of some sort of desperate calculation. She noticed this about him, and that he wasn't looking at her. When he finally reached the porch, she was growing concerned. "Will you sit down, we have chairs now, and I've made lemonade. We don't have any ice, but I have an ice-box coming from the Mercantile later today. They tell me they have ice delivery once a week, or twice weekly if we like. It's too far out for daily delivery but…"

James puts his hand up to her mouth and abruptly stops her from talking. He seems to know exactly what he's doing. "There's a preacher here. I asked about him a few days ago, and he already has come to see me."

She moves his hand away. "What are you trying to tell me, James Jenkins?"

He watched her push her long blonde hair behind her ears. Her eyes watched him too. "I got something," he said backing down the steps and piddling with what sounded like change in his pocket. "And when I get it." He pulls out what seems to be about fifteen or twenty cents. Then he stops, reaches into his other pocket, and pulls out another round object. This one happens to have a diamond attached to it. They stand motionless looking at one another. "From the time I met you I never worried." His voice had begun to rise. "Sorry, that's not what I meant to say." He hesitates to clear his throat. "I've never given you any reason to worry have I, Grace? Tell me that."

"No, James, I never worried."

He had knelt, one knee now rested on the second step of

their house. "I reckon you could have any man you wanted." His face looked whiter than usual, grave, like he was hollow with no words left in him. He looks up into the sun for a moment, and when he looks back at her his eyes are more deliberate. "For a fact you could have any man."

She was trying to hold back. Trying not to force him. "I don't want any other man, James."

"I didn't mean to keep you waiting. It's just that I have enemies. It's all taken care of now, I'm quite sure. Grace, my beautiful darling, will you marry me?"

"I will marry you." She watched him stand up and climb two steps to the porch. He places the engagement ring on her finger, then she stands on her tiptoes and kisses him on the lips.

Later, after discussing the wedding arrangements over a meal of greens and field peas, James walks outside into the yard. He waves over one of the hired workers.

A man of around twenty-five sprints up to him. "Yes sir, Mr. Jenkins, you need me?"

"Its Joe… no Jim, is that right?"

"Jim's my brother. I'm Mike, Mike Love. My Uncle once almost came to blows with Andrew Jackson. They nearly dueled. If it weren't for their seconds they would have. You might have heard about it. It was the talk of the town a year ago."

"No, Mike. I hadn't heard. I know that you're quite busy right now. The thing is… I need to send a message to town. Is there one of the workers that can do that? I'll pay him for his trouble."

"Will you be waiting for a return message, sir?"

"Yes."

"Its near eight miles, could be two or three hours getting back. Maybe more depending on how long it takes to find the recipient and retrieve his response."

"Yes, I figured as much. Can you do it, or is there someone else?"

"I'll do it, sir. Just let me get my horse. Oh, who might this message be going to?"

"Do you know the little white church west of the sawmill."

"You mean preacher Tom's place. My mother knows him well."

"That's the one. Just ask him if he can be at my house tomorrow at noon. He'll know what you're talking about."

Paralleling the house was a small garden of corn and squash. Grace had planted it earlier in the summer. Beyond that was a few nice shade trees where worker's horses were tied off. After walking with a swift gait, Mike stood a while longer strapping his saddle to his horse. Placing his left foot in the stirrup he sways back slightly and swings himself over the animal. He points it sharply toward town, and after a short distance disappears into a field of tall grass.

When preacher Tom emerges from a patch of woods the next day, he jerks the reins hard, turning onto a well-worn path and rides quickly up to the house. His horse is panting noticeably. The last two miles of the trip he had been riding him hard. He doesn't wait for the animal to come to a complete stop before jumping off. "I saw Indians," he screams, running up the steps of the porch. "They were hiding, watching me as I passed. But I saw them just as clear as I see you, James."

"How far away?" James asked looking into the distance.

"Two miles, maybe less. Over near the big poplar. You know the one?"

"Yes. That area is a sort of known right-of-way for the Seminole. After they deserted the land here they would still use it, at times crossing over from South Georgia to the Atlantic Ocean. Strange though. I was told when I purchased this land at the government outpost in Pensacola that they haven't crossed through in near four years. That would be about five years today. I wouldn't worry too much about it though, Tom. They'll probably be moved on through by the time you head back that way."

The wedding was as simple as they come. Grace stood in a pretty yellow dress that covered her ankles. It was set off by white fringe surrounding the neckline and long flowing sleeves. Her hands were cupped together and filled with wild, black-eyed Susan flowers. James was dressed in his fanciest, most posh, three-piece suit. The grand, deep blue color generously added to the beauty of the event. The young couple looked splendid standing next to one another. Other than Preacher Tom there were only Mike and Jim, along with another hired worker to witness the nuptials. There was no reception, no wedding cake, and other than tea and coffee, no refreshments. By two o'clock in the afternoon the wedding had come and gone, attention already turning to other things.

Two days later word came by mouth of the hired help that preacher Tom never showed back up at his home. He had been found bludgeoned to death with a tomahawk, scalped and his body purposely left along the trail to town. Tension was high in and around the Tallahassee area as other isolated attacks rose in volume over the next few months. Eventually, this led to the burning of twelve homesteads and the massacre of fifty people. The Seminole Nation made it abundantly clear that the uprising was a direct retaliation to Andrew Jackson's aggression against them. For the next eight years the situation would die down and start up again until an all-out war against the Seminoles started in 1837. The war lasted through 1845 and resulted in the death of many Indians. Many others were re-located to the Oklahoma Territory. Afterwards problems with the once-mighty Seminole Nation were over.

During this troublesome time of war, however, there was an incident at the Jenkins house that brought back to light the youthfulness and incredible abilities of the ageless couple. One day Grace walked from the kitchen into the living room and was instantly seized by fear. She was looking into the face of a Seminole Indian. Looking around the room she realized there were at least ten others. "James!" she shouted, "you need to come out here right away!"

"What's the matter, Grace?" He shouted back, running from the kitchen into the living room. Almost immediately one of the Indians lifted his arm, tomahawk in hand, and ran at James. In what could be labeled a reflex move, James throws up his hand, a white illumination already shooting out from him. He catches the Indian's arm just below the wrist. Without time to think, and with no strain whatsoever, he bends the arm backward, sending a sharp cracking sound shooting through the room. The arm is broken in two, a jagged bone protruding out of the flesh. Another Indian lunges at James, tomahawk up high, but in less than five seconds he endures the same results. The two red men lay on the floor moaning in horrific pain, blood running from their twisted, punctured flesh.

One of the Indians standing separate from the others, reaches out his arm as if to halt any further attacks on James. After this is made clear, he motions with his head at Grace. In response two Indians move toward her. She has already been made hysterical by what she's seen. Frightened, she swings both her hands up in the stop position and screams. "No!" Unaware that her adrenaline has spiked, and that an involuntary mass of energy has been building inside of her. All at once the energy jolts from her hands, forming a white sphere and blowing the two Indians off their feet into the living room wall. Three more Indians react, stepping straight towards Grace. Again, she throws up her hands and an even greater amount of energy is released. This time the energy springs out, floating like unsteady heat rising from a road, engulfing the three red men, and elevating them off the floor. When Grace moves her arms, the hapless men move through the air mimicking her arm's direction. They are now completely under her shaky, trembling control. Scared, and unsure as to what to do next, she hesitated, but then stepped forward. When she does, the men are hurled backward, crashing through a tall, double-sized window landing on the porch decking. The white ball of energy now quickly dissipates.

The Indian that has been giving directions suddenly drops to his knees. His face mirrors something horrific and subterraneous. When it clears he takes his finger and mimics the drawing of a man and woman. Following this he raises both hands up high, palms toward the ceiling and moves his head upwards, acting as if he's looking into the sky. Over the course of the next two minutes, he chants words that seem like an Indian ritual or song. When he stands, he takes a small hollowed out piece of wood from a leather pouch hanging around his chest and hands it to James. It turns out to be a pipe. A symbol of peace between them. The Indians mount their horses and ride away with no further hostilities.

The next day James and Grace spot smoke rising a few miles from the house. When they go to investigate, they find a bloody massacre. All the Indians that had entered their house the day before were dead, along with many others. Some of the bodies were contorted from attempting to run from the hail of bullets. The harried, desperation still clinging like wild plankton to their faces. The U.S. Calvary had caught up with them after an attack on French settlers about ten miles away. Later an Indian interpreter tells James that the drawings the Indian had made on the floor of their house meant the Seminoles believe James and Grace have the spirit of the gods.

Following the Seminole war, the two of them decide the area is now safe, and the time is right to formulate the potion so they can inject and regenerate people again. It had been eighteen years since they brought themselves and old Jack back from old age to youth. They agreed on a minimum age of sixty, unless someone was in extremely poor health, and on no more or less than five people per year. This would be the number of bodies they could house and care for while helping them integrate into the mid-1800's life in Tallahassee. They had five extra rooms in their house. After one complete year, a regenerated person would have to move into a place of his own to make room for the next. Their plan worked to perfection, and in ten short years the Tallahassee area had over fifty regenerated people walking its streets. In another ten years there were over a hundred. All their friends and every person involved in their lives were now regenerated people. The need to hide their age which for a few years had been a concern, no longer existed.

Chapter 9

The clock had just touched 1:30 in the afternoon and the sun was on high beam, flashing off the numerous cars and window fronts of downtown Lexington. In front of his immediate view Carter could see a crowd of people gathered at a bus stop. Beyond them he has a triangular glimpse of The Hub Coffee Shop.

Dropping off the curb he takes advantage of an opening in the traffic. Stepping swiftly, he sprints unwavering and with grit across the street. Once on the other side he slows down, looking back at the thoroughfare, and walks in silence a half-block farther. Just outside the Hub he nods his head in recognition of a couple of teenage girls. They are puffing cigarettes and talking slow, in a lazy, country, deep southern drawl. He maneuvers around another girl who is too busy looking into her phone to move out of the way.

Finally, he pushes open the door, his eyes already roving, searching the room for who is now officially the love of his life, Jen. He spots her behind the counter working the espresso machine and watches as she smiles, motioning with her head to a corner table. After he acknowledges her with a quick lift of his hand, he takes the corner seat trying to relax. He keeps looking over her way because he has something exciting to tell her.

"Charming woman." A man's voice said from what seemed out of nowhere.

When Carter turns to his right he sees a young man in his early twenties staring down at him. He leans back in his chair, twisting his body to get a better visual. When he does he notices the man is wearing a handsome three-piece suit. "You don't know how right you are about her."

The man's eyes stay firmly fixed on Carter. "I can always spot a good woman."

Carter leans even farther back in his chair, his face tightening in suspense. "How's that?"

"Experience."

"Really?" He gestures for the man to take a seat, which he does on the opposite side of the table. "But you can't be more than twenty-two."

"Age and experience are not always relative or... connected. An older person is not always the absolute advantage when it comes to experience. For example, a fifty-year-old man may have been single his whole life. He may have never even dated. On the other hand, a man of my age may have dated dozens of women. I'm sorry. I'm talking too much. You and the girl, it's none of my business."

"No, it's... it's fine. I was enjoying the conversation. What's your name?"

"James Jenkins. I apologize again. I seem to have made myself at home."

"I'm Carter." Carter's face naturally tilts upwards. "Where you from James? Not Lexington, that's obvious."

"Nice to meet you, Carter." He moves his hand across the table and the two men shake. "Originally I'm from across the water in England. Most of my life's been lived here though, first New York, now Tallahassee."

"That's interesting. I just got back from Tallahassee."

Suddenly Jen interrupts. "What you boys gonna have?"

"Jen, this is James. Would you believe he's from Tallahassee?"

"No way, we just came back from there. Do you live in one of those plantation houses? We saw some incredible ones there."

"No. More like an apartment building. Could I get a cappuccino?"

"What am I thinking? Yes. Carter, you want your usual?"

"Yes. Could I have a shot of espresso in it and a multigrain bagel? I didn't have lunch. You know how I like it?"

113

"One cappuccino, one caramel iced coffee with a shot of espresso, and one toasted bagel coming up."

After Jen walks away, Carter dips his head, slowly raising it, giving James and his spiffy three-piece suit the look-over. "I have a feeling you are a lot older than you look. The situation…it's too… I'll just come right out and ask. How long have you lived in Tallahassee?"

"You sure you're ready for the answer?"

"No. I'm not sure. But I need a clear picture of what I'm dealing with. I see the same characteristics in you as I did the last time I saw my grandfather. So just tell me."

"Since 1827."

"What?"

"I moved from New York to Tallahassee in 1827. That was the year I regenerated myself. I was 58 at the time, making me 248-years old today. I've fought with Indians, dealt with run-away slaves, and helped Florida transition from a territory to a state. Before all of that I fought for the United Kingdom in the war of 1812. During that war, on August 24, 1814, I helped set fire to the Capitol Building in Washington D.C. Not too many people today even know the White House was nearly burned to the ground. I'm sorry I'm not the innocent person you thought I was when offering me a seat. I was hoping we could ease into this a little slower, sorta soften the blow for you. You were quick though. Had me pegged from the near start."

"How did you find me?"

"I went to your house to start with. It was clear to me that it was not occupied. I knew you weren't at work. We have people there, but you are aware of that I'm sure. Next, we turned our attention to the girl-friend. Then it was easy. Only a short time and we were here."

"How many of there are you, in the world I mean?"

"I was hoping you wouldn't ask that. It's complicated. I wouldn't tell you at all but… You seemed to have uncovered… I'll just come out and tell you there's now around ten thousand in the United States. I can tell you more, but I need some assurances."

"Assurances?"

"What I mean is, you're either in or you're out. We're offering you the same thing we offered Dillon and others like him. The opportunity to be one of us. If you accept then you'll be privy to much more information." James glances over to Jen, who is walking toward their table with a tray of drinks. "We wouldn't leave your girl out. The offers for her, too. How much does she know already?"

"Other than what you've told me today, everything."

"I thought as much."

"I don't suppose you could tell me what the Pinnacle is?"

"No, sorry. I can't right now, but you'll know soon enough."

"Apparently it's pretty important, what with all the secrecy."

"Important, yes, but as I said…"

At first, Carter didn't let on to anything when Jen arrived with the drinks. She sits down at the table and informs him that her shift is over. However, in no time she was faintly aware that something was up. She had no reason to believe that she was involved when she asked an inconvenient question. "What are you boys talking about?" When she senses them holding back, she grows more curious. "Is it Tallahassee?" Still no response, other than a slightly embarrassed look on both their faces.

The situation was growing tiresome to James, so he eyed Carter hard. "Are you going to tell her or am I?"

"Tell me what?"

"James is older than he looks. Do you understand?"

"Do you mean he's like your grandfather?"

"Yes."

"You're from Tallahassee. You followed us here didn't you?"

"Yes, Jen. I did."

"You're worried we're going to talk. Are you here to keep us quiet, to bring us back to Tallahassee?"

James lowers his head like he's been shamed. "I wish I could calm your fears, to relax your mind from this whole crazy situation. Let me start by saying it's not what you think.

Neither of you are being brought back to Tallahassee."

"Then what? It's clear we know too much. You're not here to exchange names. So, what is it, James? If that's your real name."

"Its been my name for 248 years."

"Okay, that's… a long time, just tell us what you want."

"I can't even begin to tell you the benefits, Jen. We want you and Carter to join us."

"You mean to be regenerated?"

"You would have to wait a few more years due to your ages, but yes."

She turns to Carter. "Did you know?"

"He just told me."

"And…"

"And I haven't had time to think about it. James, how long do we have? Can we talk this over between ourselves?"

"The preliminary steps have already been taken. Approval has been granted. Yes, talk it out. Just remember that every cell in your body will be at its optimum youth. We can make it stay that way by regenerating you every fifty or sixty years. We think there's a hidden virus that's interfering, causing people to age. If we could ever find it we could develop a vaccine. Until then we must continue regenerating. The good thing is your abilities will far exceed what they are now. They will be exaggerated beyond belief. We can discuss that later. If you choose to accept you will be used in recruiting subjects. We're having difficulty hitting our target numbers. You can't imagine the difficulties involved in finding those that would not be missed. We've made mistakes. You found out and so have others. We're fortunate that it's been limited to just a few. I'll be staying at the Museum Hotel tonight if you make up your mind, or if there's anything else I can do. Otherwise I'll see you tomorrow."

Jen murmurs under her breath as they watch him walk out. Impulses like that came naturally to her, and it was instinctive for her to question possible areas of trouble or conflict.

Carter taps her on the hand breaking her gaze and getting her attention. "What did you say?"

"It's not what I said. It's what he said: 'If there's anything else I can do.' I don't trust him, Carter. I don't think he's that understanding of us. Do you?"

"I think they've looked at both sides of this, and...I think they're in the elementary stages of something big, something we're not being told about, something..." He places his hand over the top of hers. "Jen, I don't think we have a choice. The only way we're going to find out what they're up to is to go along. They assume it, expect it. I doubt they've ever been turned down. I mean it's all so fantastic. Can you think of one person who wouldn't want to be young and healthy...forever? I've been working on this for years and haven't even come close to what they have."

"What if we *did* turn them down?"

He reaches for his drink, sipping from the straw as he pulls it forward. "Wow, that's really good. You got it just right. The bagel looks good too. He takes one side of it, tears it in half, then just holds it in his hand. "If we turn them down, I think they go to plan B." He continues by shoving the bagel in his mouth and biting down. "I doubt plan B is as pleasant as plan A." He starts chewing.

"What you mean is they're going to take steps to keep us quiet. If they don't kill us they'll probably take us down to Tallahassee with that horrid little creature Dillon." Her instinctive side was taking another slant. "But if we agree, and stay here, we're not going to find anything out."

Carter takes another drink, this time downing several swallows before he stops. "Are you saying we should agree and then ask to go stay in Tallahassee?"

"Maybe. Then again they might find it easier to control us there."

"James said they needed us to recruit subjects. That entails sending us somewhere else. It could be Florida, but I doubt Tallahassee. They have plenty of help there already." Carter takes his phone and googles states with the most retirees. "We could be sent to California, Arizona, Texas, North or South Carolina. Other than Florida they have the highest number of retirees. If that happens we're just another pawn in their

117

game."

"I have an idea."

"Ideas are what we need. Let's hear it."

"What if we agree but insist on seeing your grandfather first."

"You think we can learn something from him. Don't you?"

"I think we can learn *a lot* from him."

That afternoon Carter and Jen walk passed a few solo art exhibitions just outside the Museum Hotel. The site and surrounding area have specially commissioned work by some of the art world's most exciting artists. They continue passed huge columns of molded concrete shooting out of marble foundations. Farther inside they find more than 7000 ft of exhibition space, filled with contemporary art, and rotating cultural programming for guests to sink their eyes into. What they expect to find in the hotel turns out to be nothing that they expected.

Inside James' room, they have a view passed the glass exterior wall overlooking a balcony. The skyline of Lexington is staring through the windows back at them. "I guess you've made up your minds or you wouldn't have come. Am I right?" James' voice is friendly and engaging. "Could I get you a drink first. I have vodka with tonic, including flavored. Also, whiskey, or there's beer if you go for that sorta thing." While he talks he pours himself a vodka in a short, clear glass.

Carter glances at the mini bar, which looks like an old-time street vendor cart. It has two large black wheels with red spokes. "Maybe later. James, Jen and I want to thank you for your offer. We are happy to accept it. We are... how can I find the words? We are thrilled to be included in the regeneration project. Our energy levels were soaring after you left earlier today. The magnitude of what's taking place though, I'm sure whoever your leaders are, that... well, surely you've discussed accountability."

"The world as we know it is going to change, and much sooner than later. Accountability, responsibility, liability, answer-ability? All these words apply and have already been considered. You two are not the silent type. You speak up and I like that. You'll be of great use to us. There's the matter of where we need you the most. We've been sending recruits like yourselves and a pretty big contingent of regenerated ones out west, Texas, Arizona, California, and so on. I'll give you the option of staying here if you like. If you decide to stay we would prefer you to move in here at the Museum Hotel. We own it along with six others."

"I notice you have raspberry tonic," Jen says while re-positioning herself on the sofa and pointing at the minibar. Could I have a glass with a little vodka? Would you mind too, telling us about any other options?"

"You *are* talking about where you might be sent?"

"Yes."

James takes a glass from the corner of the bar, scoops ice into it, pours in one-quarter vodka and three-quarters tonic, then hands it over. "If you want to stay in Kentucky, we could send you to Louisville. We own the Museum Hotel there as well. Also, in Nashville, Cincinnati, Oklahoma City. Then there's Durham, North Carolina, and Bentonville, Arkansas. We could use you in Florida also if that's what you would like. There are massive amounts of retirees in the sunshine state. Retirees make up most regenerated ones. But it's not necessary for you to go to Florida. It's up to you."

"I'll take that drink now if you don't mind."

"Sure, Carter. What's your pleasure?"

"Two fingers of Wild Turkey on the rocks. There's something else I would like also."

"If it's not here I can send for room service."

"That won't be necessary. Jen and I talked it over. We would like to visit my grandfather. We haven't seen him in months. Afterward, you can send us wherever you need us the most, Florida, Carolina, doesn't matter."

"You seem compelled."

"We need to know he's okay."

"I'll have to make a phone call"

"Make sure they understand, *we insist*. We can't move forward without knowing, seeing for ourselves what's happened to him."

"Beforehand, we had reasons for hiding him. Good reasons. I hope you understand that Carter. Tell me you do." Suddenly, during conversation, James' face chills with concern. Instantly it loses color with a blank, trapped look stamped into it. He looks to his left sensing someone approaching. The stranger had entered the room with all the characteristics of his profession: part messenger, part bodyguard, and part cold-blooded killer.

James pours two more fingers into his drink. "How did you get in, Jack?"

Old Jack steps from the shadows farther into the room. At the minibar, he stops, unscrewing the vodka bottle. "You never had guards worth a dam, James." He snatches the bottle up to his mouth like the vulgar man that he is, hesitating, the bottle floating in front of his mouth. "You need to be more careful." He tilts the bottle up downing several huge swallows.

"Did you kill them?"

"No. But don't go expecting any help. The two of them are in a pretty deep sleep right now."

"I suppose I should thank you for that."

"You can thank Mr. Lett." Lightning quick, old Jack pulls a bowie knife from its sheath and points it straight at the face of James. "I would-a cut their throats and watched them bleed out, and you know that." He turns the bottle up again while still pointing the knife, the stout liquid is now running down his cheeks. Bubbles are splashing around the clear, round container until it's near empty. After he finishes it off he rattles the mini bar, slamming the bottle down doggedly hard. "You've been a bad one, James. If you don't end it now there'll be a requital." Old Jack's voice is veering upwards. "You can't win. Mr. Lett knows what you're up to. It's time, can't you see that! The world has been dying freaking long enough!"

James looks away wincing. Soon he turns, glancing at Carter and Jen, his face now covered with humility. He shakes his head in disbelief, wishing the pair were not present to hear the conversation. In their eyes, he can see doubt, and questions about what his purposes might be. There is fear in them too. Fear of old Jack, of what he's capable of, and fear of Mr. Lett, whom they have only now been made aware of. He turns from the couple and gives an earnest look into the face of old Jack. He looks also at Jack's two slumbering, subordinate associates, one with a pushed-in face, the other with a scar running from his eye to his chin. "I have thought of death. Although after so long a time it seems foreign." He sips his vodka, then holds it out in front of him. "Yet, if death be in this glass in the form of retribution, then it is now at my lips." He takes a sip. "I have done nothing deserving of vengeance. Even if you imagine that I'm scheming, which I most certainly am. It is for the preservation of life. Mr. Lett's plan is murder, plain and simple. My plan may take a little longer, maybe even years, but it leaves ownership of the right to live, in the hands of each individual."

Old Jack slings his knife out underneath the chin of James. He is only a hair-width away from slicing his throat. "Then have your damn drink you fool! Because death is sure as hell what you'll get!" As he spoke his face was turning red-hot, and a white energy was already emanating out of him, forming a circle. When he notices this and sees the same happening to James he backs away. "You're a lucky one James. If we fight it out here the energy will just consume the room. And, truth is…" He starts calming down. "Mr. Lett said not to harm you. He still thinks you'll come around. He told me to tell you, one week. After that the requital. So, you think about it." For the first time, old Jack turns to Carter and Jen. "People like these are not our identicals, and they are certainly not the future. Pretty as they are they got to go. I mean it, the time has come."

"But they *can* be the future, just like us."

"That would take another ten years, maybe more and we're tired of waiting."

"But my plan could shorten that number. I've worked it out. Grace has been a big help. A year I think, maybe two at the most. After that, nothing but regenerated ones."

"You always were the simpleton. I tried to tell Mr. Lett you wouldn't listen. You got *one week.*" Old Jack snatches up a lime from the bar and starts tossing it back and forth in his hands. "Living is better than dying. You think about that. One week, I'll see you then." He turns his head motioning with a quick flip of his hand to his counterparts. As the three men exit the room there's a loud slam that rattles bottles on the mini-bar. Old Jack had slammed the door with the purpose of making James feel the reality of the moment.

All James needed was time. Time to expand his plan throughout the earth. But the days of the far-off future had arrived. The accumulating years and ensuing decades had piled up in a heap of misery at his feet. He had always been a moralist and could never be happy in the kind of world they were trying to bring about. The numbers given him at a recent conference of regenerated representatives pointed to the annihilation of possibly half the population of the earth. At that same conference there was a restructuring of leadership, and not a friendly one. James' role which had been second only to Mr. Lett was greatly diminished. His outspokenness against the plan to extinguish what was thought of as leftover people had been met with an iron fist. Everyone eighty and above would be allowed to die off unless chosen as worthy of regeneration. The thinking was that they present no threat to the project and within twenty years none would remain. Another group would be chosen by a network of computers with specific criteria previously installed into its software. The age bracket of possible subjects running between thirty-five and seventy-nine. Anyone under thirty-five was already marked for extermination. This age bracket could not be regenerated without serious health complications, including death.

"How?" Jen asked, leaning back and sinking deep into the sofa. "How are they going to kill us?"

Without looking at her, James sets his glass down. He reaches over picking up the bottle of vodka and pours himself a fresh drink, his head still tilted down. He swirls it, then slowly, smoothly, takes a sip. "I don't know how they managed it. They've created a formula that ages people dramatically." Now he looks up straight into her eyes. Tears are running down his cheeks like he's pleading with her. "I don't know, Jen. I wasn't part of the team that created the new formula. They tell me people will think its a horrible virus, worse than the Black Plague or the Spanish Influenza. The first steps have already been taken. All those chosen for regeneration have already been immunized. It was accomplished the same way the infections will be, through the contamination of food and drink. They will sleep for three days after which the poison would have run its course. Somehow they've managed to create an expiration date into the formula. After a person awakes from sleep they'll have less than a week to live. I'm sorry, but there's nothing more I can do. I had a plan, but time has run out. And as you've seen, they're onto me."

"What if you had more time?" Carter asked.

"You heard what Jack said. One week. There's no negotiating."

"But just suppose, what if you had six months to work with, would that give you the time to stop them?"

"It would be difficult, but yes. I think so."

"I have a formula of my own. I came about it while working on a solution for Alzheimer patients. My work was a complete failure, but I ended up with a formula that can wipe out a person's memory. I didn't think it would ever be worth a dime. It lasts for about three months, but I can push it to six safely by increasing the dosage. If we can infect Mr. Lett and his people, you would have six months to change the outcome."

"You're talking about a tall task. Still, if we start planning now I believe we could be at implementation within six weeks. That's important because the Lett plan goes into effect in less than ninety-days. If we can do it we could take control of Lett's global organization. There would be no plan left for them when their memories come back. I still control the U.S., all North America. And my influence in South America and Australia can negate Lett's influence. Antarctica and Africa are not an obstacle, so we've got the infrastructure to get this idea of yours rolling. The European nations and Asia will be our biggest challenge. But I know some pretty influential people there who aren't too keen on Lett's plan."

James walks with drink in hand to the edge of the room where the furniture slopes away. He stands in front of the exterior glass wall overlooking Lexington. "Have you two ever been to Myrtle Beach?"

Chapter 10

He walked beside her in silence, passed a boardwalk of arcades, souvenir stands, and restaurants. Pending the weather they had grown accustomed to a morning walk. When they reached the SkyWheel, one of the country's tallest Ferris Wheels, he grabbed her arm abruptly stopping her. "Have you seen Grace today?"

"No. When we left she wasn't up yet. Why?"

"Are you sure she went to bed last night?"

"All I'm sure of is that she was on her cell phone all evening. She was still on it when we went to bed."

"What time did she get in?"

Danny is bothered by an abrupt change in Harlan's voice. She twists her shoulder and yanks her arm, breaking away from his hand. She can see a glare in his eyes. "Nine o'clock. Why, Harlan? What's the matter?"

"Strange. She's never on the phone that much, and she's always up early unless the art association has one of those late-night events."

"The old man a few days ago, he's got you worried. Why don't I just text her?"

"Would you, Danny? You know, just to be sure."

"I'm on it." In five seconds, she has her phone out and a message already typed. *"You up yet. It's ten o'clock, the day's wasting away."*

The response is immediate. *"Yes. I meant to catch you before you left. Tell Harlan he has visitors. Tell him I worked on getting them here late into the night. They flew into*

Columbia, then drove a rental from there. They just arrived from Kentucky, from Lexington. Tell him to come home now. And I mean the both of you. It's important."

"She says you have visitors, to come home now. She says it's important, that she spent most of last night getting them here."

"Ask her who it is."

"He says who is it?"

"It's Carter, his grandson."

Danny receives this last text with a laugh. She's smiling, beaming as she holds the phone up for him to read. "We have confirmation that you really are older than you look."

"Tell her we're on our way."

"Be there in a few." She finished the text in a flash. "Come on, let's go."

He stiffens up and just stands there.

"Aren't you coming?"

He is mutely resistant.

"You can't just stand here. If you won't go back, then I will. Don't make me leave you."

The glare is still in his eyes like he senses something.

"You really can't stand here all day!"

"Something's wrong. I'm trying to think."

"No! Nothing's wrong. It's your grandson."

"If they're letting him come here, then there must be a problem." He swings around, changing direction suddenly and taking Danny by the hand. "Thanks for being patient with me."

"But I wasn't being…"

"We need to go." He pulls at her hand and they both brake out running like a flash, their invigorating youth and physical strength sustaining them all the way back. When they reach the apartment, they are breathing heavily.

After pausing to catch her breath, Danny reaches to open the door.

"Don't…don't." Harlan whispers emphatically.

She tries to give him a smile of sympathy, but her face has a puzzled look. "What's the matter?"

He drops down on a bench near the door, fearing a

dreadful hour has come, gazing into the air. The actual glare in his eyes is now so penetrating it seems it could scorch or sear. It wasn't that he had a premonition or glimpse of something bad about to happen. But rather because, here and there throughout the last few months, the surface of his dreams had been trying to alert him to an ominous situation. He could sense as clearly as the vapors entering his lungs, an upheaval approaching. His sense of being involved, his sense that it was lurking behind that door, that if they entered the apartment everything was about to change. He looks up at Danny, the glare in his eyes turning to one of fright. He wonders if he pleas with her to leave with him if her ears would be open to listening. Or would she coax him, drag him inside, conscious as she was that nothing was amiss.

He was so wound up, that when a neighbor walked by, Danny feared she would think Harlan was in the middle of a panic attack. Thank goodness after breathing deeply a couple of times he couldn't sustain his frenzy. He sighs heavily and settles down. Their eyes are now locked in a gaze, lingering on each other, their human bond growing second-by-second. All his stress and troubles melt away into her face.

Danny broke the silence with the clearing of her throat. "We don't have to go in if you don't want to. If you want to go back to the boardwalk…"

Suddenly the door swings open. Caught by surprise Harlan jumps up from the bench, swinging around distrustfully. "Carter? Is it really you?"

"It's me, and I'm not calling you Gramps anymore. Just standing here seeing you makes me feel old. You're even different from the last time I saw you. Have you stopped growing younger?"

"For the last month or two, yes."

"Your southern drawl. It's completely gone now. How is that possible?"

"It's changed almost every day," Danny spouts out while taking Harlan by the arm.

"I haven't met you before, but I have a feeling you're older than you look. Am I right?"

"I just turned ninety-nine." She holds out her hand. "I go by Danny."

"It's good to meet you, Danny. What else can you tell me, because he's not acting anything like my grandfather? By now he should be scolding me about something, and I mean that in the most affectionate way."

She squeezes Harlan's arm pulling him tight against her. "There's lots to tell. For starters, his voice and accent have changed, but it's more than that. He's using fewer and fewer... I guess what I mean is his vocabulary, his word usage has changed. It's like he's being educated without having the schooling. Both of our senses are much sharper, but with him there's another aspect to it. I'm convinced there's something shaping him. I don't mean his personality. He's still the same person, except...he's becoming a more polished... more advanced version of himself."

By now Jen had walked outside along with Grace and James. They're all listening carefully to Danny's description of Harlan. "Whatever it is hiding inside him, that's changing him, it's a marvel. It has its own personage, the wisdom of a much older person that communicates on a different level with him. He senses things ahead of time. He knew somehow, that if we came back to the apartment, that things were going to change dramatically. We were about to leave when Carter opened the door."

"One thousand five hundred years!" A voice from behind in the shadows shouts out. "That's how often the phenomenon comes around." A figure moves from the shadows into the light and is the wearer of the brown hood. "The marvel you spoke of Danny is in his brain. I discovered it with a brain scan during the regeneration process." She walks up close aiming her eyes at James and Grace first. "I came as soon as I received your message." Quickly her attention turns to Harlan. "I'm Angela. You met me at the hotel pool. Can you remember everything about me now, including the injections and our conversation in the operating room?"

"I remember."

"Everything, until you fell asleep?"

"Yes."

"Continue using your vocal cords so that everyone can hear."

He repeats himself. "Yes, I remember."

"You now know that you're different from other regenerated ones. It's time I explain why. After I tell you, your life will change. But you already know that, don't you?"

"Yes, but not the details, just that it's a critical situation."

"You are correct. We will get to that later, but first, you need to know why you're different. Let me start by telling you a surprising truth. Man has been on this planet for far less time than he believes. He thinks because the planet itself has been here for millions of years that he has also. However, the vegetation has been here much longer, along with the animals. They were placed here ahead of time by an advanced civilization of beings from a different realm. Afterward, they placed man here, to enjoy the earth, to take care of it, and to be guardians over it. There is more to it, but that will suffice for now.

That said, the brain is an amazing thing, especially for regenerated ones. But yours, Harlan, is even more so. My father was a scientist who studied in the field of anatomy. Specifically, the anatomy of the nervous system. The famous German, Franz Gall. He spent most of his life studying the brain. As a kid I grew up trying to understand, investigating the brain. We have come a long way from my father's time. Back in the early 19th Century, many people believed that you could accurately judge someone's personality, character, and intelligence, simply by feeling the shape of their head. My father pioneered that thinking, and although he was wrong, it did lead to an approach that later helped us to map out the different areas of the brain. Now we know that certain areas of the brain deal with memory, other areas decision making, and so on, including all the senses. One of those areas deals with instinct or intuitiveness. It's what we often refer to as intuition. Brain scans show that this part of the brain is sleeping when compared to other parts. In most people it's almost or completely dormant. Those lucky enough to have a bit more activity in this part of the brain, end up being considered brilliant people because they can maneuver through life seamlessly. They intuitively go the right direction, make the right decisions. It's as normal to them as going to sleep and waking up. This brain function, when it's as alive as yours, Harlan, and paired with other abilities such as you have, makes you an extraordinary person. You could rule the world, and it's probably what you were meant to do.

That is if a rebellion hadn't broken out after the first 1500 years of man's existence. Because of that rebellion, those who placed us here have long since left us to our own devices. They won't return until a set time has passed. We believe that time is approaching. Meantime they're watching, waiting to see if we're going to prove ourselves worthy of their attention again.

There are two others in the world like you, Harlan. There were four, but the first two died fighting each other during the rebellion. Each successive 1500 years brings about another. The selection process is called *the Pinnacle*. You are the fifth. A man by the name of Lett was the third. He is 4500 years old and the oldest living man. Everyone before him grew old and died off. His remarkable abilities allowed him, because he was a chemist, to come up with a formula that could reverse the aging process. He now believes that eliminating all aging people and replacing them with regenerated ones will be the proof those who placed us here are looking for.

There is a reckoning coming. You already sense it, that there are two sides pitted against each other. It's the reason we've brought you to this location. I'm going to step aside now. James will continue. You can trust him. He regenerated me back during the civil war. Listen to him. Ultimately, the decision to join us will be yours. However, *the Fifth Pinnacle* is here. You have been chosen. Nothing can change that."

Harlan nods, sits back down on the bench, and just as Danny starts to follow suit with him something extraordinary begins happening. A bright, fluorescent illumination suddenly emerges on the skin of his body. It alternates going from a bright orange-yellow to a dull, almost muted but perceptible white. He resembles a torch-light that is being thrust between the darkness and the light. His arms lift outward as he looks closely, analyzing himself.

"Has this happened to you before?" Grace asked.

"Nothing quite like this. Never thought I'd be a human glow stick, but it's supposed to happen. Don't ask me how I know. I just do."

After about a minute the back and forth illumination starts toning down. It slowly changes to a faint throbbing of white light, then dissipates altogether. Oddly, he is left more relaxed but in an obvious state of contemplation. After Danny sits next to him he lifts his face, his eyes searching out James. "Before you continue I have a question."

"Anything you want, Harlan. The time for hiding things from you has come to an end. What would you like to know?"

He lifts his arm and places it around Danny's shoulders, then he stretches out his legs and crosses them with one of his running shoes lying over the top of the other. "I want to know why you believe Lett is wrong, and I want to know why you believe *you* are right. So please, James, go on. Explain yourself. I need to hear this in your own words."

"We just don't think half the population of the earth should have to die."

"But aren't they dying anyway? In a few years won't they be dead and replaced by more dying ones unless it's stopped?"

"Gracious God, Harlan. You can't be on Lett's side of this. Your own grandson and his girlfriend would die."

"You're asking me to choose a side, your side. And yet you haven't answered my question."

"The answer should be obvious."

"Then make it obvious to me. You just said people shouldn't die. But they're already dying. The cycle of dying has been here for thousands of years. I want to know why you are right and he is wrong."

James turns away walking a few steps. When he turns back he resolutely bends down on one knee. "I suppose he's right, in a way. The cycle of death needs to stop. I think we all understand that. So how do we go about it? Ending the cycle quickly is desirable, I give him that. But eliminating death by

131

creating more death is absurd. Mass murder has never been acceptable, and it shouldn't be now."

"Are you telling me your plan, when put into operation, will cease people from dying?"

"You got me there, Harlan. No. My plan will take too long to complete. In the meantime, people will still be dying. Mr. Lett has brought this to my attention time and again. With the technology we have right now his plan would be much easier to implement. It would work, yes, but at a great cost."

"Then what do you plan on doing about it?"

"What do I…" James stands back up abruptly. He turns again pulling his hand through his hair. When he turns back he has a surprised look.

"I'm going to fight." He scans his eyes around the group. We're all going to fight because of the principles of right and wrong, of goodness and badness…of the human character for heaven's sake! Everyone gets to decide, not just one group of people. No… wait, that can't be right. These principles have been here all along guiding us like a built-in-compass. Which means they were put into us by the civilization that placed us here, to begin with. So, they're not *our* original values, but the values of those who placed us here. It's the only explanation. We all naturally understand basic right and wrong, that no one has the right to take another person's life, and that's why *we're* right and Lett's wrong."

"Is that your answer?"

"Yes, because in the end, it will always come down to the same issue. Mr. Lett believes that the quick results justify the means and that it will appease the other realm."

"You are almost there, James."

"If Lett gets his way it will only make things worse. They're watching us. Murdering billions of people would be another rebellion, going directly against our moral compass. Those who put us here would probably interfere again. They did something back then, planted something in us, possibly a hidden virus that started the aging process. They'll interfere again like they did thousands of years ago, making the formula ineffective. Even regenerated ones would start growing old again. The cycle would restart. The whole process would be in a holding pattern for another 1500 years, until the next pinnacle."

"Yes, James."

"We can stop Lett and his people. Carter and I have come up with a plan."

"You are overlooking something, James."

"No. It's a good plan."

"They have two with the same instincts I have. Maybe they don't know your plan, but they sense you've got one, and they sense it's powerful. You won't fool them easily."

"But we have you."

"There are two of them and only one of me."

"True, and it's our biggest obstacle, but there's something you still don't know. Surely you've felt it. After every Pinnacle, the succeeding chosen one's instincts are more powerful. You, Harlan, are more powerful than Lett and his accomplice. They know that the Fifth Pinnacle is here, and they have been searching the globe for you. We found you first, and with your help, we can negate their abilities and implement our plan."

"Then where do we start?"

"In five days, they want my answer: am I joining them or not. I've arranged a meeting in Lexington. That's where you come in. If we can keep them guessing long enough, we can infect them with a memory loss formula Carter has come up with. We can wipe their memories for six months giving us time to undermine their plan and implement ours."

Harlan stands up with no sign of the unsure, frightened man he resembled earlier. He turns his attention back to the wearer of the brown hood. "Angela?"

"Yes, Harlan?"

"I'll need your expertise with the brain. Can you help me?"

"What exactly do you want me to do?"

"They're hoping for the best, but they sense a problem, anticipating that James has a plan that could foil them. I meant it when I said they won't be easy to fool. We need a diversion, and with their instincts we need a good one. You understand the mind, how it works. We need a diversion of the mind. Can you do that?"

"I think so. When do we start?"

"Now."

Chapter 11

(The Summer of 1863)

"My dear Beatrice, I am writing you this letter in fear that I will never see you again. I have just returned from a visit to my Landlord, who is my solitary neighbor for near two miles. He informs me that the war has come to our door, but he needn't have said it because like most I recognize the sound of cannonballs. Gettysburg is such a beautiful rolling countryside. My first trip to Pennsylvania, I fixed my eyes on it as a place I so much wanted to live. Now my dearest sister, this horrid, costly war it appears will completely remove it from even the stir of society.

This morning a blue-coat soldier banged at my door. When I opened it, his voice was hardly intelligible. In short order, he fell dead at my feet. A musket ball had ripped through his leg, and consequently he had lost too much blood. Deeply saddened I covered my face in the presence of such grief. My eyes warmed toward him when I beheld his blue eyes. They looked so like our father's, Beatrice. You would have been amazed. In times like these I miss him so. Do you remember when we used to sit, both of us at the same time, on his peaceful, loving lap? My beautiful, only sibling, I never used to think of the aging process so much as I do now. With father long since dead, and us now so quickly old and gray. He always suspected a hidden infectious disease was the cause of aging but could never prove his theory. There have been times when I cried, yearning to be in his lap again, yearning to be with you, wanting desperately to experience that wonderful feeling again. In my heart right now I'm hugging you. Can you feel it like I do? Close your eyes my dear beautiful sister, and I make a promise that you will. I want you to recollect how happy we were, as I do now.

Yesterday during a hail of cannonballs, I encountered the nauseating site of two other blue-coats running past my house. I'm told they will eventually be caught and hanged for desertion. I have thought about writing a letter to President Lincoln, pleading for their cause. They are nothing more than scared teenagers running from desolation as all men should.

Right now, as I am writing you this letter I am looking out the window at another blue-coat. He is trying to take my horse, but I have him chained up thanks to my landlord's instructions. The sight is almost more than I can take. His breaths are like suffocating sighs, and it's clear that tears are running down his smoke covered cheeks. He's leaving now, running away, the third since yesterday. He can't be more than eighteen or nineteen, just a boy trapped in the depths of agony. I have heard it's the same for the confederates. Do you think they have actual grown men in this war?

Because of such said dangers, I am thinking of moving. That is if this contemptible war will allow it. I have received a letter of invitation quite unexpectedly from a man in Tallahassee. If this city is unfamiliar to you it is in the state of Florida. Currently, it is the state's capital due to its proximity to the Atlantic Ocean and the Gulf of Mexico. This once wild territory has settled down considerably since its statehood which was official in 1845, some eighteen years ago. Its Indian problems have all but disappeared now that the Seminoles have been sent out west to the Oklahoma Territory. So, if you've heard any talk of Florida's Indian problems, you can now disregard it.

The man that sent me an invitation to move there is a wealthy scientist and landowner by the name of James Jenkins. He owns two sugar plantations, one cotton, and many commercial buildings, some of which he rents out to the state government. However, he says his real interest lies with the brain. He has studied some of father's theories as well as my own and has become intrigued with us. When he read in the Tallahassee paper that one of Franz Gall's daughters who also studies the brain was still alive and living in Pennsylvania, he took action to find me. He has made me a lucrative offer to teach and train him extensively in the goings-on of the brain. The opportunity also allows me to further my research. I at first replied with very little interest to leave this beautiful area that the locals call 'God's country.' But I do, so desperately, miss my work. Due to my heavy leanings in renewing my brain research, and of course the hostile environment I now find myself in, I have made the decision to accept his generous offer. If Florida turns out to be less than expected it will still be better than the shell Gettysburg is being turned into.

I think that the Tallahassee newspaper gave me more credit than I deserve. To quote them, they say that 'Gall's daughter, Angela, is still one of the foremost authorities on the brain.' They even have a diagram of the brain I published two years before I left Germany. It's the one where I mapped out the different areas of the brain. I thought the diagram was rather crude at the time, but others seem to like it. It's being used in hospitals now and in training surgeons. It's even found its way into universities. All I've really done is continue the great work father started.

I'll end this letter by asking that you pray for my safety. However, I would be remiss if I didn't ask you to pray more so for all the boy-soldiers in blue or gray. Blessed be the God of all comfort, who sustains during times such as these.

When this dreadful war is finally over I will once again venture over that great mass of fear-inspiring water to visit you. I hope I am not too old and worn out by then. Maybe I will write you first, and send you passage fare to St. Augustine. After all you are younger than me by almost two years. I could meet you at the ships docking and we could ride coach to Tallahassee. To see you again my dearest would be like breathing the air of heaven. Until that most desirable day.

Your sister, Angela Rena Gall

The blinds of the Hotel Casa's sitting room were drawn down due to the oppressive August sun. In the dim, sultry atmosphere Angela's face resembles one of disappointment as she sits knitting in a soft cushioned chair. When the door swings open, she hardly stirs from her knitting or notices the handsome young man entering. He quickly recognizes her from the description she gave in one of several correspondences. To get her attention, he clears his throat. She looks up with a distant faraway expression, her working hands resting in her lap.

"Miss Gall, I wish to express the hope that I have not inconvenienced you by my tardiness. Please rest assured that our agreement to meet at the ship's docking was important to me. I was delayed at a ferry crossing for almost a full day due to inclement weather. I shall reimburse you for any monies you have put out for food and carriage these last four hours. You were right to come to the Hotel Casa, where you could be comfortable until my arrival. Again, my apologies ma'am."

"Do you represent Mr. James Jenkins, boy?"

"I understand your confusion, Miss Gall. I haven't been able to shed my baby face looks yet. I'll have to ask your patience with me, but I am indeed him, ma'am."

"But you can't be more than twenty-one or two. If I could control it I should not allow you to inconvenience me any longer. But as it is you've already got me here. The least you could do is tell me under what false pretense you have done so."

He sits down on the edge of a sofa directly across from her. "It seems I have underestimated my boyish face. However, I assure you to the best of my abilities that my sending for you was with the most honorable intentions. I wish to study the brain, and I wish it to be with the greatest teacher on the subject. Your father, God rest his soul, and you, ma'am, are at the forefront of brain research. If you will indulge me I promise to be an attentive student. You will not have to repeat yourself twice. If you need time to think about it, I will pay for your accommodations here at the Hotel Casa for as long as you need."

"You don't look like a man who could pay what we agreed to by letter."

"Nevertheless, I can pay it and more if you desire it to keep you here."

"I think that circumstance requires me to accept the invitation. You should know, however, that if there weren't a war raging in the states north of us, I would be more inclined to board another ship."

"I'm sure, Miss Gall, I don't have to tell you how happy I am of your decision to stay."

"Would you please call me Angela from henceforth. In the presence of such youth I'm starting to feel like an old maid."

"If it pleasures you, then Angela it is, and Angela it will always be. I have taken the liberty of arranging a room for you in a large building adjacent to my house In Tallahassee. My wife has furnished it with suitable bedding and furniture. It's nothing extraordinary but I think you'll find it to your liking. Anything else you need we will purchase upon arrival. You will have a domestic servant to attend to your needs, and you will take all your meals with me and my wife, as this is only a short walk away. Our cook of many years prepares nourishing, tasty meals three times a day. I hope this meets with your approval."

"As long as the ventilation is good, all of your efforts sound acceptable."

"I have made sure of the ventilation with a large double window on the west-facing wall and a push out transom over the door. The air is more humid than you are accustomed to, but in a few months you will not notice it as much. The summers are hot, but the winters are reliably nice. I'm sure you will not miss the ice and snow so much as a minute."

"No, I should guess not."

"Has your luggage been moved to a room?"

"No, it's here in the sitting room, over there in the corner."

"I'll procure a room for each of us, then send the bellhop for it. There's plenty of time, but they won't move to assist unless I've shone them my keys and waved a few coins at them."

"When I arrived here there was an attendant both rough and uncultivated. His dress and speech were rude, devoid of the superiority I would expect from an establishment like this. I don't want him carrying my luggage or coming to my door."

"Most certainly not, Angela. I won't allow him to encroach on your patience a second time. What did this attendant look like?"

"He'll be easy to spot. He's the only one here with whiskers."

"I'll see to it they keep him away from you. Before we withdraw to our rooms, do you have any questions for me?"

"Nothing that can't wait until we dine. Oh, but there is one thing I've been wondering about."

"And what might that be?"

"Tallahassee is such an unusual name. If I'm going to live there I shall like to know what the meaning behind it is?"

"Tallahassee is an Apalachee Indian word meaning 'old town' or 'abandoned fields.' Not very romantic. Is it? Nor clever for that matter. The area became an abandoned Apalachee village. In 1656, a Spanish deputy governor and his crew settled in the Apalachee town that they called San Luis in what is now West Tallahassee. When they abandoned it, the Indians started calling it by its current name."

"Thank you, James. It seems silly but I always wonder about names. Why some that are so obvious a blunder can remain so. Why are there never any attempts to correct them? Tallahassee lies halfway between the Gulf and the Atlantic, so why not change it to a more fitting name."

"What would you propose?"

"How about Midway or Middleton, or maybe Junction City."

"Say, your good at this. I do quite like Junction City."

"Yes. It has a nice ring to it, doesn't it?"

"Angela, when do you usually dine.?"

"I prefer seven o'clock."

"I'm sure that's the European in you. Would you mind if we make it six? Around here they dine earlier, most around five. By seven they may be starting to clean the tables."

"Then six it is James. It's strange how customs mold our taste and ideas. But I don't mind, really. What I do mind, at least a little, is that others will think there is too great a disparity between our ages. They most likely will think you are my grandson."

"I will attempt to correct them if you like."

"Oh, and now you play the comedian. I think we both know how that would go. I do like that you are purposely making me laugh. After such a difficult start we seem to be getting along very satisfactory."

"I *can* be the clown sometimes. Whatever the case, it did occur to me while you were talking, how beautiful you are at your age."

"And now you flatter me. A sad pity, too. Because my reflection whispers to me that I have the appearance of retirement. And it is true."

"If you're up for new treatments, I can make you look much younger."

"Don't tell me you're that kind of a scientist. A chemical scientist I presume."

"I am. I've developed facial tonics that work wonders. But my revitalizing injections are astonishing. They will make you feel young again. We could discuss it later while we dine if you like."

"If you've been using the treatments on yourself then I should like to hear what you have to say."

"I have indeed and look forward to the discussion. Now, if you can wait a few more minutes I'll see to the accommodations."

After being led upstairs, Angela fastens her door and glances around the room. She notices a poster bed with mosquito netting, something she's not used to seeing. The netting is tied up with white ribbon and connected to a frame protruding inward from its post. The whole room consisted of an old-fashioned couch, a small writing desk with chair, and a large oak chest with squares cut out near the top. When she approached the chest, she could see that the squares were covered in glass and that it formed a little closet. Next to the writing desk, there was a ledge with books piled up for the occupant's convenience. One book was a ledger opened and covered in writing. There were all kinds of characters crudely drawn like a child had been here. She leans against the wall, smiling, and looking at them. A note next to the ledger asked for pen and ink commentary, so she starts flipping through the pages. Some were no more than detached sentences while other parts took the form of a regular diary. She notices more words and characters scrawled in the hands of a child and this strangely prompts her to amuse herself with her own words.

"Today started with an awful flood of rain. It came just as all passengers were leaving deck to the mainland. If I had not had an umbrella I would have caught the brunt of it. The day has since gotten much better as I now find myself in a comfortable well-equipped room. My voyage here was the initiatory step of a great change in my life. Tomorrow I leave by coach to Florida's capital city, Tallahassee. I have my prayer book and will refer to it heavily. If things go wrong, I will knowingly answer for it. However, I have always been invigorated by a terrific challenge. This move into the unknown may be the most noteworthy of my life. I am hoping it will be a last sought after blessing and not a final downfall. I would like to say to those in charge of this fine establishment that you should dismiss the attendant with the whiskers at once. Any man who would steal the face of a baboon and take it for himself is not worthy of such a position. Rest assured he'll not change his crude ways. You'd as soon squeeze a fart out of a dead cow. I hope you don't mind my humor on this last matter. I couldn't think of a better way to address my concern. Thank you for arranging this wonderful room for my rest.

Angela Rena Gall
Gettysburg Pennsylvanian
August 21, 1863

She began to nod drowsily over the dim pages of the ledger. Noticing this, her eyes wandered from the print to the room's singular window. She walks over and pushes the drapes apart to give more light. Her brain tired and only half-conscious, she sits on the edge of the bed, sinks back and falls asleep. As soon as her head touches the pillow she starts to dream, wearied from worry and travel.

Hours later to her relief she is awakened by a gusty wind and the tapping of rain on the windowpane. She preps herself, then hurries from the paradise of her room to the Hotel Casa's dining room. Almost immediately she spots James waving to her. Sitting quickly, she sounds somewhat out of breath. "Sorry to keep you waiting. I lighted on a spot where it was close to impossible to get up."

"So, you fell asleep?"

She smiles with her whole face, a tinge of pink filtering to the surface. "Yes. I was compelled to rest. It was out of my control."

"The apologies unnecessary. I'm glad you've rested up."

"James, have you lived in Tallahassee a considerable time? I believe you mentioned eighteen years."

"I may have mentioned eighteen years in referencing Florida's statehood, but I don't think so."

"That's right, my mind's a little fuzzy from sleep. Surely you weren't raised there though?"

"I've lived there for a long time, but it could hardly interest you."

"No doubt times are greatly changed since then. You've seen many alterations haven't you?"

"Yes, and a good many troubles, too."

"You don't sound like a native of the country. I detect an exotic English accent."

There is a pause, and then an interruption by the waiter. "Today we have roast beef or chicken. Both come with an assortment of vegetables and fresh rye bread. To drink, we have coffee, tea, cow's milk or, if you prefer it, goat's milk. Will the gentleman be ordering for both?"

"No. Please start with the lady."

"The chicken and the tea. And I should like some ice water please."

"And you, sir?"

"I'll have the same."

"Very good, the wait won't be long."

"Where were we, James?"

"You were asking about my history."

"I'm sorry I didn't wait for an invitation. You seem so companionable I felt it okay."

"Before I came to live in Tallahassee I spent time in New York."

"And your birthplace?"

"England, Liverpool to be exact."

"What of your parents?"

"Both my parents died of consumption while I was in college."

"Do you mind if I ask where you got your money at first."

"Growing up I learned the management of land from my parents, who themselves had inherited an enormous amount. They were in fact extremely wealthy landlords. I have no siblings, and thus at the age of twenty-one found myself rich beyond my wildest imagination. I still have holdings in England, and as you know already, many holdings in and around Tallahassee."

"You don't seem hardened by it, perhaps to the mistreatment of others. It's common with those in your situation. So much so that your story would appear suspect. It's a good thing I'm taken with you, believing all you've said. If we have trust, we won't be saying the wrong things to each other. Do you wish it so?"

"I do, and I sympathize with what you're saying. Because of my wealth, I've had access to a good many like you've described. It vexes me to see it, but as you've said, it is common."

"James I have one last question you've smoothly wriggled your way around. Would you mind if I asked your age?"

"The age of a man has never been important like the age of a woman. However, if you insist then I must warn you that I

145

cannot be exact on the matter."

"I've never met a man so mysterious about his age, especially one obviously still quite young. Maybe we could make a game of it."

"If you desire."

"You are not in your twenties are you?"

"I am not."

"Then how far in your thirties is the mystery."

"It's your game, continue on."

"Is it under thirty-five or over?"

"Over."

"Then you are between thirty-five and forty, and I dare say closer to thirty-five."

"If you are happy with that then we will leave it as it is."

"You're not going to help me anymore are you?"

"Of course, I will. I am considerably under three hundred."

"I see what you meant about the clown in you. Since you have a face almost half your age I should like to hear of these age-defying treatments you mentioned earlier today. Looking at you I find it compelling and am already considering testing them. Would you mind amusing me with more information?"

"I can give you a series of injections that will make you look and feel much younger. You will have a fresh complexion with eyes that sparkle as bright as diamonds. Truth is you will be altered considerably in only three days."

"But how does it work?"

"I wish I could tell you I have all the answers. To make a long story short, I don't fully know how it works, only that it does. Looking into my face you know that it's true. Currently, my technology is ahead of my education. It's the main reason I brought you here. It's my belief that the injections affect areas of the brain that control aging. I need to understand the brain on a different level than I do now. I am hoping between the two of us, we can figure out exactly how my formula works. Also, why it doesn't continue to work. Every so many years it's necessary to repeat the injections. Something's interfering, but I don't know what. You can see now why I am so thrilled that you are coming to Tallahassee."

146

"Let me express my pleasure that you brought me here for something so important. To affect the aging process even a little is thrilling to think about. I can set up a series of tests. The first thing we need to know is, does your formula literally affect the brain. There are plenty of senior people that would gladly volunteer as subjects. Do you plan to keep this secret?"

"Yes. I don't want to rouse the attention of the wrong group of people. Only a few words could make us look entirely negligent. They may even want to reprimand us. So, we can't afford to be careless."

"I was thinking the same thing. The world's a fickle place. Often they punish a person that should be given an award. Better to keep strict confidentiality until all documentation is complete. It will take some months, maybe a year, but if we *can't* prove the brains being affected, people will think we are witches injecting spells with red hot needles."

"I see your point, no pun intended, well maybe a little."

"I'm really starting to like you."

"If we were in New York and word got out, we could be throttled quickly. As it is though, Tallahassee is the perfect place for our experimentation."

"Oh, James, our supper has come, and it looks like such a treat."

Chapter 12

One complete rotation of the earth glided away. The rapid transformation of Harlan Landcaster was now at the center of everyone's talk. The dramatic changes in him during the previous months were now being matched or surpassed by the revelations of the last twenty-four hours. As was Harlan, so too the universal human aging concept was changing. The past day was connective, bringing to Harlan's understanding that he was the next chosen one, and the hope of all mankind. The Fifth Pinnacle had arrived, and now Harlan would be the key to the survival of humankind, and possibly the key to every person living forever. He now understood the consequences of Mr. Lett's plan, the scope of which Mr. Lett himself could never comprehend.

Inside Harlan's brain was an awakened transmitter to another realm. The cycle of time in this realm was by definition a different concept than the unit of measurement used by man. Since death didn't exist in this realm, time was less relevant. One solar day was no more than a blink, a thousand years a short vacation. Time was counted with threes, fours, and fives instead of one as the starting point. Five hundred years times three brought about each successive chosen one. The fifth chosen one could be the complete solution or possibly the complete end of not just humans, but all physical matter. Included in this matter were many other inhabitable planets. The purpose all along had been the procreation of man without death, and his gradual spread throughout the universe. Those in the other realm, who placed man here 6000 years ago were watching closely.

It was a golden, refreshing morning. Every inhale and exhale of breath from the beach is so full of life. Angela's face was just like the landscape. The sunshine was beaming, and shadows from clouds were moving over her in rapid succession. As Harlan watched her and the few early rising tourists walking barefoot in the sand, it appeared the cycle of life was endless. However, no matter how beautiful the scene was to his eyes, his brain was being candid with him. Eight in every one-thousand people die every day, which amounts to 151,600 or 6,316 per hour. People are dying constantly and unless someone is affected, it's rarely thought about. Every one-hundred-years most of the population of the earth turns over. This is what he's thinking when he feels a face lean against his shoulder.

Danny was standing next to him, one of her feet pressed backward against an aqua colored block wall. "What are you thinking?" She asked while pressing her face farther into his shoulder.

"I was thinking Angela and I need to get to work. There's a lot left to arrange, and not much time."

"Can I come? I won't be a problem! I'll just sit and listen! Really, I want to be with you!"

"You'll probably be bored. But if you wish."

One hour later they sat in the office of Angela's apartment. Harlan's face seemed intense like he's being threatened. He grips his hands and fingers together on the desk in front of him, giving out a dreadful gasp. "I dread going through with this. I'm going to need everyone's help. It will take everyone working together."

Danny puts her hand over his to settle his nerves. "You're no coward, and you've never been afraid. You're here to work it out, so work it out."

"Yes, I suppose your right." He looks across the desk at Angela. "Time to go to work."

"Fine by me. Are you ready to delve into the secret world of the brain?"

"You've got my attention."

"We're going to have to give Mr. Lett an altered state of consciousness."

"There will be others in the room with him, I can promise

you that."

"Doesn't matter. He has the strongest mind. I promise you the others will be easy."

"Sounds reasonable. Where do we start?"

"We start by giving you a brief education on the mind. Consciousness exists in many different forms. What we think of as our normal, waking, rational consciousness is just one of them. What we want Mr. Lett and his associates to experience is one of the others, an altered state of consciousness. In doing this, they'll think that what they are experiencing is completely normal. If things go according to plan we can inject them with Carter's memory formula without any interference. They may even want to help us."

"I thought an altered state of consciousness had to be drug-induced. Are you saying we'll have to slip something into their drinks? Because Mr. Lett would see it coming as soon as we arrive."

"Drug taking produces one very specific experience of consciousness. In these cases, most people know that there's been a slight deviation from the normal waking state. It's generally why they drink too much or take other substances. They want the high it gives them. This is not what we're talking about and wouldn't work in the first place. Being light-headed, or having your senses sharpened or dulled, possibly with a distorted sense of time would not be effective enough to accomplish our plan."

"How can something that alters one's consciousness be more powerful than narcotics?"

"Not more powerful, just different. I want you to think of our everyday consciousness as an iceberg. The visual part of the iceberg on top of the water is only a small portion of what's there. Underneath the water, there is about five times more ice if not more. So, what you are looking at is only the tip of the iceberg. Its the same with everyday consciousness.

In some cultures, entering a trance state is considered quite normal. There are several ways to induce it, including the use of lights, humming, and meditation. Some believe that when this altered state happens you're being possessed by gods.

None of this is true. It has to do with the area of your brain that deals with various or altered states of consciousness. All of this is at the front portion of the brain: Starting at the top with the prefrontal cortex. Below that is the area that deals with attention, just in front of that is the emotional response, and underneath is behavior and judgment. Some people believe hypnosis affects this area and creates an altered state of consciousness. However, this is still a pretty big debate among scientists. I personally feel that hypnosis leads only to an altered state of unconsciousness.

On the other hand, sleepwalking is considered a state of unconsciousness, but is it really? Sleepwalkers have been witnessed driving a car perfectly, using a knife without hurting themselves, going up and downstairs, even swimming. What this means is that functions associated with waking consciousness are being used. Eyesight, muscle coordination, memory and so on. So, what's happened is they've fallen or possibly wakened into an altered state of consciousness, the kind that we need to induce on Mr. Lett and company. Even during a normal waking day, it is quite common for the brain to drift into brief moments of sleep-like activity. When this happens, we have reduced control over thoughts and actions, thinking what's taking place is normal, even if it's total day-dreaming. When we've done this to Mr. Lett, it will be like he's sleepwalking or day-dreaming. He won't suspect a thing because he still has awareness. He just won't be able to comprehend what should and shouldn't be happening."

"This is fascinating, Angela. But if we can't use hypnosis or narcotics, and we certainly can't invite him into a deep session of meditation, then how do we induce this altered state?"

"That's where your new abilities come in. You must disrupt his sensory perception. You can do this by focusing on his eyes and forehead. Behind those lie his consciousness."

"So, you're saying I have to take control of his mind?"

"No. If that were possible Mr. Lett would be using it himself. My understanding of the brain seems to dispel that rationale. In fact, I think taking complete control of one's mind

151

might cause damage to it. We're not computers or robots. We're living, breathing flesh. What you can do is affect it, place it into a state of altered consciousness. When you first enter the room, you will need to start with the others, then finish with Mr. Lett. He'll take longer because of his unique abilities. But you are much stronger, so it should work. Remember you can't just glance, you must focus. The eyes will tell you when it's worked. After that start setting up and injecting them, acting like everything is normal. You might even tell a joke or two to keep a relaxed atmosphere.

Oh, and remember you have a limited amount of time. I can't say for sure, but sleepwalking lasts about ten minutes on average, sometimes a little less, sometimes more. That's pretty much it, Harlan. You've got several days to practice on people. I'm here for you. You're going to do fine. Any questions?"

"Is there a plan B?"

"They don't know what's coming. What could go wrong? Other than Carter and Jen we'll all be with you in the room, supporting you."

"I just got a feeling is all."

"It's normal to be nervous in stressful situations. By the time the day arrives, you'll be fine."

"I keep thinking all our efforts will end with only a consolation. But I can't think of anything to be done that hasn't already been done."

"Relax, Harlan. Getting used to a new awareness will take some time. You're going to do fine. We all are. You have an amazing brain, the most amazing of any man who came before you. You are the chosen one. You know that, right?"

"Yes. The other realm? They've already made a connection with me."

"Then don't be so hard on yourself. Give yourself time. You've changed so much so fast."

"Thank you, Angela. I'll work on that. For now, though, I'm going to the beach."

"What for?"

"By now there will be lots of people there. I want to practice over and over until I'm completely comfortable with it. I want it to be natural, not at all noticeable when I use it."

"Maybe you should eat some breakfast first, you too, Danny."

Solomon Ray Lett stood at the edge of the room over-looking Lexington's skyline of high-rise buildings and elongated, silver clouds. His three-piece suit had a deep gloss to it, tacitly emphasizing his importance. His brilliant looking wife appeared bored holding a partially filled champagne glass. Her emerald-green gown proclaimed her insignificant interest and disregard for the important matter at stake. In total there were eleven people in the room, which was on the fifth floor of the Museum Hotel. Three sat on a large sectional sofa, three more in tall bar-like chairs, the others standing at various locations sipping drinks and blending in with the nicely arranged chrome outlined furniture.

Soon there is a rustling of bodies, heads turn announcing the opening of the door. Two female faces are the first to enter, that of Angela and Grace. The next are James, then Harlan and Danny. Behind them, old Jack leans his head in holding tight to the doorknob. "He brought his whole darn entourage. If you like, I can remove them."

Solomon hesitates while looking at Harlan. He takes a sip from his glass, then waves a dismissive hand. "No, Jack. No need to interfere. Shut the door behind you." Next, he twists his body, turning directly at James. "Everyone needs their friends with them when making important decisions, don't they, James?"

"Friends, yes." He glances around the room. "It seems you've filled the place with yours."

"Nevertheless, I'm pleased you brought your own. It shows you're not play-acting. You *are* ready to swear your allegiance to the cause and not your contempt. Tell me I'm right about that."

"There are words for how I feel, but I have no contempt. As for you, Solomon, I have a great deal of admiration. It saddens me to think of where man's hope would be today without the formula, which was of your invention. Not only that, but you were flawless in how you opened it up to others like me. It was a display of sheer genius."

"I think it was my greatest accomplishment, splitting the globe seven ways. Revealing the formula to seven people on the seven continents. Now here we are all these years later, the final stage in putting the earth back to where it started."

"Do you mind if I ask, why now? You could have done this at any point in the past, hundreds of years ago."

He takes another quick sip, this time finishing it off and jerking the glass back. "You think you know, don't you, James? It's the scientist in you, so I'll try to overlook it." In a fleeting pass, Solomon glances at Harlan. "I am *constantly* reminded of the past!" A white glow is quickly streaming outward, forming a circle around him. Temporarily his body pulsates in a colorful display of light.

"Settle yourself down!" His wife shouts sarcastically. "You'll blow the whole freaking room up with all of us in it."

"I never came close to where I am now!" He starts calming down. "It was always kept at a distance from me. They never helped me. I would've been so grateful. But they never offered, not even once."

"Who never offered? Who are you referring to?"

"You know exactly who I'm talking about. Our inventors, those who placed us here. The other freaking realm, Zion! I think they chose me because I was trained extensively in the art of mixing potions, and in the science of the day which didn't amount to much. They've visited me many times. Until recently they've watched me. For over a decade I was tested. They filled my room with mathematical problems. I spent year after year solving them. In total twelve years, and not once did they ever help. It all started when I was first inaugurated as King. As soon as I was situated in my new accommodations, the math problems started appearing. No one could see them but myself. When I cracked the formula, I thought they would be satisfied. I thought maybe then they would do away with death forever and bring things back to the way they were in the beginning. Instead, they acted like it was nothing, and they just kept watching me."

"I can see why you're troubled. Still, they knew you would eventually crack the code and make the formula. What you did with the formula is what they were really interested in."

"How could I be expected to know what the objective was? For decades I wouldn't even use it on anyone but myself. I thought they wanted me to rule the world, to be a better ruler than any who came before me. Did you know my father was a king?"

"No, I had never heard that."

"That's because its been a very long time. You've heard of Solomon in the good book?

"His stories based on you?"

"Not exactly. I'm one of his many sons. It's how I ended up a king, at least for a time."

"People adored your father. What about you?"

"Some yes, but others not so much. Unlike my father, the Queen of Sheba didn't care for me. We knew her as Queen Makeda. She came from modern-day Ethiopia. She was a prissy petite thing who visited my father when she was young and later, when she was older, she visited me. She wasn't at all what people think of her, and not nearly as beautiful as she wanted to be. She didn't come to hear my wisdom like my father, although she did put me to the test. She came to scout out the land for a possible invasion. That kind of thing was common in those days. I even once sent a huge caravan to visit her for the same purpose. I was still miffed about her attempt. Some say I sent the ark of the covenant along as a show of good faith. Some even say that's where it ended up and is there to this day. None of that is remotely true. Anyway, during her visit, she found out I couldn't be tricked. It miffed her and she left never to return. Before she left she did talk me out of some pretty nice things I have to admit. She was witty, which I admired about her. Nonetheless, what she left with was nothing compared with my vast fortune at the time. There were others like her that came and went. Being King keeps you busier than people realize.

For a couple of years, I didn't even try to solve the

mathematical problems that had been given to me. When I got back to it and subsequently broke the code I had to spend decades covering up my age. Everyone was far more religious during that time. When I didn't appear to be aging, there were rumblings that I had made a deal with the Devil. The royal guard foiled several attempts on my life. I became a master of disguise, using my chemical mixing abilities to produce makeup that helped me match my age to my number of years. Eventually I had to fake my own death. After that I fled into Arabia and started a new life. Naturally I had lost the favor of the other realm by then. It was a long time before I got back to trying to figure out what to do with the formula.

James, you remind me of the Queen of Sheba."

"Why do you say that."

"You underestimate me just like she did."

"I don't think I've underestimated you at all."

"I won't be tricked, I can't be. She came on a pretense. She was really looking for trouble. You're looking for trouble, I can sense it."

"Yes, but in a good way."

"No, and I'll prove it. How are you with dreams, James?"

"Dreams?"

"You heard me. Or maybe I should ask how are you with *sleepwalking, or an altered state of consciousness*? As I said, you underestimate me."

"What did you expect?"

"At the end of it all I expected you to do the right thing, and I still do."

"I am doing the right thing."

"No! You're trying to prolong the agony. You haven't spent years seeing death the way I have!"

"Who told you? And don't tell me you just sensed it. I know better than that."

"You think you know things, like how deep this really goes, but you can't even begin to know the half of it."

"I know your abilities don't reach that far. I'll ask again. Who told you?"

"Tell him, Solomon. He deserves to know, everyone does."

Solomon jerks his head around to his wife. "You could die for this. Is that what you want?"

She sits her glass on a small table and walks over to him. "I'm just drunk enough not to give a damn anymore. You've kept me alive for over 2000 years. I'm tired of watching you walk around in those fancy suits like the sun shoots out of you. When what you really do is use people. You use them and dump them, hundreds of them for thousands of years."

"I never let go of anyone who didn't deserve it."

"That's a lie and you know it!"

He grabs her by the arm and shoves her backward. "Sit down and shut it up or I'll send you back to where I found you. Moscow's not an easy place to live these days."

"Moscow's never been an easy place to live. You should apologize for all the secrecy."

"You don't want me to apologize with ice on my tongue do you."

"Tell him. Tell him or I'll tell him myself."

Solomon glances a moment at Danny, making direct eye contact. Then in quick succession, his eyes go to Harlan, then back to James. "Your perception of everything you think you know is about to change James. I'm not even sure you can take it. You've always been so many steps behind. I don't know what made you think you could compete with somebody like me! How *arrogant* of you!

We've known about the chosen one from the exact moment of his appearing. We knew to the day when he would appear, and I sensed that you had him immediately. After that it was easy. I give you credit for using Angela to test him. She's been a big asset to you. I would've liked to have had her by my side. Did it never strike you as strange that you never knew who the fourth chosen one was?"

"Never. You told me it's the way he wanted it, that he was the reserved type. You told me he was more comfortable with assisting than leading. I had no reason not to believe you."

"For starters, James, he's not a he, but in fact a woman. Out of the previous four chosen ones two have been women, and two have been men. The latest of the chosen, the fifth, is

157

of course as you already know, a man." He glances at Harlan. "The first chosen couldn't give up his power after his time was up. He fought the second, a female. Their battle is what started the rebellion. When one killed the other, that one was put to death by Zion. It's never been allowed for a chosen to kill another chosen. I was the third chosen, and although I didn't know it at the time, it was thought a chosen one could right man's plight. Some of these things you already know, but what you don't know is that the fourth chosen one is also in this room. You look surprised, James... That brings us to the fifth chosen one. You actually thought you could bring him here, and I wouldn't know it?" He glances again at Harlan. "You seem surprised a second time. Something else you don't know is that the fourth chosen one, being the more powerful one, is in charge. She orchestrated everything. I'm only a cover. It shows her brilliance, wouldn't you agree?"

James looks around the room. There are three women other than Solomon's wife, one standing, the other two sitting. They were already in the room when he arrived. "Are you going to tell me which one it is, or is she going to tell me herself."

"Again, you disappoint me. Still, you think you know how deep this goes, but you have no real clue. You never even thought about looking at the women that came in with you." Solomon turns to Harlan. "Are you starting to get it now? Your powers aren't what you think. They won't be complete for years to come. We were able to keep her a secret from you, and right under your very nose. Your own girlfriend, or so you thought. Daniela, darling. It's been 1500 years, but the cat's out of the bag. It's time for you to take center stage."

She turns to her left and whispers into Harlan's ear. "No matter what happens, I did fall for you. But I can't change, I never will."

He remains silent as she walks to the center of the room and begins talking.

"I remember when I came out of Russia, the part that's now Finland. Sorry, Harlan. I can't recall even once ever visiting West Virginia. You were so easy to fool, like a young schoolboy. And in a way you are. Your powers are so new to

158

you. Anyway, I went into Caledonia, which was part of Britannia ruled by Great Britain at the time. Solomon tutored me there for years. All told we stayed on that Island for some fifty-years. He helped me understand my powers and to reach my potential. We can do the same for you, Harlan. You need it, you just don't know it yet."

A space opens around Harlan as the others start moving out of the way. No one is standing between him and Danny. "What happens if I don't join you?"

"That's your first question for me? I can see this is going to be a memorable conversation."

"And another thing. Have you used your powers to kill before?"

"You've got to be kidding me."

"Answer the question. I deserve that much."

"If you must know… then yes. But it's not what it seems."

"Doesn't matter. If you've used your powers to kill you'll kill again."

"Yes, but it's for the good of man. It's always been for the good of man."

"Are you planning on killing someone in this room today?"

"There's a rule. A chosen one can't kill another chosen one. If they try, our watchers will intercede. If we try to kill you, we will lose our own lives. It's happened before, you know that. So, relax."

"I'm not worried about me. I never was."

"None of your friends will be harmed if they join us. But time's running out. We're almost ready to implement our plan. I can't hold off much longer, it would jeopardize certain regions, set us back another year. I beg you, Harlan, all of you. Don't be stubborn. No, there's no time for protest or struggle. In the end, this is going to happen with or without you."

"You look puzzled and tormented, Harlan."

"Shut up Solomon! And wipe that grin off your face."

"But he doesn't know you, Daniela. Let me have my fun. You don't know this woman, Harlan. Someday I'll tell you, but there's no time now. You're starting to see her now though, aren't you? Inside she's really laughing herself sick.

159

She tore your heart out by the roots."

"Stop it, Solomon! It's too much!"

"It will be impossible to believe her now. Put an end to your torment. Join us and everything is all well again. Don't let James and Angela fill your mind with innumerable doubts, some picked up and some invented. Act quickly and firmly. Do it now."

"That's exactly what I plan to do. I won't be a part of your mass executions." He turns to Danny. "The two men at the beach, under the pier. You were testing me?"

"I needed to know how far along you were with your powers. So, I made sure those two rednecks saw me take the money. I knew they would chase me. The look on their faces when the energy came out of you. You were spectacular. There's so much more. Let us help you reach your potential. You'll be amazed, I promise."

"Amazed? Yes, I suppose so. An interesting word, amazed. It's the past tense of amaze. It's more than being surprised. It's being filled with astonishment like your breath is taken away.

While it's true that we underestimated you and Solomon today, it's also true that you two have underestimated us, or maybe I should say me. Since I'm the latest chosen one, and the powers of the latest are always greater than the previous ones, you don't really know what my powers are. What you've seen from me to this point is only what any regenerated one can do. I have been given understanding, and abilities that have not been afforded to any prior chosen ones."

"No, we've been watching you for months."

"You, Danny, are the one who will be amazed! You have no idea what a direct connection to the invisible realm can do. And that's what I've been given. What you perceive on this earth is only one-quarter of the reality. The Universe is not alone, it has brothers and sisters. There are in actuality three other dimensions. You've heard terms like alternate realities or parallel universe? A more accurate term would be multiverse because there are actually four universes including our own. The physics and mathematics involved are staggering to the mind. Am I taking your breath away yet, Danny?"

"You're bluffing. It can't be. We would've known."

"And yet you didn't until I just told you. And that's not all. I can move between these dimensions and, if I choose, to take others with me. So, we might not have won today, but we certainly haven't lost, not yet. What you are about to see, I promise you, will take your breath away." A slight rumble starts up. At first it seems distant like a huge tank is moving toward them. Straightaway the room starts to agitate.

"What's that vibration? What are you doing? Stop it, you're going to shake the building down."

"No. I'm just sending notice to you that you're up against more than you've imagined. The next time we talk, I hope you'll be more agreeable." All at once there is a high-pitched shrieking noise and the room is instantly filled with a striking blue fluorescence. The building wobbles violently like they are amid an earthquake. The vivid, bright blue glow hangs in the air and seems painted on the furniture, the artwork, and the walls. The atmosphere, now determined by the brilliant fluorescence, begins to lose its visibility. It's impossible to see, and the sound of things thrusting up then crashing down causes panic to set in. Everyone is reaching out trying to grab hold of something to brace themselves. As the shaking starts to lessen and the air slowly begins clearing, remnants of the fluorescence pulsate a dull blue out of the bodies of all those in the room. Finally, when the air clears and the pulsating stops, it's quickly obvious that there are four people missing: James, Grace, Angela, and Harlan.

"My God! What just happened, Daniela?"

"Zion is helping them, that's what."

"Are you sure?"

"No. I need to think!"

Chapter 13

(The 1800's)

The door is propped open with a cool breeze coming through it. It brushes briskly against James' dark-brown, three-piece suit. Without the feeling of privacy, he takes it upon himself to step just inside the room. There is no one present, but he can hear a faint rustling sound behind a dressing partition. Beyond that he can see the window fully open and the curtains blowing continuously like the ripple of waves from a beach. He reckons she must be behind the partition, but at first hesitates to speak. Then it hits him that she might walk unclothed and unsuspecting out from behind the partition. He clears his throat loudly.

"Is someone there?"

"Miss Gall, do you have a certificate of birth or any other papers that identify your age?"

"Is that you, James?"

"Of course, who else?"

"Don't come in any farther. I'm changing."

"I wouldn't dare, but did you know you've left the door open?"

"I see your point, but it is July, and I do love the breeze. My privacy seemed secure. Other than my chambermaid there's not a soul in the house. What I mean is, well without the understanding that you were paying a visit. Now that it's come to my attention, maybe I should close the door whilst dressing from now on."

"Yes, I would hate to hinder you in this way again."

"It's been near a year. When are you going to start calling

me Angela?"

"My apologies. I must start remembering to do so."

"What was it you needed?"

"I only just thought of it a little while ago. Your regeneration was completed months prior. You're a young woman again. Obviously, you can't be walking around with the same credentials as before. Your certificate of birth or any other papers identifying your age must be modified. Grace and I made the decision long ago to counterfeit ours every ten years."

"Do you mind if I wait until tomorrow, to dig them out, I mean? It shouldn't be too difficult to find."

"I don't mind at all. Tomorrow's fine."

"It's just that I've been readying myself for the gathering this evening. I wanted to look my best. It's not often all regenerated ones come together at the same location."

"Not all, Angela. Only those we've regenerated here in the Tallahassee area. We're not sure of the numbers worldwide. Maybe someday we will be. In fact, I'm certain of it."

She walks out from the protection of the partition, smiles and gives a curtsy. In a sudden gasp, James' breath is almost taken by her beauty. She is draped in a red dress that flows to her ankles and is outlined in fancy white lace. A white hat, completely round, bowing slightly at its edges, is tied with red ribbon and crowning her head. She holds a lightweight parasol umbrella with mixed colors of lace covering its fringes. She tilts the point of the parasol downward, pointing its wooden tip at James. "How do I look? And be honest."

"Unlike any scientist I've ever seen. You look like a painting out of one of those French street scenes. Really, you're absolutely, stunning. What time can we expect you?"

"Not more than an hour. I'm too excited to wait any longer."

"There will be about a 120 guests total, the majority of whom you've never had the opportunity to meet. About half of them no longer live in the Tallahassee area. You needn't be in a rush to meet them. The gathering lasts for three weeks, so relax and give yourself time."

"The only thing that's going to relax me is a vodka tonic."

"There will be plenty for that, too."

Later, while Angela was outside making the rounds meeting some of the guests, she hears a peculiar sound. When she walks to the edge of the yard, she sees an unusual animal meandering slowly with its nose down as if inspecting the grounds. She waves for James to come over.

He walks over along with a man named Johnny; he was regenerated several years ago.

She points out the strange creature. "What is it, James?"

"We have an occasional problem with wild pigs."

"Do you mean boar?"

"Yes."

"Would you like me to shoot it?" Johnny asked with a tinge of duty mixed with excitement in his voice."

"You wouldn't mind?"

"Not at all. We could roast it at the bonfire later tonight."

"That's a splendid idea. Would you mind shooing it into the pine forest before shooting it, due to all the guests?"

"I'll get some help and do it right now." He dips his head, then runs off in a rush.

"Angela, Johnny just came from Atlanta. I think you might be interested in the report he gave me a few minutes ago."

"Do you mean with the war?"

"I do indeed."

"Then please, tell me what's happening."

"As you have heard already, General Sherman has Tennessee under the control of the Union Army. Some weeks ago, he marched his troops south into Georgia. He crept slowly through the mountains being hindered only a little by snipers along the way. North of Atlanta he began destroying every building he deemed capable of supporting the Confederates. Everything from uniform processing operations to munition depots, including farms capable of providing food. He's gone out of his way to knock down and burn even the smallest of towns along his march. A few days ago, he leveled the great city of Atlanta and set it ablaze. Johnny reports that General

Sherman is now marching toward Savanna and the Atlantic Ocean. He reports that the Confederates are in short supply of money and the war may very well be over shortly."

"I see. That's incredible news."

"You only came here because of the war. You made no bones about it. I suspect you're already thinking of moving back when it's finally and mercifully ceased. Am I correct in my thinking?"

"I will admit that Tallahassee is raw. And compared to what I'm accustomed to, it's quite vulgar. But I'm young and strong again and can endure so much more. Really, truth be told, you and Grace have made life for me more than compatible. My housing is nice and so too are the acres and acres of well-kept grounds. You have a lot to be proud of here. You're helping to civilize the area. I've gotten used to the weather. The winters here are so temperate, although I do miss a little snowfall now and again. Pennsylvania? The summers there are just as amazing as the winters here. To have both in my life would be heaven-like. Yes, I would very much like to go back to Pennsylvania, and I would also like to visit my dear homeland Germany. But neither of those things are possible." While she spoke, she looked over a field of green grass, and watched three vigorous men chase and shoo a 100-pound pig out towards the forest. She laughs at the sight of it. When her laughing subsides, she turns facing James. "I'm so grateful for what you've done for me. Have I told you that?"

"About a dozen times if my count is right."

"Just the same, it can't be said often enough. Truly, I mean that."

"You are the finest of women, Angela. I'm very lucky to have you as my teacher. It's my desire that you stay and continue my education of the brain. Since your regeneration, you can see more clearly why it's so important to me. I envision everyone on the earth being young again. With your help I may one day understand how the formula works on the brain. I think it's possible to unearth the mechanism to endless life without having to be regenerated. It's all there in the extraordinary brain, and eventually, working together we shall find it. That being said, I don't want you to think you owe me anything. You are most certainly free to go at any time. It's why I brought it up. You've already taught me so much and lived up to your end of the bargain."

"What are you trying to tell me, James?"

"I do have a devil of a time getting to the point sometimes." He looks her straight on. His face resembles a child about to confess to his parents. "If it's your desire to leave, then as much as it pains me, you must leave and be happy. Otherwise, being young again won't mean a thing."

"I'm not at all surprised by your entreaty. Your kindness grabbed my attention from the first occasion we met in the Casa Hotel. Your seeming selflessness has subsequently proved itself sincere. Grace is the same, and she's already like a best friend to me. If I leave here I could never make myself known to any of my old friends or relatives. What would I tell them? How could I explain? So, there's nothing to be done. Pennsylvania and Germany are out of the question. I shall have to be content with writing letters.

Your cause is now my cause. I want the same things you do. I'm staying here in Tallahassee. I don't care if it takes a hundred years or two. It doesn't matter because we have all the time in the world now. At some point we're going to break the code to the formula, we'll release that mechanism and bring everyone endless life. I want to be part of that, really, truly. I believe in the cause, James. From now on you and I are connected, partners. That is if you're agreeable to it. Regardless, I won't be separated from you and Grace. You are my family now."

"If this is how you feel, then I agree immediately. Still, you're free to change your mind at any time."

"I won't be changing my mind."

"All the same, you're your own decision-maker. Do you mind if I leave you unattended now? I'm so excited by your decision, I want to run off and tell my dear Grace."

"Feel free to scurry. I've got three men and a pig to keep me entertained."

Late that night Angela watched from a considerable

distance as a huge bonfire blazed unabated. Its flames reach so high that it appears to be scorching the moon. From where she stands, under a stately pecan tree, a blue coolness in the air is whisking between its limbs, firmly blowing against her legs and causing ripples in her dress. She can hear the occasional outburst of laughter around the fire, and the sound of speeches, toasts, and what seems a constant stream of jokes. She feels wonderful and happy as she sips heavily from a bottle of white wine. It was at this moment that she became aware of another voice, this one familiar to her. It was Grace, and she was giving Angela congratulations and good wishes.

"James has not been able to stop talking about you. You have *made* his day and mine, too. We are overjoyed that you will be staying indefinitely." The two friends stood speechless, hugging and crying. Suddenly they were reminded of the great number of guests standing around the fire as a loud outburst of laughter erupted, filling the glowing night with a lively happiness. There were gasps of delight and astonishment as one of the guests, drunk out of his mind, ripped his clothes off and went running completely naked around the fire.

"That's different," Angela said half laughing. It wasn't a dark night due to the huge bonfire and a full moon. As the night deepened, each individual star looked like a light being lit in a distant window. The back of the house was visible, as was the lawn and a patch of lemon trees. Men and women's faces shone with a reddish glow, their bodies intermingled and set off by the bright fire.

"Are you lonely, Angela, without a man I mean?"

"No, Grace, I am not. There is plenty to think about with the work James and I are doing. He has an extraordinary capacity to store up the knowledge he picks up in my training, so he keeps me on my toes. I no longer seem as well-informed to him I'm sure."

"Yes, he soaks information up quickly. I think because he's done so much reading in the past. It sharpens the mind. But he has high regard for your expertise. So, you don't feel the need to marry?"

"No. Should I?"

It's just that you're a young woman again. There is a large contingent of regenerated men here. There's no worry about having something in common. I'm sure whomever you chose, you would get along quite nicely with. That is if it were your desire."

"The ordinary feelings a woman has for a man. They are nothing new to me." She bit her lip in silence, hesitating. "I still have half-forgotten passions from my former life. I should like those to die away completely before I re-engage my heart in that way. For the time being, I'm married to mathematics and science. I used to have the reputation as a knower and explainer of the brain. But the brain is so undeniably complicated that no scientist or Doctor of Medicine should be given these labels. I find out new things practically every day. Sometimes it causes me insomnia. What I'm trying to tell you, Grace, is that you don't have to be fussing over me. I'm busy with my work, and perfectly happy without a marriage union."

"If you're sure then I won't fret over it any longer."

"I'm sure."

"Some of the men who have already noticed you will be disappointed."

"I'm not the only regenerated woman here. There must be fifty or sixty others."

"Yes dear, but none more beautiful than you."

"You flatter me, Grace."

"Try to keep in mind that some of the men here badly miss the wives of their past life. They will no doubt seek your attention."

"I hadn't thought of that. I don't want any misunderstanding, but I'll try not to completely ignore them."

"As long as you grasp the situation, do as you please. They are much older than they look, and in no way need to be coddled like they are babies."

"I've made some mistakes in my past relationships. I once gave my heart to a man who didn't deserve it. I'm embarrassed to say that he never really gave it back. If I do ever desire that kind of friendship again, I hope to eliminate them, the mistakes I mean."

"We all learn from our mistakes. Your acknowledgment in these matters of the heart shows that you have, but don't expect too much of yourself. No matter how intelligent you might look, or how old you eventually get, mistakes will still happen. They are as a part of life as the sugar cane fields or the hot Florida sunshine."

Angela nods in agreement, and the two friends turned their attention back to the bonfire which had since died back a little. There was quiet. A calmness had settled into the evening. Fireflies floated in the night air, drifting across the grounds and along the edge of the forest. Somewhere far away a dog barked. It seemed a sad, mellow announcement that the night's festivities were coming to their end.

James walks out of the shadows and tips his hat in the soft glow of the moon. "Are you two ladies as ready for sleep as I am?"

Grace takes him by the hand and kisses it. "I can't speak for Angela, but I've been ready for the better part of an hour. I think we should go inside and allow the stars and the night some time alone."

"First I have something I would like to tell both of you." He stood looking at them, but his voice had changed. It was quieter, more serious; his face, sullener. Then he was so quiet, it was as if he had changed his mind or wasn't sure what to say.

Angela, detecting the change, quickly takes a step closer to him. "Are you going to leave us hanging? What were you going to tell us?"

"Grace has told you the stories of Old Jack, and how we came to be here in Tallahassee."

"She has indeed. He's a terrible man, the worst."

"He's come to Tallahassee. He's out there somewhere looking for us."

"How do you know that?" Grace shouted. "You can't know that!"

He didn't answer for some time.

"You heard your wife, James." And then in a softer, more subdued voice, Angela spoke again. "I'll repeat her words.

How do you know that?"

"I don't know it!" Again, he goes silent.

Angela looks at Grace, her eyes widening. She looks back at James. "You're not making any sense."

"I can feel it. And for me, it's the same as knowing it. If I'm not damned then I don't know the meaning of it. It's been almost forty years, but he's found us. I've had Johnny prepare ten men with muskets, just in case."

In the distance, at the edge of the pine forest, the faint glow of a light could be seen bobbing up and down, moving in their direction.

"Is that one of the guests?" Grace asked.

The light stopped temporarily, then proceeded. It did this same sequence, stopping and starting several times until it had come within fifty yards of the bonfire. Voices coming from the light could now be heard arguing. Then suddenly a commanding voice with the distinctness of Old Jack rang out. "You betrayed me! I never was the lets-get-along forgiving type, although my mother, the old bag would've loved that!"

About fifty guests standing around the fire, walk to its north end, turn around, puzzled by the single glowing light and the sound of voices. The others were either too drunk to stand or had fallen asleep and didn't know what was going on. There were other much fainter voices coming from the light, and it sounded like they were arguing again. And then they fell silent. A stillness at once takes over the atmosphere. With no breeze blowing, the thick air of humidity is causing a stickiness to cling to the faces of all the guests. They are all quiet as they stare into the darkness at the single glowing light. The whole situation was playing out like someone had invented it to entertain the guests. That was in fact what some of them were thinking.

What happens next happens very quickly and in succession. Suddenly the light goes out and the sound of fireworks cracks through the heavy, dark air. For a split instance it appears that entertainment is indeed in play. However, the thought is wiped away with a horrific scene of agony. A volley of fifty shots, discharged from six Henry repeating rifles was the actual sound at first thought to have been fireworks. At the inaudible command of Old Jack, the riflemen had mowed down about twenty men and women, killing most of them outright. As the rest scatter, several more are picked off. All those asleep or drunk jump up and begin to run along with those being shot at. Several women fall and are trampled. There are inhuman shrieks coming from the wounded, some of which are laying on the ground holding their injuries, some stumbling, trying to run. Everyone has lost his self-control. The indescribable scene continues playing out as all the guests able to do so run for the house or the barn. There are sixteen dead and another eighteen too injured to run. The light from the bonfire hovers around them as Old Jack and six other men walk up. The men and women laying injured on the ground swear loudly, begging the executioners for mercy. One is shot through the head, falling over dead. "Please, you don't have to do this!" One of the injured men shouts. "I want to live a little longer. I want to date a girl again, to get married and..." He is shot through the heart, his body instantly going into convulsions as he dies.

Another round of rifle fire rings through the night. This time three of Old Jack's men fall, shot with muskets through the chest. Old Jack raises his own rifle, but before he can find someone to aim it at, it is shot out of his hands. "Drop your guns!" A voice shouts. It's Johnny and he has nine other musket toting men with him. As they walk into the light of the fire, James is walking with them.

"I'm not the murderer! You are, Jack, but you're going to have to pay for what you've done here today. You have massacred innocent men and women, and all regenerated ones like yourself."

"It's of your own making, James. You knew Old Jack would find you someday. I have to say though, I needed a little help and got it from an extraordinary source."

"Okay, Jack. Go on, I'm listening."

His name is Lett, Solomon Ray Lett. He's the man that invented the formula. I work for him now. I'm his new head of security. By the way, just for your information, he found me, I didn't find him."

"How did he know where to find me?"

"You're going to be surprised by his powers, James. He's known about you and your whereabouts since you picked up on the trail of evidence he left to find the formula.

I give you credit. Didn't think you had it in you to double-cross me. A few years after you ran to this less than civilized place he came to me. I've been with him ever since."

"You've killed people regenerated by his own formula, why?"

"It was important he get your attention."

"Are you telling me *he* ordered this?"

"You're starting to catch on. I already told you, I work for Mr. Lett now. The few we've killed here today can be replaced a hundred times over, the next year if we like. You're not alone in the regenerating of people. You need to take ownership of that. Mr. Lett is your boss now. Do you understand? Do you accept that?"

"Why now? Why not years ago?"

"He's been watching you, keeping up with how successful you've been. Now he's decided to bring you into the worldwide program. This country's growing by leaps and bounds every day. He wants you to lead a panel of twelve men and women. The panel with you at its head will oversee the United States, and all of North and South America, which includes the Islands in the Caribbean."

"So, I'm just supposed to believe a murderer like you?"

"No. Since I've gotten your complete attention, and I think I did a great job of that didn't I, James? In three days, you'll meet Mr. Lett in person. That should give you plenty of time to clean up the mess here. He'll give you further instructions leading to the development of the panel. The scope of your regeneration project just got a lot bigger."

"What building do I meet him in, and what time?"

"There's a large room upstairs from Delmonico's Steakhouse. Seven o'clock. After dinner. No double-crossing this time. If you run, he'll know where you are right off."

"I won't run, Jack. I want to hear what he has to say. This

172

sounds like an incredible opportunity."

"Then I will be leaving. And I'm taking what men I have left."

"Don't move an inch, Jack, and keep your hands up where I can see them. Johnny, have your men keep their muskets aimed."

"Mr. Lett wouldn't like you picking off his Head of Security."

"I'm sure he knows the pathetic person you really are. You and your men can be replaced a thousandfold this next year if he wants it. I can't let you massacre these innocent people and just walk away from it. Johnny, when you're ready."

"Yes, Sir, Mr. Jenkins. On the count of three, men. I'll take Old Jack, and you men take the others. One, two, *three*." Johnny was an excellent marksman, but his hand shook with excitement and nervousness, and he only grazed Old Jack's side. While the other three men fell dead, Old Jack ran and disappeared into the darkness. Johnny throws down his one-shot musket, runs and slides boots first at the feet of the three men they had just shot. He grabs up one of the Henry rifles and starts shooting and screaming wildly into the darkness.

Afterwards James, Grace, and Angela walk into the field where Johnny is still agonizing over his missed opportunity. The grass is glowing eerily from the moonlight, so too are the faces of Old Jack's men as they lie dead. Angela notices an object lying next to her shoe. When she bends down to pick it up she hears Grace's voice from behind her. "How weird the light is tonight. The fields look covered in snow." When she lifts the object it's a large red-handled knife, its blade covered in blood.

"James, what do you make of this?"

He takes the knife from Angela. "Looks like Old Jack's bowie knife. He's been hit. One of the musket balls took it right off him. And look there, I see its pouch too."

Angela touches the blood with her finger, then rubs it in her hand. "Is it possible I could have known about this?"

"That doesn't make sense, Angela?"

"Couldn't someone have tried to warn me, but I just wasn't

listening."

"No, child. No." Grace leans into her, hugging her. "James, the sight of this is too much for her."

The moonshine was coming in through her window leaving a sort of white gloss halfway across the room, and a dark silhouette across the other half. She stood in the doorway propping herself up against the casing. Her arms are crossed, her mind in deep thought, her breathing slow and labored. A voice near the tone of whispering sounds behind her.

"Will you be needing anything, Miss Angela?"

She turns her head and her face has the look of someone who does not expect to sleep tonight. "Heaven's sake, at this hour? No, Julie, you are free to go to bed. But thank you, dear, I know you mean well. With the constellations still burning so bright and beautiful, it's hard to comprehend what just happened only a short while ago. Go to your room and pray. We need all the prayers we can get tonight."

"Yes, ma'am. I've refilled your water bowl and will check on you first thing in the morning."

"Very good. You're excused now." Angela leans forward, walking farther into the room. She tosses her hat atop the bed, rests one hand on its post while slipping off her shoes. Then as she walks around to sit on the bed, she soberly notices an elongated box with a note beside it sitting on the nightstand. As she picks up the note and starts reading, it is apparent it was left well before the hellish bloodshed had broken out. It was in the handwriting of Grace but was from her and James. The note makes it clear that the gift in the box was James' idea. When she opens the box, a sparkling necklace filled with diamonds is shining at her. The note said it was in gratitude for her generous decision to stay on and continue working with James. The note finishes by saying, *You're a dream come true.* She lays backward across the bed biting her knuckles and wondering about this Mr. Lett. How he could possibly justify killing innocent people.

She didn't remember when she fell asleep, but she was

awakened early the next morning by loud voices and the sound of a wagon and horses. She felt well-rested as if she had slept several hours unbroken. She looks out the window and sees dawn breaking. Next to the wagon was James and Johnny talking heavily. She rushes out into the gray and red dawn, only to see the wagon pulling off and James standing in shoes wet from a heavy dew.

"Hold on there, Angela! Why are you running?"

"I don't really know. I thought you and..." She stops a moment to catch her breath. "You and Johnny were talking about something important, weren't you?"

"I should say so. He and some of the other men are gathering up the bodies to bury. We've decided to cut the gathering short. It's been ruined and there's nothing to be done about that. Three more days will give everyone some time to discuss what has happened and when to have the next gathering. After that, they can all go home and, hopefully, come to terms with it.

I want you to understand something, Angela. I don't trust this man *Lett* even if he did invent the formula. No matter what oversight he gives me, I will still be focused on our work. However, he and his people are the powers to be, and we will have to find a way to exist with that."

"Yes, James. It's reasonable. I understand." She looks out to the distant field where the dew was glistening from the early sun. James follows her lead pointing his head in the same direction, and they both catch sight of the wagon, and the bodies being loaded.

Chapter 14

(The Reality of Multiverse)

For the third day in a row, the weather was wretched. The rain poured down with a depressing steadiness. Nothing seemed to be able to slow it down or speed it up. Adding to the indifference of the weather were the expressionless faces of Harlan and Angela as they sat peering out a cafe window. The other two of their party had not yet shown for breakfast. As two of the four escapees sat motionless waiting for the others, the surprise of what they had found upon their arrival was starting to wear off.

This version of earth was called Loam and was in the second year of a war. In terms of progressive history, Loam was decades behind their own earth. The dimensions were not aligned. The war being fought was World War II. Technology in terms of computers and advanced wireless communications had not yet begun. Canada was part of the U.S. and the U.S. was tied in treaty to England as part of a dual world power. This was in part because the revolutionary war had ended with misunderstandings leading to a second war three years later. With money reserves spent on the U.S. side, the next war was decidedly going to the British. With French help, a surprise invasion caught the British completely off guard. When the invasion reached London a treaty was suggested by its Queen that became the basis for a dual world power. The two nation's currencies would be different leading to a freed America. But in terms of military force the two, in essence, remained one nation. Two nations with one army was, in itself, revolutionary.

Loam's version of World War II was in its second summer. It had seen the tide turn several times already. Now it was leaning heavily toward the Germans with Russia taking most of the casualties. Germany was much more formidable in this version of the war. They had taken an extra decade to prepare which gave them time to create the largest military in the world. Their armaments were unequaled by all the other nations put together. France had fallen under Nazi control at the outset and Britain and the U.S., in the middle of an economic depression, both struggled to build their military. Talk of a worldwide German language was front-page news.

In the distant background, artillery fire could be heard which roused the attention of several people in the cafe. Suddenly a gust of wind shook the coffee house windows violently as if it were attempting to end the war with one quick shot. Just behind the unexpected wind trotted James and Grace. James was holding a newspaper above his head while Grace struggled to hold onto an umbrella. When they reached the door of the café, another hard gust ushered them inside. The wind blowing through an opened door momentarily whisked napkins across tables, ruffled skirts of ladies and tipped the hats of gentleman up into the air. "We're safe! We're safe!" James shouted, not understanding what a man had asked him as he entered.

"No, old chap. That's not what I meant. I don't care about the weather. Can't you hear the gunfire? Oh, I'll go check for myself." The man opens the door and there is a quick repeat of the wind blowing through the cafe. He runs outside and disappears down the street. Word of invasion was spreading, and most people were filled with anxiety over it.

"Have you heard the news?" James asked as he and Grace seated themselves at the table with Harlan and Angela. "If I were you, Harlan, I would send us back home now. It seems the prudent thing."

"What have you heard?"

"Why did you have to send us here to London anyway?" Grace interjected.

"Hold on now, we need to keep our wits about us. You two

act as if I played a role in what's happening, like I actually had something to do with it."

James continues. "Of course not, but you did send us here in the middle of a war. There's talk of London being bombed at any moment now. Already the hospitals are desperately overcrowded. Soldiers are being put in passageways and on landings."

"Did you know there are no antibiotics, that penicillin hasn't been discovered yet?"

"No, Grace…"

"In the lobby of our hotel, we've just heard stories of soldiers dying from infection."

"I agree that's terrible, but…"

"Germany's sending warplanes to London as we speak, and hundreds of tanks have been spotted heading this way. The wars turned lopsided. They're not even hiding plans for an invasion of New York. They want control of New York Harbor."

"But James, it's unlikely that anything will happen before we leave."

"Unlikely!"

"If we stay here we'll be under the control of the Nazis."

"No, Grace, I would never let that happen."

Angela, who has stayed quiet and looking out the window, now turns her head. "Harlan had no way of knowing what life would be like here. None of us did. If we were in New York or anywhere in the U.S., it would be just as frightening. Before he sends us back we need a plan. If you're in such a hurry to go back then I suggest we get to work on that plan. One thing I do agree on, if we stay here much longer, we'll all be learning another language. Not to mention in four days Danny and Solomon implement their plan."

Harlan taps his fingers on the table. "That's not entirely true."

"If that's not true, there must be something you need to tell us."

"Yes, Angela, and I'll get right to it. Their plan is still a week away. While we're here in this world, we are only losing time in this world. When we go back, we will be in the same room with the same people, only minutes after we left. I can stretch that to about ten minutes if I concentrate."

Quickly pulling a handkerchief from his vest pocket, James jumps up from his chair. "Heaven's sake, Harlan, are we really in that bad a predicament." He starts patting his forehead. "The last time we dealt with Solomon and Danny it didn't work out too well. If we stay here, we'll be bombed to death. And if we go back, we're right where we started."

"I'm open to suggestions, but that's about the whole of it. I do think they'll have a little more respect for my powers this time. Especially after seeing us disappear in a mini earthquake."

"You need to play on that then."

"I'm listening, Angela, go on?"

"I mean put some fear into them as soon as we show up in the room again. Startle them, throw them into confusion. They'll be caught off-guard, so I think it'll work."

"And then what?"

"Then force them to agree to meet for negotiations. Pick a time and place that's within 24-hours. It buys us time and is still days ahead of the deadline they've given us, so they probably won't argue the point."

"Solomon and Danny will see through the deception in about 30-minutes."

"That's the beauty of it. We leave before that takes place. As soon as they've agreed, we come back here to Loam, only not London, somewhere safer."

"That won't work because when we return here the next time, we'll be in the same room, within minutes of the same time."

"Right, I forgot that part. Then we still must get away from them fast. By that, I mean out of the building, and we must make sure we're not followed. After that, we start working on our original plan of altering their state of mind. I guarantee it will work as long as they're not suspecting it. This time they won't know what we're up to because they have no spy among us."

"How can we be sure they won't suspect it?"

"We've got to really make them believe that we've got a new idea, one that will bring our two sides together. If they think we're working toward that goal they won't suspect a thing."

"Any thoughts on what that might be?"

"I think if we could sell them on the idea that we're ready to compromise our stand, to meet them somewhere in the middle, then I don't think they'll be suspicious. We need to give them a new plan that they can mull over, keeping their minds averted for 24-hours."

"I don't suppose you have the new plan in mind?"

"I'm afraid I haven't a clue right now." Angela looks back through the window to the outside. The rain is still coming down at the same dreary persistent rate. "But we need to come up with something fast."

She sees a man running frantically waving his hands toward her from down the street, the same man who had earlier rushed out. The door of the cafe flings open. The soaking wet man slips as he enters, falling to his knees. He looks upward from the floor. "They're coming! Do you hear me? They're driving tanks as big as houses. I spotted them only four blocks away. Run for your lives now my countrymen, or you'll soon experience a horrible death." Artillery fire that could be heard in the distance was now growing louder. A thick cloud of smoke from the gunfire is ebbing its way down the street, decreasing the already poor visibility. As the smoke traverses in front of the cafe windows, it swirls and mixes with the rain, turning the entire atmosphere a translucent pale green. "Run! I said run! You damned fools! Our airplanes can't stop them! Don't you understand? Run! The monsters will be here any moment!"

With those words an unimaginable sight punctures the cloud of smoke revealing one giant singular tank. It stops with its 18- foot cannon nearly touching the glass front of the cafe. The metal treads and compartment of the enormous machine are 35- feet long and over 12-feet wide."

For the second time, James stands up from his seat and

starts patting his handkerchief across his forehead. Placing it back into his suit pocket, he lightly touches the tips of his fingers on the glass window as though it was alive and breathing. The breath backs up in his throat as he peers through the glass making a visual examination of the tank. After about a minute he shifts his shoulders uncomfortably, tilts his head down and sighs as he lets out a long breath. He jerks his chin back up as if he had forgotten he wasn't alone. He turns to the others, his fingers still on the glass. "I've seen that tank before, but only in photographs. It's the largest tank ever built, nicknamed the German Mouse because it can go anywhere. It can even travel underwater through rivers using a long snorkel. In our version of World War II there was only one prototype completed, and it never saw action before the Soviet forces invaded the construction site. They found it sabotaged along with several others that were incomplete. It was suggested to Hitler by Ferdinand Porsche. He also built the savage thing after its immediate approval."

"Just what kind of danger are we in right now?" Harlan asked sliding his chair back like he's getting ready to act.

"Extreme danger," James answers looking back at the massive tank, his fingers slowly falling from the glass. "Even in our world this tank stretched the technological achievements to the very edge. This imposing vehicle carries an equally imposing weapon. It shoots double loading ammunition, consisting of two 6-inch wide by 2-foot long, shell propellants. They shoot simultaneously one behind the other and can penetrate eight inches of solid steel armor. This tank can waste an obscene amount of resources in short order. Several of them together can destroy whole cities. Nothing standing in its way is safe. It was built to turn the tide of the war. My guess is it's doing just that."

He looks across his shoulder at Harlan, and as he does he realizes that everyone other than the four of them have evacuated. "There's one of those rent by the hour places about two blocks behind this building. It may not be the ideal place, but its safely away from any main street, and we can decide what to do next."

Harlan nods in agreement. "Let's see if this place has a back door." Suddenly a loud cranking sound draws their heads back to the window. The tank's cannon is being aimed at a building across the street, and its movement is shaking the building. "Everyone on the floor!" Angela shouts. And then the blast, which instantly sends the cannon backwards on a sliding shock absorber. The immense sound warbles outward in waves shattering the window front of the cafe and sending fragments of glass flying over the tops of the four horizontal figures who are now strewn out over the floor.

"Let's move!" Angela shouts. "Before that heartless creature turns its weapon on us!"

There is no hesitation. The four of them jump up and run to the backside of the cafe, flying through a door into a smoke-filled alley.

"This way," James shouts. "It's not far." They disappear into swirls of greenish-gray smoke, rapidly, desperately running for safety.

Hours later, Harlan sits in a dreary, dank room thinking quickly, silently, ravenously. Going over the words, changing them, going over them again, and translating them as to how they would sound or be interpreted. After a while, his head snaps up looking at the only other one in the room, Angela. Grace and James had gone out looking for food. "I've got an idea that seems logical enough to work."

She looks over from a bed where she has been resting her eyes. "I'm listening."

"They're going to want to know *why* we're willing to settle. I'll tell them the powers above us, the other realm insists we work this out together. I'll tell them I'm being forced to settle and so are they."

"And the plan? You *are* going to pitch them a plan?"

"Of course, it's the starting point. It's simple, but I think we need simple. Otherwise, it may get too confusing. If they grow suspicious it could ruin everything."

"And?"

"Our original plan, which they've already turned down,

would take at least a year to implement. They feared that so long a wait would lead to losing what is already shaky support from the leaders of each continent. They're not risking such a long wait. So, I'll ask for a few months instead. Six months and I can cut the number of deaths to about half. I'll suggest they run the numbers to see for themselves that our compromise is possible."

"Is it possible?"

"It's a stretch, but that's good. It'll give them more to think about. I'll tell them to take 24-hours to appraise the situation, and we'll meet back at the same location. Then I'll tell them if there's still doubt, we can discuss it at that time. When they come back to us the next day, their minds should be completely focused on the compromise. My guess is they'll be ready for a debate. That's our opportunity to draw them into an altered state of consciousness."

"You mean *your* opportunity."

He hesitates. "At that point, you've said it yourself, we can inject them and wipe their memories. If this works, we win."

"It's a good plan, Harlan. Really, a great one. With the city collapsing around us, we haven't much time. Do you think you're ready?" Her chin tilted upward as she felt confident.

His expression matched hers. "I believe so, yes."

"You need to be certain. You're the only one living that can make this happen. If it fails, then everyone except regenerated ones will die."

"I know. No pressure, right? I have traced everything in my mind to see as close as possible how this will go. My conclusion is there is a 95-percent chance that the plan will succeed."

"And the other 5?"

"The other 5-percent makes up the unknown factor. There's a small chance that something unexpected will happen. In the event that it does, we'll have to act extemporaneously."

"You mean improvise?"

"Or ad-lib, yes. If it comes to that our chance of success falls considerably."

"I guess that's it then."

"I guess so. When James and Grace get back, we'll have something to eat. And then, we'll see what's in store for this generation of people."

"Since we have some time, I thought I would ask, why did you never tell me?"

"I was wondering when you would get around to that. You do mean my being contacted by the other realm, and my knowledge of the four dimensions, notwithstanding my new abilities."

She bit her bottom lip and her eyes tensed up. "You can imagine my surprise when the room turned blue and started shaking."

He looks down in pause, then back up but beyond her, his eyes roving uncontrollably. "In a way, I did tell you."

"No, you didn't tell me! But it was my job to make things easier for you, so you should have."

"I told you. I didn't tell you. I don't know. What I told you just wasn't enough. Maybe that's the truth of it."

"Okay then, let's go with that. What did you tell me?"

"That I had a feeling our plan would end with a consolation."

"I remember. So, you knew we would escape to another dimension. That was the consolation?"

"Partly."

"Are you going to tell me the other part?"

"I don't know."

"Try again."

"I'm not sure if I should."

"It's simple. You should. Now tell me."

"No!"

She grabs his shoulder. "Tell me!"

He looks at her with fiery eyes. I'm the last of the chosen line. Did you hear me? Do you know what that means? Because of that, we will be successful like I said. However, there is always the chance of the unexpected. The other part of the consolation is that we would have this opportunity. The first chance was doomed from the beginning because of

Danny."

"You knew ahead of time?"

"Yes, but there is still more to the consolation." He hesitates again.

Her eyes are now locked onto his. "Don't stop. For God's sake, Harlan, tell me!"

"If I tell you now, it changes everything for you. Are you ready for that? Can you accept it? Because I'm not so sure its the right time."

"No more secrets. Tell me!"

"Don't say I didn't warn you. I am the last of the chosen line, and you, Angela, are the beginning of a new one. I have been instructed that now there will be two co-chosen ones. You and I will act as partners, something that's never taken place before. This has been their plan for a long time. They picked you out even before your regeneration. You will have similar powers as myself, but I'm not clear exactly what that means, at least not yet.

Now you know, so now it begins. When we transport back to that room in Lexington, you and I will be working together to alter their state of consciousness. Unless something unexpected happens, we have a 100-percent chance of success. Angela? Angela, are you alright? I knew I should've waited. You look like someone cast a spell on you."

"You knew my father was a famous scientist, right?"

"I've heard a little about it from James."

"What you haven't heard is where my father came from, where I came from."

"Where might that be?"

"My grandfather was a deserter in the Napoleonic wars at the beginning of the 19th Century. He was thirty-nine at the time and later was shot by a firing squad. He wasn't shot for just being a deserter, but also for stealing anything valuable he could fit into his pockets. He was known as a bully, a thief, and a drunk. Before the war he bounced around from town to town, dragging his poor wife and son, my father, along with him."

"Sounds like a real winner."

"Oh, he was real cute alright. He used to team up with other losers like himself. I once heard they liked to sell their talents to the highest bidder."

"Talents?"

"Strong arming people, debt collecting, even killing for a price. Most thought that my father was being groomed by him, that it was a godsend when he was executed."

"Is that what *you* think?"

She rubs her arms, then looks at the center of the room where a single glowing bulb hangs motionless. "I think there are just as many examples of sons *not* following in their father's footsteps as there are that do. I think my father made better choices because he was a better person. I wish my father were here today to see what I'm a part of, what we're trying to accomplish."

"I'm sure he would be proud of you."

"Do you really believe that?"

"It's not every day that your daughter helps save the world."

"Do you think it's possible that I could have dreamed what's happening now, as a kid I mean?"

"I think it's not unusual for childhood memories to be very vivid and long-lasting. Do you think you dreamed this as a kid?"

She shrugs her shoulders. "I don't see how, but it gives me goosebumps." Her voice sounded dry, and then her eyebrows shot up. I remember seeing it before dreaming it! I remember telling my father about it!"

"What did he say?"

"He said that it's called an imagination and that I have a wonderful one. But I couldn't have been imagining it because it's all coming true."

"You saw this and dreamed it while you were still living with your father. Are you're sure?"

"I don't want to believe it either. It seems strange."

"Have you always had these memories?"

"I suppose so. No, no they only just started while we've been talking."

"Your powers must be starting. It appears you have the ability to see into the future, but to what degree I'm not sure. I think they're giving you new childhood memories that are actually future events."

"No, Harlan. That's crazy, its…"

"What else can it be. Be sure to inform me of any new memories, and most importantly don't tell anyone else. Not James, not Grace, not anyone."

She nods, turns and looks out the window where she has a view of the street. A large moving truck is blocking part of the view, but she can still see enough, too much. This part of town was a shady exhibition of filth, and the shady people were out in droves. They were too scared to do business, too scared to run, and too scared to stay indoors. They were like trapped rats swarming together.

She looks over her shoulder. "Harlan, it's happened. I've just been contacted by the other realm." She walks over to the bed, picks up a bag containing the formula to wipe memories. "Follow me."

"Now, but James and Grace aren't back…"

"If you wouldn't mind, we've no time to argue. This building's about to be bombed."

"I have a bad feeling you're not joking."

"And I have a bad feeling your right. If we wait much longer we die, and we can't finish what we started if we're dead."

He walks behind her out the door to their new grimy surroundings and suddenly catches sight of James and Grace.

In one sweeping motion, Angela points a stretched-out arm behind the approaching couple and starts screaming. "Run! Now! Everybody, run!" As she continues screaming a steady high pitch sound suddenly interrupts, quickly growing in volume, morphing her screams, and sending pandemonium into the lewd crowd. While the crowd looks up the four of them are running like wild animals being hunted. Turning the corner behind another building, they hear the bomb detonate and are shaken by the subsequent shock wave. Smoke filters down the alley while ringing in their ears has numbed them from any other sounds.

After a few minutes, Harlan wipes at a wet feeling on the side of his face. Blood is oozing out his ear. He reaches out to Angela, pulls her up away from the brick building, then watches as James and Grace do the same. Together, all of them walk through the thinning smoke and look back where they just came from. A glittering of fire and smoke shoots upward over the burning heaps of rubble and carcasses. Buildings that once stood for 100-years or more, now lie in waste.

Still shaking from the near-death experience, Angela falls to her knees, placing her hands over the sides of her face. "I dropped the bag. I'm so sorry. I dropped the bag Carter gave us, the one with his formula for wiping memories."

"Where?" Harlan asked nervously.

She didn't answer, just pointed to the pile of flaming bricks that only a short while ago was a building.

Chapter 15

The next five hours were spent wandering down smoky roads under the light rain of a dank sky. The foursome was thoroughly frightened by the horrors of what they had just gone through. Occasional bombings from earlier, gradually and mercifully disappeared.

The atmosphere had faded from the gloomy green color to a pale yellowish-gray, much the color of straw or flaxen. The German resolve to crush and subdue London was now fully clear. Still, the idea of moving a second time back through the multi-verse to Lexington, pinned in a room with Solomon and Danny was not being talked about. That situation had been their worst set back and had chased them into this other dangerous dimension. Their position would have been catastrophic had it not been for Angela's new, amazing powers, alerting them to run. Regardless, had the radius of the encirclement of the blast been larger they would have surely died.

What to do next seemed impossible to figure out. For now, they needed a dry room in a building not under siege. The foursome, at the end of their tether, needed to figure things out and fast. Being inaccessible to Solomon and Danny no longer felt like an advantage. However, although in a precarious circumstance, they were afforded time to organize their thoughts before making the inter-dimensional return trip.

Already there was a shortage of food in the city. James and Grace were able to secure only a bag of bagels due to the hoarding of all foodstuffs. With all public transportation suspended, moving around was strictly by foot. All those in need of medical assistance were being denied entry to hospitals. The Germans had moved quickly, seizing control of them and turning away any English-speaking individuals. Within a day's time, London had fallen, and a fearful dread had taken hold. Drunkenness and fights were breaking out on street corners due to the enormous tensions of losing their city. Word spread of children being separated from their families and sent to indoctrination camps hundreds of miles away. Back through alleyways the foursome walked, their situation hostile and pressing in on them. Time, not on their side, was marching like savages to a battle.

Finally, they cautiously approach what appears to be a deserted building partially damaged by a blast. Harlan reaches for the brass doorknob. With one motion he turns it, hears the latch click and pushes. As soon as the door is open he has an ax blade shoved in front of his face and a voice shouting at him. "I just sharpened this, so don't try anything!" The man has an intimidating soot-covered face. "If you know what's good for you. you'll turn right around and leave!"

"We're friendly, mister," Harlan answers back with his hands up in a defenseless position. "We just need a dry place to rest awhile."

The man who appears to be in his mid-thirties gives them the look-over, slow and deliberate. "You got any food?"

Grace holds up a bag. "We got a dozen bagels with a bit of cheese." She smiles while waving the bag.

"Somebody cleaned me out while I went to check on my mother-in-law. Ransacked the whole house. Went through it like a stiff wind. I was only gone for twenty-minutes. They took the only gun I had too." He relaxes, lowering the ax to his midsection. "Come on in. You stay out there you're likely to get killed. The brutes, all of em. How quickly they turn on each other." Once inside he shuts the door behind them.

"Shouldn't you lock that?" James asked.

"I can do my own thinking, thank you!"

"Right, of course, I didn't mean anything by it."

"It's fine. I'm just a little on edge. I found my mother-in-law dead. You might have noticed we had a bomb fall on us, two to be exact. The lock doesn't work. Whoever broke in earlier jimmied it and messed up the mechanism. I've been wondering what to do about it ever since."

"Sorry about your mother-in-law. My name is James. This is Grace, and this here's Harlan and Angela. You mind me asking yours?"

"Timothy."

"You sound American, Timothy."

"That's correct. Sarah, my wife, is British. She died four-months ago from tuberculosis."

Grace whispers to Angela. "Since there are no antibiotics, people still die from that."

"What did you say?" Timothy asked.

"Nothing. It's not important."

"Anyway, this building held up reasonably well." He tilts his head motioning upwards with his eyes. "Above me, there's a lawyer's office and a couple more flats. They're fine, just some bricks busted away on the north-facing wall and lots of cracked windows. I haven't noticed any rain getting in, so all-in-all we're good. The bombings are done for now at least that's what they're saying. The bombs were just to strike fear into us while they took the city. Worked too. In 24-hours all the good citizens of London imploded on themselves. I'm still seething over it." He lowers the ax to the floor. "Just so you know, I'm originally a South Alabama farm-boy. They raise us to be respectful and tough in that area of the states. The respectful part didn't take as well as the tough, so if you got any bright ideas of rushing me you've been warned. And this ax goes where I go."

"Its all right, Timothy," Grace said calmly. "We're just thankful you let us in."

Angela points down a hallway. "Is there a room Harlan and I could use? We need the rest, and… there's a private matter we need to discuss."

He motions again with his head. "Suit yourself, lady. Last door on the right." He looks back to James and Grace. "You two others got any requests?"

"No," James responds nervously. "This rooms fine. Grace, why don't you offer Timothy a bagel. I bet he hasn't eaten all day."

"Now that you mention it, not since yesterday."

She sets the bag on a table. "You mind if I wash up? I don't want to contaminate the bagels."

"The kitchen's right there. Meantime I'm gonna press a chair underneath the doorknob. Don't wanna be surprised while we're eating."

Inside a backroom, Harlan and Angela were just getting settled in. After she reaches to shut the door, Angela starts speaking forthright, without hesitation, but quietly. "Maybe it would have been better if we hadn't come here."

"Do you mean here in this house?"

"No. I mean this dimension. This version of earth is a disaster."

"I had to do it. If we would have stayed there with Solomon and Danny…"

"So, what would've happened?"

"I'm not sure but… they knew our plan."

"We've almost been killed here, Harlan. You should have told me what you were planning. We could have worked together. Coming here was a mistake. From now on we have to work together."

"But… I had to do it."

She folds her arms. "No, you didn't. You just wanted to because you could. You wanted to send a message, to display your powers, and you did. The truth is nobody was going to get hurt. So, they figured out our plan. So, they had the upper hand. So, what! We still had a week to work with. A week to come up with something else. You should have told me you had Danny pegged. We could have used that to our advantage." After she spoke, she was still, quiet.

Harlan leans back against a chair looking down at his feet. He can hear the stroke of a clock ticking away. The sound ceased and died away but returns as his mind drifts in and out. Only a few months ago he was old and sick with cancer, ready to die. But that was in another time, another life it seemed. All that had ever been was now so different from what was to be. For the first time, he was thinking of this with quiet astonishment. He moves his head a little, then tilts it back up and moves it around the room in a sort of flat pattern. Although he wasn't trying to be, he was silent. He knew that Angela had been right about him. He could feel her in his mind like the two were not really two, but rather one. It was like there was a frequency that connected them, not with words, but with understanding. They were now looking at one another.

"Harlan, I didn't mean to upset you. Will you say something?"

He saw her arms unfold. They fell to her side. They looked soft, just as her face now did.

"Please, will you *say* something?"

He rises from the desk and a light from a lamp spotted him sending his shadow shooting against a wall. "There's just one other thing left to do."

She didn't ask what. She didn't have to. Their minds were now connected. They were going back through the multiverse, back to Lexington, back to being trapped in a room with Solomon and Danny.

"Do you remember when I was first teaching you about the mind, about altering Solomon's consciousness?"

He watches as her right hand comes forward. "I

192

remember."

She rests her hand on the side of his face. "That's when you first suspected Danny was a spy. I can sense it."

"She was being too eager. She just *had* to be there while you trained me. Once I focused on that, it became completely clear to me."

She pushes her hand farther back, brushing it through his hair. "I have a confession to make. After your training, the day before we were to meet with Solomon, I heard voices."

"Really?"

She moves her head, leaning forward to lightly kiss his cheek. "Yes, but I was confused and... I didn't know what was happening."

"When *did* you know?"

She moves her face again, this time kissing him on the lips. "In that house, just before the bomb destroyed it. I heard them another time, too. It was right after James regenerated me. Even before then, now that I think about it. But, I didn't understand what was happening, and eventually dismissed them." Although she was completely unaware of it, she was holding him in her arms.

"The first time you heard voices...it was probably important."

"Hush, shut up." She kisses him again, pressing hard against him. "It's our chance. Will you hush now and kiss me back?"

He only thought for a second about the importance of what she had just told him, and then he kissed back. When they had finished there was nothing to do but hold onto each other a little longer. Soon they had let go and started talking again, their muscles still tingling, their hearts panting from the encounter. They continued to talk, not fast, but slow and comfortable.

Their relationship had turned a page, then another, and now another like the steady progression of a book. Only this page had their minds lingering on one line, or perhaps only one word. Their minds had melded, they were talking without the use of their vocal cords. Their earlier conversation about the voices was of profound significance but had completely slipped their minds.

Soon they started talking about staying the night to dry out and get rested before facing Solomon and Danny. That's when they hear other voices and the rustling of feet. At first, they appear to be body-less voices, murmuring and complaining in British English, like they are under the desk or in the walls trying to find their way out.

Angela walks to the window. Through it she can see an alleyway behind their room that backs up to another building where it ends abruptly. There must have been two hundred people with more coming, crowding in on them.

By now, Harlan is standing at the window. He looks beyond the glass into the crowd. Focusing, he looks into the face of one of them and sees desperation.

"What could be happening out there?" Angela asked. "Look, Harlan! Look over there where I'm pointing. No, my dear. Look with your eyes, where my fingers pointing. That's right! What's that?"

"I'm not sure but there's a Nazi emblem or flag on it."

"That's not a flag. It's stamped or painted onto what looks like a machine."

"A huge machine that walks like a man."

"Yes."

"You mean a robotic machine."

"Yes, someone's probably inside it, operating it. There! There's another one! Do you see it?"

"I do and there's two more! I wonder how long the Nazi's have been working on these things?"

"They're herding these people into the ally. That can't be good."

There are now countless people crammed together, rubbing arms, chests, and heads in a scene of intolerable crowding. In no time they're pulling and climbing on top of one another, roaring and screaming. The situation turns chaotic as those being climbed are trampled and crushed.

"I'm going out there," Harlan shouts, turning for the door.

"I'm going, too."

"No. I need you here. It may be to our advantage." He scurries out the door, and Angela watches through the window until she sees him being forced into the alley-way with the others. Suddenly he is hemmed in with the crowd, the buildings on one side, a tight horizontal line of red and black robotic soldiers on the other.

The machines are massive, streaming upwards, towering three times the height of a man. They look like shadows reaching toward the sky. They hold out their weapons which look more like miniature aircraft guns. They are in an offensive position, ready to fire, ready to annihilate the crowd of people like they are helpless sitting ducks.

Harlan, standing between the crowd and the mechanical soldiers, turns his back to the soldiers, stretches his arms up and outward, and faces the sky. His body suddenly lifts, floating, hovering off the ground about a foot and a half. As this is happening a white circle filters out from his body, then a second one forms--full of color like a 360-degree rainbow. It quickly forms an outer circle.

Just as the bullets start to fly, a translucent congealed-like substance shoots out from Harlan's hands, shooting a wide swath, creating a horizontal, rectangular wall. Hundreds of bullets scream out of the automatic guns, blasting toward the wall. Dozens at a time are caught in the thickness of the gel, stopped instantly, they lay hovering in the rain-laden air.

After their failed attempt, the machines turn all of their weapons on Harlan.

Angela pushes up the window, and she can be heard screaming out to Harlan. Already surrounded by an inner and outer sphere of white and colored circles, she throws out her hand, palm up and a ball of lighted energy shoots out toward the soldiers. Before the ball of light reaches them it suddenly spreads out forming a wide field of illuminated energy. It smashes into them, breaking them into pieces. It sends them spiraling backward's across a street into the adjacent buildings. Flying into the bricks, the mechanical soldiers are left looking like worthless, useless metal parts. The bodies of those inside the machines operating them lay groaning, their injuries mostly superficial.

After destroying the machines, Angela looks as though shes caught a chill. She has expended a sizable amount of energy and is breathing deep, long breaths within the murkiness of the white circle. While looking outside at the terrified people, who are now scrambling to get away in the falling rain, she hears a faint sound. Not knowing what to expect, she turns from the curtain-less window and sees Timothy standing at the doorway, motionless and quiet. Their eyes squarely fixed on each other, she watches as he begins fumbling his hands beside him, reaching against the wall where the ax is leaning.

He is scared, thinking hard, his eyes bulging like a startled animal. He starts thinking out loud. "You're not human, you can't be."

The outer color laden circle disappears. The inner white illuminated circle flashes brightly, then fades slowly like a fog lifting. "Please leave the ax be," Angela says in a low soft tone. "I don't want to hurt you."

He halts, making a sound like a choking cough, fright beaming from his face. His legs tremble fiercely. He thinks about sitting down at the desk. He needs to sit. Suddenly he is hunting wildly with his eyes around the room, uncertainty plastered all over him. "Are you hurt?" he suddenly blurted out. He coughs hard like he's trying to catch his breath. "I don't know why I said that!"

"You don't have to be afraid of me."

"Yes, I do! How did you do that?"

"Let's just say, '*It's a gift*,' and leave it at that."

Feeling a tingling heat moving up his legs, he tries to stay balanced but suddenly falls. Peering upwards from the floor, he wants her to see him, to see what has happened, to see what she has done. "Sorry, I guess I'm a little dizzy."

"You have nothing to be sorry for." She helps him into the desk chair. "You're going to be fine. You've just been frightened by what you've seen."

He looks back over his shoulder at the window. "What did I see?"

"If I tell you, it won't make sense. It's going to sound crazy. Can't we just call it a gift?"

He nods. "There is still heat coming off you, like the heat from a hot road."

"It'll be gone soon. I promise. It won't be long."

"It doesn't bother me. I was just making an observation." He looks back into her eyes. "The bombings are over, and we're in a building of bricks, but we're not safe, are we?"

"No, Timothy. We're not safe. The Germans have weapons unseen before now. Machines like giant robots. They're using them to exterminate people. I've just destroyed twenty of them. But chances are they have a whole army."

"The Russians have talked about them. It's been said that at the onset of the war they decimated France with them. Now they're going to do the same here."

"It would appear so."

Harlan, James, and Grace come scampering through the doorway. Once in the room, Harlan, who still has illuminated remnants of the white circle emanating from him, starts up. "Angela! We have to leave. I've just seen hundreds more of them. We've no more time. We have to leave now!" He glances down at the desk. "Timothy, I'm sorry we've no time to explain. You're going to have to step out of the room."

"Are you all like her?"

"What do you mean?"

"He saw me, Harlan. He watched."

"Well, there's nothing to be done. We have to go."

"We can't leave him here, he'll be killed. I think we should take him with us. I think he could help us."

"You haven't thought this out, Angela?"

"Yes, I have."

"Then how could he help us?"

"Our leverage with Solomon and Danny will be much stronger when they see we've brought someone back from another dimension. They'll take us much more seriously. They'll have to with the proof staring them in the face."

"We've not much time. Timothy, how do you feel about this?"

"What makes you think they won't attack us when we leave the building?"

"We're not leaving like that, that's how I know. We're leaving through a portal that moves between dimensions. I'm about to open it and send us through it. Look, I already told you there's no time to explain. Are you going with us or not?"

"The way I see it, I don't have a choice. There's nothing left for me here anyway. But later, you people got some serious explaining to do."

"Alright then. When we arrive in Lexington, it'll take some time for the air in the room to clear. You might feel a little shaking, or maybe a terrible shaking. No one says a word except for Angela and me. Everybody got it? Good. This is it, try not to tense up. I'm opening the portal."

Chapter 16

(Childhood Trauma, The Civil War, and Foreign Voices)

When she was ten-years-old her mother died during a summer of intense heat. To this day she can still feel the sweat that was on her mother's forehead after kissing her for the last time. She can still see it, can taste it on her lips.

"Take care of your father and your sister," she had said. "Your sister's younger and less capable. Remember that, she's going to need you." And then she was gone, like a wonderful breeze that blows for a while, then leaves without much notice, quiet without commotion, leaving you in want.

When she was gone Angela looked around their modest wood plank house. Its totality was three bedrooms, a narrow hallway, kitchen, and living area with a fireplace. Its walls, filled with tiny cracks of white plaster, were smooth like new leather. Its floors of yellow pine, dented and marked, displayed some sixty years of boots, broken dishes, animal paws, and embers.

The next day they buried her. The next week they departed the house forever, the pain burrowed inside her.

Due to his work as a well-known brain surgeon, her father had been mulling over a job offer to teach at the 'Royal College of Physicians.' He had been mulling it over for months. However, after the death of her mother, he quickly accepted and moved his daughters from the rolling countryside of Surrey to the massive city of London. By today's standards this was no more than a rock's throw away, but in the early nineteenth century it seemed a million miles.

Later she was educated at the same college, and after

twenty-five years as a physician, she came back as his peer and fellow teacher. Together they blazed a trail in brain research, setting the accepted standards, and catapulting them to fame.

Through all those years Angela never lost her love of the countryside, nor the pain of leaving it. When her father died she did something she had dreamed of for years. She took a ship across the sprawling ocean waters to New York, then onward to Philadelphia where she had a job waiting for her at the Perelman School of Medicine, where she was allowed to continue her research. During her off time, she would take long trips to the countryside, eventually falling in love with Gettysburg. Shortly after her retirement she rented a house and moved away from the city, hoping it was her last home.

She squatted next to the soft, fresh-smelling garments. Just plucked from the clothesline, they were sitting folded on the seat of a sofa. Her arms slid comfortably under them, she stood up, pointing in the direction of the bedroom, and then heard an unexpected knock at the door.

The visitor, Mr. Simmons, her landlord, did not wait for her to answer before pushing it open. He began talking at a fast pace. "Forgive me for intruding, Miss Gall. I just came from town where I heard rumors of fighting north of Gettysburg. They say the war's converging right on top of us. Others say it's just a skirmish like they had in Virginia two weeks ago. I'll keep you posted when I hear more. But right now, I have a cow to rescue from the creek. It may take me until dark, so I wanted to drop your mail off first. You've got a parcel from your sister and another letter from that fella in Florida. Tallahassee, I believe it is. I see you have your hands full, so I'll just set them here next to the coat rack and be on my way. Sorry for the rush." And just like that he was gone, gone before she could even say thank you.

She turns away from the door towards the bedroom, but then stands silent. After a moment, she looks over her shoulder peering at the mail. With the clothes still in her hands, she looks back at the bedroom door, then again back over her shoulder at the mail. When she realizes that she's been standing there for over a minute, she dumps the clothes back on the sofa, rushes over and picks up the letter. Ripping it open with her bare fingers she starts reading.

"Dear, Miss Angela Rena Gall."

Never taking her eyes off the letter she walks with an anxious restlessness and sits on the edge of the sofa, next to the haphazardly placed laundry. After only the introduction, she has drifted hopelessly into its words, subconsciously giving away an already rooted desire.

"I am writing you this correspondence with the hope that you are doing well. It has come to my attention only just moments ago that this deplorable war has advanced closer to the safety net of your beloved Pennsylvania. I've said a prayer for you and your beautiful, quaint town of Gettysburg. Possibly you will be spared the savage nature of advancing troops. Be they of blue or gray coats, they will undoubtedly be of determined, even desperate minds. This cannot be held against them, as they are--all of them--loyal to their cause, and only want to finish the thing the higher-ups have sent them out to do. I fear that many of them, mixed and intertwined with wars warm bravery and cold dirty tricks, will never see their families again. I hear General Lee is a brilliant tactician, fearing nothing, and continues pushing his troops northward. The signs are not in place telling us that we might see a quick solution. Neither do we expect a peace treaty to save the divided country its impending huge casualties. May your faith, which you have in earlier correspondence discussed, sustain you in such difficult times as these.

As you may be aware, the war has not as yet reached the fresh new state of Florida and is not expected to do so. I have written you twice already, and I do so again in a sincere effort to persuade you to move here for the purpose of assisting me with my studies on the brain. I would be remiss if I didn't point out its proximity to safety. I hope you do not see this as an underhanded way to prod you into giving in to my pleas. It's just that I desperately need your help, and you are living in wars perilous pathway. At this time, it is not known to me anyone living in the states that has even near the accomplishments regarding brain research like that of yourself. Although you have previously made it clear to me that you are happy living in retirement, I once again, embarrassing as it makes me feel, entreat you to accept my offer. Please consider semi-retirement as a viable and fulfilling option. You will be afforded a comfortable place to live, and a handsome stream of income largely surpassing your esteemed teaching days.

If I have not in earlier correspondence made it clear to you what the area I am asking you to move to is like, let me, with enthusiasm, do so now. Where I have my house, and adjacent buildings, (one of which you will reside in, others of which I lease out to the state government,) is a mix of rolling hills and flat land. The wildness of the area, once galloping out of control, has been corralled and tamed over the course of the last two decades. Its incredible beauty has emerged like the birth of an infant child. Its acres of grass fields spiraling in green and golden tones, resemble the color of sunlit wheat. Much to the delight of local Floridians such as myself, the areas freshwater is abundant, its soil rich for farming. There are areas nearby where water bubbles from the ground, forming rivers so clear that their depth cannot be understood with the eye. Where fish on the bottom look as though they are only at a hand's reach, although in reality they may be more than ten or fifteen-feet away. It is believed that the water travels in underground springs from far away places in the Appalachian Mountains. The city of Tallahassee, of which we are adjacent to, has two large mercantile trading stores. Both of these have a woman's boutique. There is also a stand-alone dress shop with a seamstress known for her fine quality. I'm quite sure you will lack nothing in your usual standard of clothing. We will attend to any of these kinds of needs promptly after your arrival. This is with the joyful hope, of course, that you will with the spirit of a pioneer accept my offer to be my teacher. I will explain more about my work, which I believe is of great importance once we have ample time to sit.

As for my daily goings-on here, my work with you on the understanding of the brain will, I give my word, take precedence over my other many ventures. In addition to my leasing interest, I own two sugar plantations and one cotton plantation. Five years ago, I purchased and installed my own cotton gin, which I hire out to other plantations when I am done with the harvest of my own. I am telling you this, so that you will know that you will lack for nothing if you should decide to move here. My income would rival any businessman in the southern states and, I have been told, would surpass all except three of them. If I included my interest in Europe there would be no contest whatsoever.

As far as transportation goes, we have steamboat navigation on the larger rivers such as the Apalachicola and the St. Johns. There are railroads planned, with some already being installed. However, if you accept my offer, you need to understand that there are no railways between Tallahassee and St Augustine, the place which you would be arriving by ship. From there I would meet you, and we would travel by coach for the final duration of your trip.

I just have one other matter to discuss with you. I have heard that many people outside of the southern states have a great concern about Indian hostilities in Florida. Also, the perception that Tallahassee is a haven for runaway slaves, many of which are violent. Let me put your mind to rest if you indeed have heard the same said conversations. The Seminole Wars have been long since over. Under President Andrew Jackson, the U.S. government spent twenty million dollars and the lives of many U.S. soldiers, Indian people, and U.S. citizens to force the removal of the brave Seminole. The ones that were not caught have left voluntarily or escaped to the everglades far away. As for runaway slaves, most of these are good family men and hard workers on the areas many plantations, including mine. I will stay neutral on the debate about slavery, which along with high tariffs have for some time now divided this still young and fledgling country. I can tell you that I own no slaves. Everyone under my employ is paid a fair salary. I have seen no more threat of violent slaves in Tallahassee than in any of the states above us. I felt I should address this subject, as it has kept a good many people from moving to the beautiful, sunny state of Florida.

I suppose for the time being, my attempts to sway you have come to an end. Please give yourself time to consider my offer. If I have not heard from you in a month's time I shall take it that you no longer want to correspond with me. At which point I will, along with my wife, pay you a visit. Maybe my presence would be more convincing. If nothing more, at least I would be able to look into your eyes and see if they are filled with fortitude to remain in Gettysburg. What I really expect to find is a sparkling glimmer of the adventurous person I think you are. You and your late father are one and the same. Trailblazers in your field, unafraid of the unknown. Miss Gall, you will find that my wife and I are of the same sort. I believe that we will all get along in a superior fashion. And I believe that given the chance, we will blaze our own trail, possibly moving your brain research to a completely new frontier.

With all sincerity,
James H. Jenkins

Finishing the letter, she presses it tightly against her chest. Then closes her eyes and inhales a slow deep breath while thinking about her father. She remembers everything about him. All the details seem fresh in her mind. How he dipped his head slightly when he was in deep thought. How he would always hold the door for women, no matter their color or age. How in a grieving situation, he was never afraid to cry in front of his family? She remembers after the death of her mother, how he would always help her with the housework. And she remembers how he talked with graceful, straightforward words, like this man, Mr. James Jenkins.

Though she did not know this at the time, she had made her decision right then. She *was* going to blaze that trail with Mr. Jenkins. And she *was* going to traverse new, unknown ground, like the adventurous unafraid pioneer she knew in her heart she was.

Still thinking of her father, she kisses the letter, folds it and slips it back into the envelope. Tilting her head down, her eyes are looking, her face smiling at the laundry. Scooping it underneath her arms a second time, she walks it into her bedroom. Once inside, she hears the first far away blast from a musket and turns toward the window. Peering outside she hears another and another until there are so many they seem as fireworks mixing together.

Little does she know the Union soldiers have just retreated through downtown Gettysburg. They were now in a violent skirmish with the Confederate gray-coats, attempting to make a defense at Cemetery Hill, just under one mile from her homestead.

She places the clothes on her bed and begins putting them away while fidgeting and rotating an eye at the window, keeping watch outside. She had heard musket shots before from hunters and nearby neighbors who would sometimes target practice. But this was strikingly different, and she knew it.

Once finished with the laundry she walks outside to the front porch and stares in the direction of the gun blast. They hadn't slowed down, and she was growing antsier when she noticed a man riding hard down the dirt road that leads to her house. She recognized him as her landlord, and when he comes close he jumps off the horse before it has even come to a complete stop.

He runs up to the porch, pausing, out of breath, leaning his hands on his knees. He is still breathing with difficulty when he looks up at her, his eyes bulging, filled with torque like they will explode at any moment. "The rumors are correct, Miss Gall." He hesitates again, breathing heavily. "The war has reached Gettysburg. The fighting's not far away, and there are tens of thousands of more soldiers reported to be coming fast. There's no time to escape to Philadelphia. The east road is already blocked. There's no way out. Everyone's staying put, so lock yourself inside, but first chain up your horse. There are already reports of deserters. If your horse isn't chained, they'll surely take it. Do you have a chain?"

While glancing at the barn she lifts one hand up over her eyes attempting to block the glare of the sun. At the same time, she is stretching and pointing with the other. "Over there, under the lean-to. You left one hanging on the barn wall when you helped tow my buggy a few weeks ago."

"Do you have a lock?"

"A lock?" She looks back at the door to her cabin, places a hand on her forehead and stares. "A lock?"

"I thought as much. Never mind, we've no time." He rushes over to his horse, slaps at the underneath side of his saddlebag. Flipping up the leather cover he reaches inside. Then he rushes back. "Take this. Chain your horse, Angela. Do it now! After that get back inside and no matter what happens for God's sake stay there! I'll check on you as soon as it's safe." Again, he rushes to his horse, mounts it with one sweeping jump, quickly kicking up a cloud of dust. In no time he is again riding hard down the road.

With alternating feelings of lightheadedness and clarity, Angela backs up, half-sitting and half-falling into a rocking chair. Oddly, she is intrigued at the sound of musket balls more than she is frightened. As she focuses on the commotion of the guns blasting away, momentarily she wonders why she has no necessity of silence. Quickly dismissing the thought, she becomes deeply engrossed in the spectacular sounds coming from the forest.

She had first moved here because the area was the definition of simplicity itself. It was a garden-like environment filled with larger trees than she had ever seen before. And a whole world of creatures: a variety of birds with colorful, gorgeous plumage, plentiful deer, bear, fox, racoon, and rabbits. The noises now echoing from the forest seemed a new species as they unexpectedly become mixed with emerging cannon blasts. Smoke rises over the distant trees making the scene have all the strangeness of a dream. The rising smoke mixes with the soft currents of the air, drifting eastward so slow that a dragon's tail is being left in its wake.

She hadn't really imagined the war would come so close,

or that she would not see it as an imposing, threatening force. She could not make herself be scared and couldn't remember any truly fearful moments streaming out of her even when she was a child. If there had ever been any fright in her, it was positively clear now that it had been left behind decades ago in the beginning years of her adolescence. The battle of Gettysburg now so completely underway and taking shape, seems to her a horrible yet natural event.

She shakes her head, stands up and starts out across her yard. She walks over a patch of hay thrown down to curb mud from a hard rain some two days back, lifts a looped rope, unlatching a gate, and enters the coral, a rough circle made of wood-rail fencing. Her horse gives no trouble as it walks with her toward the barn. Under the lean-to she lifts and pushes at the chain, noticing it's not as heavy as it looks. Once the horse is secured to a large support beam, she makes her way back to the house. Walking onto the porch, she without hesitation goes inside, locking the door behind her in obedience to her landlord.

Her mental excitement of the letter she had only a short while ago read, along with the war so suddenly and surprisingly within reach of her cabin, was making her amazingly alert. Sitting at a small writing desk adjacent to a large window, she perched herself like a cat looking out over her front yard, barn, and pasture. She was now in a state of calmness, the house silent, the scene outside one of peace with the sun shining brightly over the barn.

Unrestrained by the battle's close proximity, she sits back in her chair resting comfortably. This is when she becomes afraid for the first time. Words from a foreign voice meet her ears with astounding clarity. *"When winter comes and the snow spouts blow through the pastures, you must not be here."*

She is startled and turns to look behind her to the back of the house. "Who is that? How did you get in?" She stands up, keeping her hands on the desk. "Answer me! Who are you and what do you want?"

"Mr. Jenkins is waiting."

"How the devil, do you know about him? Have you been

reading my mail? Show yourself!" She raises her right hand slipping loose strands of hair behind her ear, then sucks in a quick breath, spouting it out her nose attempting to build a small amount of courage. Heat building in her face is forcing her to sense her own building panic. The palms of her hands are now pressing hard against the desk. "Show yourself, I said! You, miserable coward! Do you hear me? Say something!"

Blasting cannons and musket balls that had seemed to her lost and faded to the back of her consciousness, now come roaring back into her ears. For just a moment she tilts her head down, squeezing her eyes together, trying to silence the surreal battle taking place less than a mile away. She waits, focusing, wanting to hear the voice, but there's nothing. Almost giving up, she opens her eyes, raising her head with a fierce expression beaming from her face. "I don't believe in ghosts, and I know I'm not crazy, so talk to me whoever you are, and wherever you're from." Just when she thinks the voice has left, it confronts her again.

"Out of snow-covered fields comes the red blade of a knife. From then forward you will restlessly go from one task to another."

"What task? Who are you? What do you mean?"

"You will reach your hand out, into the field of snow, desperate from tragedy. A red blade, Confusion, they are lurking. Tallahassee is waiting."

"If I agree to go, will you tell me who you are?"

"Dimensions are separating."

"I still don't know what you're talking about. Who are you?"

"You have everything we are looking for."

"I said who are you?"

"Dimensions are separating. Remember your father's work."

Immediately after those words, she sees a Union Soldier through the desk window running hard toward the barn. Stopping at the lean-to he taps and rubs the horse frantically, jumping atop him bareback. His blue coat, fully buttoned and half covered in mud, flaps in a sudden burst of wind.

208

Squeezing his legs, he turns his shoulders quickly attempting to lead the horse away. Angela notices his hair is of golden tint and pushed sharply to one side. His suit is a plain shell cut, devoid of officer rank either on the shoulder facings, collars, or cuffs. Across his chest is a blue shoulder-strap attached to a pouch with dove-gray piping. She figures it to be for personal items or possibly food. When the horse doesn't budge, it suddenly brings to the soldier's attention its unmovable circumstance. Leaning forward he shakes sharply and vigorously at the chain. It is obvious to Angela the soldier's boyish face. She figures him to be no more than eighteen. Jumping to the ground he splats and kicks his way over the hay sprinkled mud, runs out from under the lean-to, high-tails it across the pasture, jumps a wood-rail fence and eventually disappears into the forest.

She relaxes again, sinking back into the desk chair. Any possible danger from the blue-coat deserter now disappeared. So too has the foreign voice, now completely died out in the cedar scented air of the cabin. How strange the voice differed from the grimmer reality of war that lay just outside her windowpane.

She sits still and silent at her writing desk, her mind now set off to wanderings. She pushes aside the war again, thinking exclusively about the amazing paradox of the voice. It was her estimation that the voice came, not from another person hiding inexplicably somewhere in the cabin, but rather from the confines of her own consciousness. She does a brief examination of the order of the mind, quickly running through each supposed area of particular usage. After years of study, she had drawn the conclusion that the brain was like a large city in miniature, each area of the city for a different purpose, so too the brain. She had mapped it out, did a colorful diagram of it, and had become famous for it. Was there as yet another undiscovered section, one that might be capable of communication without the need of talking? She thought this idea possible, but the brain as its source, unlikely. She along with her father had spent years studying and testing the boundaries of each section.

In this moment of deep thought, it hits her; the body survives by its senses, each separate but working in unison with the others. It had always been her father's assertion that since the senses were separate with no apparent connection, there must be a part of the brain that acts as a coordinator. This hypothesis could never be proved. After years of study it was abandoned as conjecture, shelved, but never forgotten.

Now Angela's encounter with the foreign voice has her thinking of a new, similar explanation. Although due to her extensive research she had ruled out the brain, she was now delving into a new, plausible possibility. Could there be another not yet detected bodily organ, one with the single function of coordinating the senses? One that has a unique skill. An organ with its own inherent sense of order, with the capability of aligning, and directing like a conductor of music, a maestro of art. An organ with its own personal communication skills, one of which needs no vocal cords but only sensory perception. It could take the brain's interpretation of events, identification of people, and understanding of the environment, combine it with its own sensory information, use the nervous system's neural pathways to vibrate a pulse that can be received by the same organ in others. The communication going back and forth like a ball on an elastic string. An organ so powerful in its communication function that when on the rare occasions it's used, it appears an illusion.

She sits thinking about the many documented cases of people hearing voices. She now knows that they are real, and not just the dreams of mentally disturbed patients.

Later in the day came a lull in the ragged rumble of the battle. For Angela, it would prove to be a false alarm, as she took it to mean it was safe to venture out. Suddenly she thought of going to her landlords to discuss her options for leaving Gettysburg. More afraid of the voices she had heard earlier than the battle cries raging for most of the day, she changes into riding clothes. After attaching her horse and buggy she casually rides off acting as if the war is completely over.

Her landlord is furious. "Have you lost your senses, Miss

Gall! There are still skirmishes on the western border, and just down the road at Cemetery Hill, it's about to erupt with even more intense fighting. Hundreds have already died and it's only the start! Reports are Generals Meade and Lee are close to arriving. Earlier this afternoon the Union's eleventh corps had arrived, and the Union position was in a semicircle from west to north of town. The Confederate second corps under General Ewell began a massive attack from the north. The assault was repelled at Chamburg Pike, but the Federal's General Reynolds was killed. Other divisions were attacking from Oak Hill and across the open fields north of town. Barlow's Knoll was overrun. A third phase of fighting with the Confederates attacking at Herbst's woods and on Oak Ridge finally caused the Union line to collapse. They then retreated through town to Cemetery Hill.

Miss Gall! Angela, the war is in our backyard! Haven't you any fear? You don't know what it's like out there. The whole town is groaning. Those poor soldiers. They're like a chicken someone has snatched up to cut its throat. I swear to God they haven't any better chance. The shootings been like bands of wind cutting across the fields, sticking like honey to the faces and shoulders of soldiers. Haven't you seen the clouds from cannon blast rising up like hopeless prayers?"

"I have indeed, Mr. Simmons. I don't know what I must have been thinking to come out in all this."

"Go back home, Miss Gall. Lock your door and stay inside till you've heard from me. Is your musket loaded?"

"Yes but…"

"If a deserter gets inside sit yourself in a corner. If he threatens you don't hesitate to shoot. Are you in need of anything, food, water?"

"No, I just…"

"Then go, get back in your buggy and go. And sakes alive, Angela, don't try this again!"

On her way back she is stopped by a regiment of Union soldiers. One with the obvious markings of a high rank maneuvers his horse next to her. "Madam, the fighting is about to escalate. Are you close to home?"

"I am, sir, and was just on my way there."

"Would you mind telling me how large your house is ma'am?"

"If you will first tell me who you are?"

"I am Major General George G. Meade.

"Good day to you, Major."

He tips his hat. "Good day to you, ma'am."

"If you're looking for a headquarters post you may take my cabin. I'll turn back around and stay at my Landlords. My cabin has four rooms and is just a piece farther down the road."

"Indeed, ma'am? I was thinking of that very thing. You keep your cabin though. I need something much larger. We'll be on our way now. I've got a battle to oversee." He tips his hat a second time, and the regiment crosses a road into a field headed for Cemetery Hill.

When Angela squeezes the reins, readying to prod her horse, she is stunned by the scene in front of her. She leans back with the knowledge she will be sitting a while longer. Thousands of impressive Union soldiers are crossing the road, spanning a distance as far as her eyes can see. All with faces bristling with determination, pouring like a river into the fields.

"Hello stranger," one soldier shouts out as another sea of them plods their way out of the woods beside her, engulfing her carriage in a mass of blue.

"Is this the way to the battle?" Another shouts, laughing as he adjusts his kepi-style forage cap.

"I have first-rate news for you, Miss," still another shouts. "Billy Yank is gonna put a licking on Johnny Reb today. You'll hear them crying clear through the forest." This soldier's remarks are followed by a barrage of momentary laughter.

It took twenty minutes for the blue-coats to clear the road. They look eerily beautiful, traipsing and scratching in an uneven march, mixing, and swirling with the broad golden fields. She didn't know if they were being sincerely brave, or if they were just too young to know any better. She thought to herself how they couldn't see any further than their nose.

It would be close to six months later, and she would be having dinner with Mr. Jenkins and his wife in Tallahassee when she would hear the gruesome report. The Union suffered 23,049 casualties: 3,155 killed, 14,529 wounded, 5,365 captured or missing. The casualties on the Confederate side was harder to estimate, but it was believed between 23-28,000.

The following morning, she is awakened by pounding on her door. She rushes from her bed and before thinking opens it. Standing before her is a tall, solid built soldier with striking blue eyes. His face is grimacing, distorted by pain. She listens as he groans and cries pathetic, unintelligible words. Even so, she understands clearly, he is asking for help out of desperation, anguish, and fear of death. Before she can make a reply, he stumbles towards her, startling her, and falling dead at her feet.

Astonished at seeing someone die, she leans down over the soldier, trying to think of something to do, realizing at the same time, there is nothing *to* do. "He didn't kill himself," she whispers out loud, gazing at a huge hole in his leg. Because he was a deserter, no one would feel sorry for him. So, she leans farther over him, looking into his sky-blue eyes, tears dripping from her cheeks. "You're so young," she whispers out loud again. "Did you ever even get the chance to kiss a girl? I bet you did at least once, and I bet she was pretty."

After using her horse to drag his body to the barn, she locks herself back inside, now with a whole new concept of war. Sitting emotionless and quiet for most of the morning, she is now more determined to leave for Tallahassee. Watching through her writing desk window she sees the occasional deserter run through her yard. Finally, she picks up her ink pen, spots another soldier attempting to steal her horse, and begins a letter to her sister, Beatrice. She will tell of the tragedy of Gettysburg, about her impending move, even of the deserter dying in plain sight. But she will not tell her of the foreign voice. For the time being, she will simply try to forget about it. For now, there are more pressing concerns.

Chapter 17

(Modern-day, 18-hours earlier)

The distant sound of music could be heard drifting peacefully, gliding low on the breeze across the deserted beachfront. The bright and broad rim of the sun had been sinking slowly throughout the afternoon. Now appearing motionless, methodically it slips beneath an even broader ocean of water. In a sudden blaze of glory, an orange horizon burst onto the scene. With sprays of ocean mist touching his face, Carter watches the beauty and listens as a steady shrilling of locusts from nearby shrubs and palm trees blend delicately with the music. With the sun nearly gone, he looks southward in the direction of the music. Earlier, against Jen's wishes, he had decided to forgo a concert now being blasted in full tilt about a mile away at the Myrtle Beach Boardwalk. He wasn't up to going, just not in the mood, or more accurately the right frame of mind. He stands barefoot in the sand, his hands poked into the pockets of his jeans, still steaming that he was not invited to Lexington for the all-important meeting.

Behind him, beyond the hotel swimming pool, came the sound of a voice, and instantly the steady pulse of the insects turns to silence. When he turns, he can see Jen shouting and waving for him to come. Dusting the sand from his feet, he slips them into his rubber sandals, steps onto the wooden walkway, and starts heading her way. While he strides along, the locusts start up again, so he claps his hands, and for the second time they instantly stop. When he reaches her, her forearms are parallel and crossed just above her waist.

"You still pissed?" She asks while reaching out touching his arm.

His face, already tense and rigid now takes on the look of denial. Trying not to look at her, he struggles for something to say.

"You *are* still pissed. I can tell."

He couldn't meet her eyes with his own, or look at her at all, so he fixes his stare on the hotel building behind her. He can feel her watching him, contemplating him. It made him unhinged, like something was inside him that he needed to get a handle on.

"You going to say something? Or do you think I don't want to hear? Because if that's it, you're wrong. I do want to hear. I want to know what you have to say."

He gives a quick glance into her eyes, then back to the hotel building. "I'm fine, really."

"Heaven's sake, Carter! Of course, you're not fine! It's written all over your face! I don't blame you. You have a right to be mad after being left here."

He fidgets with his hair running his hand through it and rubbing the side of his head. "I think the worst part is I never even suspected, just assumed I would be going." He turns around looking out over the ocean, and simultaneously the lights around the pool click on with a brief buzzing sound. Darkness is amplifying, pushing away the last rays of light. Without looking he reaches out, feels for her hand, taking it into his own. "I thought that I was a part of it all, that they needed me."

"They do, Carter!"

"Then why am I still here?"

"It's not like they lied to you. They never made any promises. They must have believed that leaving you here was the right thing to do. Or maybe it was... *the safe thing*. I mean you and I aren't like them. They've got powers, like really incredible superpowers."

He rubs his eyes, then looks up into the sky, now not looking at anything. "I gave them what they needed, played my part. How quickly they forget."

216

She presses her head against his shoulder. "No, that's... No! They didn't forget! You're just upset is all. They wouldn't blow you off like that. Everyone agreed that your solution was the best way to go."

"So, what do I do now?"

"Now? Oh God, I almost forgot. Someone called our room. It's why I came to get you."

"Who was it?"

"I'm not sure exactly. A girl, hotel staff I guess."

"What did she want?"

"She said to tell you there's an envelope waiting for you at the front desk. And to come first chance you get, it's time-sensitive."

"Time-sensitive!"

"I know, right? I thought it was strange, too. After everything that's happened, it seems something...I don't know, might be off. Do you think its some kind of trap?"

"Maybe, then again maybe not. I know one thing though."

"What's that?"

"It's time we find out."

With the sun now completely down, a deep gloss from the moon shined across the pool reflecting off the water. Carter could see it dimly lighting Jen's face. He could see her amber hair, too. It still mesmerized him. He tilts his head forward lightly kissing her on the lips, then turns pulling her by the hand, walking to the inside of the hotel.

At the front desk, they notice a girl with electric-blue hair, matching lipstick and mascara. She's humming a pathetically bad eighties tune as she opens a wide set of blinds; it seems she's in a dream-like state. The sultry beaming moon shown through the window in all its glory shining its light on the parking lot.

"Excuse me!" Carter shouts.

The girl flinches, jumping backward's. She inadvertently drops the string, watching as the blinds, shrieking loudly, come crashing back down. One side of them appears a twisted, mangled mess. She turns around, red flashing across her face giving her a bizarre psychedelic skin tone. "You scared the

217

crap out of me!"

"Sorry I…"

"Forget the apologies, just be more careful next time!" She walks towards him. "What do you need that's so important anyway, pretty boy?" She looks at Jen, who is giving her a smirk.

Carter shifts uncomfortably, placing one arm around Jen. "Maybe we should start over. I was told there's an envelope waiting for me here."

"Your name?"

"Carter Landcaster."

"Just checking. You never can be too safe. There's thieves, druggies, perverts, weirdos, sex-starved…"

Jen's head goes slightly up and backward. "Did you say, weirdos?"

"That's right. You need to be aware of your surroundings."

"Really!"

"If you been doing this as long as I have you can spot them right off." Turning her attention back to Carter, she reaches her hand out of sight below the counter while putting on an artificial smile, the electric-blue lipstick and mascara widening across her face. She lifts up a small, white envelope. "This is yours." Her eyebrows relax as she loses the smile, her lipstick and mascara wrinkling like a sail losing its wind. "You mind if I go back to the blinds now?"

Trying hard not to laugh, he just smiles while ripping at the envelope. Turning, he motions with his eyes for Jen to follow and walks to a sofa in the lobby. While reaching into the envelope he glances back at the girl fumbling with the blinds. Smiling again, he looks at Jen. "Have I told you lately how beautiful you are?"

She punches his arm. "Just tell me what it says, lover-boy."

"This is strange, it's just a piece of paper. It has room number 116 with the word, *URGENT*."

"You're thinking about going, aren't you?"

His eyebrows raise as he moves his eyes from the piece of paper back to Jen's face. "I don't think we have a choice."

"Yes, we do! We could just leave! This could be a trick."

"If they wanted to harm us, they would've done it already. They obviously know where we are. If we leave, they'll probably just follow us."

"So that's it then? We go to room 116, like now?"

"The paper says: URGENT. It could be important."

Since the room was on the first floor it only took a minute to walk down a hallway, another minute to walk a second hallway and knock on the door. The man answering, surprises Carter. "Ansel, you're here in Myrtle Beach?" The two friends briefly hug. "What's going on? Your note said, URGENT?"

"It is, very," he says while scratching the side of his head, then he moves his arm out inviting them in. Almost immediately they see another figure standing toward the back of the room.

"Is that Dillon?" Carter asked, walking passed Ansel. "Okay, now I am confused. Somebody needs to tell me what's going on."

Dillon doesn't waste any time answering. "Your regenerated friends have been tricked. Danny's not who they think she is. She's a plant, a really good one. She was just gathering information, setting your friends up. She knows about the plan, about everything. They're in some deep trouble."

"That sounds ridiculous. And if it is true, why are you telling *us*? Why do you even care?"

"They double-crossed me. That's why. They double-crossed a lot of people. They've reached their quota. They're not regenerating anyone else. They're going to kill every aging person and repopulate the earth with only their precious, perfect regenerated ones. Because of their new and improved bodies, we're calling them the *Naib*. And right now, the Naib have two opposing sides. If we don't help your friends, the ensuing civil war between them is going to be over fast."

"You haven't seen Harlan lately? He can stop them."

"You're wrong about that. Your new and improved grandfather doesn't have a chance."

"How do you know that? How do you know any of this?"

"They made a critical mistake by trusting me and letting

me get too close. So, I eavesdropped, like a lot. Oh, I was careful, only a few minutes at a time. More than that and they would sense something. I've known that for a long time. If they had sensed something, it would've been all over for me. You know me, Carter. I take care of myself. I was always in this for myself. It's why I agreed to join them in the first place. I thought if I did what I was told I'd have a free ticket to immortality. A few days ago, I finally put all the pieces together. And in a few weeks their plan goes into action. Everybody will think a super virus is wiping out the whole freaking population. And your friends can't stop them, not without help."

"Why not? It's the Fifth Pinnacle. Harlan is the chosen-one now. He's more powerful."

"In time, yes, but that Danny, she's strong as hell. It'll take him years of practicing his powers to surpass her. Someday he'll be stronger, of course. Maybe even a lot stronger, but not now."

"Why Danny? I Thought Solomon was the strongest, the last chosen one."

"I thought so too until a few days ago. I told you I've been eavesdropping. While Danny was here in Myrtle Beach cozying up with your friends, she was managing to communicate with Solomon."

"I don't believe you! They would've known. *Harlan* would've known!"

"You never could admit being wrong. Face it, Carter. Your people made the same mistake with Danny that Solomon made with me."

"No! You're up to something!"

"Yes, but it's not what you think. I overheard one of their conversations. He had her on speakerphone while he looked out over the Lexington skyline. He's always doing that like he's a god or something."

Carter suddenly lunges at Dillon, pointing a finger in his face. "You always were the conniving one. What are you up to? Tell me! I should just beat your face in right now and be done with this! You're stationed in Tallahassee, have been for a long time. You don't know chicken crap about the goings-on in Lexington!"

Dillon slaps at his finger, steps back in a defensive posture readying himself in case Carter takes a swing. The two sworn enemies are on the verge of fighting for the third time in as many months.

"You need to back away and calm down. And Ansel, you need to update your friend on a few things."

Ansel reaches out covering Carter's outstretched hand with his own. "I know how you feel about him, Carter, but he's telling the truth. They brought him back a month ago. They consider him their brightest Chemical Engineer. These last few weeks they wanted him close."

Dillon smiles while shaking his head, then starts laughing. "Who do you think's been working on the formula to kill everybody. Course I never realized they were going to use it on me."

Carter shakes Ansel's hand away. "Why you son-of-a..." He lunges again, this time wrapping his hands around Dillon's throat. Dillon snaps his knee up, plunging it deep into the pit of Carter's stomach, forcing the two men off-balance. They fall hard against a set of shades covering the window. As they slide along the wall in a rugged fit of rage, the shades explode loose plowing to the floor with them. Almost immediately, Carter rolls on top of him, slinging the shade off him he swings his arm back in the launch position and lets it soar into the jaw of Dillon. When he draws back to hit him again, Ansel snatches his arm, pulling furiously until Carter is standing up next to him.

Rubbing at his jaw, Dillon spits blood onto the floor. "You really don't believe in casual talk do you, tough man? I've had about all I can take fighting with you." He reaches down to his ankle, pulls back his jeans revealing a small handgun. Quickly he unsnaps the holster and takes the gun. "I don't plan on getting my butt whipped again, so back away!" Pointing the gun at Carter's face he climbs to his knees, pressing his free hand against the floor he stands up. "You don't like me, Carter. You got plenty of reasons, no question about it. But here's the cold hard truth. Tomorrow morning in Lexington there's a meeting taking place which you are well aware of. What you're not aware of is that the crap is going to hit the stratosphere. Technically speaking, they're going to kill James, Grace, and I didn't hear for sure but possibly Angela. Then they're going to bring Harlan to a holding location, basically imprison him, and put him through years of programming. If they handle it right, which they will, then they can control him for hundreds of years. That's what Solomon did with Danny, so she knows the game well. At some point Harlan's powers will just be too much. Then, and only then, will he be the true leader. I don't really care about any of those things, but what I do care about is living, so I've switched sides. Call me a defector, a traitor, a Benedict Arnold, I don't care. I'm a survivor, and that's what I plan on continuing to do. Ansel and I are going to try to do something to turn the tide. You know I hate having to ask this, but are you with us?"

Carter's lips compress and his face tightens up even more in an act of disbelief. He jerks his arm loose from Ansel. "You're still an ass, Dillon. That will never change. I'm in, and you know how much I hate having to say that. Now first things first. Apparently, you have access to the building their meeting is in, but what about the rest of us? How do we get in?"

"You can walk in like anyone else. It's the Museum Hotel."

"My guess is the room they're meeting in won't be as easy."

"You're so freaking smart. You should 'a been a detective, you know that?"

Carter tilts his head looking down trying not to explode. "Just cut the crap and talk."

"The 5th floor is blocked. Actually, it's always blocked. We call it Solomon's Little Temple. I've spent a lot of time there this past month, so I've got the elevator code to the floor. I know the room, and I know the timing of the meeting."

"You talk like we can just walk right in with guns blazing."

"You haven't seen their powers have you? But I have. That would be grossly underestimating them. Not to mention their head of security. They call him Old Jack but don't let the name fool you. He's really smart and tough as they come. There'll be two thugs that never leave his side and at least one other. Altogether there'll be four of them, all of them Naibs.

The good thing is Old Jack won't see us as a threat. After weeks of seeing me coming and going with Solomon, he shouldn't even flinch."

"Makes sense, but what happens when he sees the rest of us?"

Dillon's cynical laugh starts up again. "Do you really need to ask that? Not one of you even remotely resembles a Naib. They can be hundreds of years old, but they all look about eighteen. As long as he sees you with me, he won't blink. Compared to him and his security team, we're powerless. If we're smart, we can use that to our advantage."

"Since I really prefer not hearing that asinine laugh again, I won't ask if you have a plan."

"We need to incapacitate them without making any noise. To do that it has to be a complete surprise. We'll only get one chance. If we botch this we're probably dead, so if there are any doubts?"

Carter looks around to Jen, their eyes meeting in that reflective way. She hesitates, then gives a nod of approval. "I can't ask you to do this, Jen. It's just too dangerous."

"Stop trying to protect me! I hate it when you do that! I'm a big girl, and it's time you start treating me like one! She turns to Dillon. "Count me in."

"Okay then." Dillon points to a black briefcase. "Now that we've got that out of the way. I've purchased four of the smallest tranquilizer guns I could find, then modified them to make them even smaller. They can be concealed in a purse, a pouch or a small container, but I'm afraid not in a pocket. With all the work I put in modifying them, they're still not pocketsize. We can equip Jen with a purse that holds two, and two more will be in a vodka box I'll be pretending to deliver to Solomon. That's not out of the ordinary. I've done it several times before, so it shouldn't arouse suspicion."

Jen swings a hand up in the stop position. "I don't mean to be the bearer of bad news, but my father works for the forestry dept. Once in a while, he has to tranquilize a problem bear. They don't fall instantly. They go a little loopy right off, but the drug has to work its way to the heart and brain. Then they fall unconscious. He just usually sits down and waits for the bear to fall asleep. It takes about 15-30 minutes."

"I've done my homework, and you're spot on. So, I've prepped the anesthetics myself. I don't have a chemical engineering degree for the title. The drug will work, and it will work lightning-fast, but only if we shoot them in the heart. Anywhere else and it might take a second or two. Even then I think we're good. I think I've made it clear how dangerous this is."

Carter leans his shoulder against the naked window casement. "Lexington's a long way off. When do we leave?"

"If we made good time it would take nine hours by car. That won't do. We'd have to drive practically all night. Not a problem though, because your good friend Ansel has arranged for a private jet. The pilot's on call at the Myrtle Beach Airport whenever we're ready." He points to the corner of the room where a punching bag is propped up with a small red circle drawn onto the vinyl. Then he flips up the chrome-colored latch of the briefcase, reaches in, and pulls out a tranquilizer gun. "Before we leave I thought we'd do a little target practice. We got plenty of time. The flights only an hour and twenty minutes. He hands the gun to Jen. "Why don't you go first?"

Chapter 18

(Back to Loam)

To Harlan's astonishment, there is a knock at the door, and it swings open instantaneously. Surrounded with illuminated white energy, he is on the verge of sending the five of them back through the multiverse to their own dimension in Lexington, Kentucky. He is startled to see another man enter the room. His appearance is of a glowing copper-like metal that's so bright it instantly causes all five of them to painfully squint their eyes. While they watch with difficulty, they see his eyes blaze with reflected light resembling gold gems. His body pulsates, radiating, and illuminating the entire room with the copper-colored light.

"If you do this now, it is essentially very ignorant of you," the man said. Then he gives a quick, hard shake of his body, and the brightness reflecting from him dims and disappears. "Sorry about the shine, it always happens when I materialize."

Harlan gears back down his attempt to enter the multiverse. "Materialize!" He shouted, the white aura of energy surrounding him now dissipating as he steps forward toward the man. "You obviously know something about us. Who are you? Why are you here? And..." He gives the man a cold, hard stare. "And what is that you are wearing?"

The man cringes while looking himself up and down. "No, no, no, this is not right. This is not even close. It's a Union Soldiers uniform. I was supposed to have khaki pants and a blue button-up shirt. It's the dimensions. They're growing further apart, and… causing all sorts of problems."

"I've seen you before!" Angela says while moving up next to Harlan. "And your voice, I remember that voice. Tell me if I'm wrong."

"Of course, you're not wrong."

"It was during the war, right? The civil war before my regeneration?"

He takes his Union coat off looking all around as if he doesn't know what to do with it, tossing it across a small wooden chair. He looks at Angela. "It happened as you say. I'm your watcher."

"My watcher?"

"Yes." He points to Harlan. "And his, too." He swings his arm to James, then Grace. "And his, and hers. Then on to Timothy. "But not his. Never saw him before."

"But you died! I saw you die at my feet!"

"Oh dear, this won't do. This won't do at all. I never died. I'm not even sure if I can die. It was the body. I materialized taking the form of a soldier. When I talked to you with only a voice you got really upset, so I thought if I materialized. Well, a darn farmer shot me, then ran like a scared dog. It all went bad. When I left the dead body, I unexpectedly shot through the multiverse. That was my own fault, but I won't try to explain the regulations regarding the spirit realm. So, I ended up on Planet III in Russia of all places. Then I was called to headquarters to give a briefing. By the time I got back, you had already moved to Tallahassee. Mr. Jenkins was in the process of regenerating you. I was called back to headquarters again and told to leave it be for the time being, but just to observe."

"Why are you here now?" Harlan asked.

"We usually don't interfere, but like I said, the dimensions. Trouble has been building since the civil war. By that time the killings on earth and Loam were starting to cause serious problems. In the multiverse, everything's connected. What happens here affects the other dimensions and visa-versa. I tried to warn Angela way back then because it had already been decided that she was the next chosen one. She had everything we were looking for. But it was her understanding of the brain that tipped the scales. She doesn't know it just yet, but one day, we believe she will do things far surpassing the regenerating of people. Course, you all may kill yourselves first.

Anyway, you can see why we were trying to make sure that she went to Mr. Jenkins. That was my sole purpose for contacting her at that time. Later the idea of a two-fold leadership was brought up. Soon after it was agreed on. The wait for the Fifth Pinnacle continued on until now. It's clear that Mr. Landcaster was the other choice. We ran billions of individuals' DNA, along with their functional tendencies, and innate qualities to find the perfect match. But back to the dimensions. If you would've left here without my help, I can't say for sure where you would have ended up. In Lexington probably, but even that's not certain. The Museum Hotel, in just the right room, doubtful."

"But I specifically brought us across dimensions to the Intercontinental Hotel here in London with no problems."

"Not exactly, Harlan. There are two Intercontinental Hotels in London. Your powers should have brought you to the one on London Park Lane. It's much safer there, none of those giant mechanical, killing machines. Instead, you ended up in the Riverside area, where a lot of the German forces were invading. Your powers are enormous, Harlan, but your knowledge of using them is limited. You're like a child who hasn't learned how to walk yet, but once he does there's no keeping up with him. It's the same with Angela, but she's a month or two behind you. The power to travel the multiverse, it won't be long now before she has it, too.

Now let me get to the main reason I'm here at this particular moment in time. I've just come from the Museum Hotel in your home dimension, where I made a thorough examination of the structure. It's a well-built building of that you can be sure. But there are some concerns. Points of highest pressure run extremely close to the room in which you will be addressing Solomon and Daniela. I've determined that although structurally sound, it won't remain standing if you

227

enter into a direct power to power conflict with them. The resulting energy being released would be too much for the support system, which is mostly made of concrete and steel. Normally they keep me tightly tethered. As is my title, I'm only a watcher. However, in this instance I have received permission to pass along this communication. I believe at this point you understand the reasons."

Harlan wraps his arm around Angela's shoulder. "It's not our intentions to physically battle with them."

"We understand that. You and Angela have a wonderful plan, which you no doubt expect to have a non-violent outcome. Tricking them by taking control of their waking consciousness, then injecting them with a memory loss drug, although not a peaceful solution, would not incur any damage to the building itself. Nevertheless, we have calculated an 80% chance that something will go wrong, resulting in the release of extraordinary power. Hypothetically speaking, between you and Angela, along with Solomon and Daniela, there's a hundred times over enough power to destroy the building. All told, there will be nineteen regenerated one's present--eleven of them, four of you, and four more handling security just outside the room. If a battle breaks out, and everyone gets involved, it's possible that the building with all its occupants will be vaporized."

Angela rests her head against Harlan's shoulder. "What do you suggest we do?"

"Suggest?"

Her head jerks back up. "Yes! You must have some kind of recommendation! Surely you're not just here to advocate peace! Don't you have a proposal?"

He picks up the vintage Union coat, looks at it with disgust, raises an arm out, and puts it back on. "There is no suggestion, recommendation, or proposal."

"Then why are you here?"

"To inform you, and I've done that. We've covered this. I'm only your watcher."

"But...you're not being any help!"

"If we asked you to disengage, would you?"

"Of course not."

"And neither would Solomon and Daniela."

"But we have a good reason. They're going to kill billions of people. What will that do to the precious multiverse?"

"You know exactly what will happen, and so do we. But they believe in their cause the same as you believe in yours. Unless our parliament convenes and changes age-old laws, we are not allowed to interfere, at least not directly, in your battles. Your fate has to remain in your own hands."

"But that's absurd. You *made* us!"

"Angela, you know more about the brain than anyone in all the four dimensions combined. You should know that allowing your emotions to take control of you at such a critical time as this will only... Tell you what, I'll take a little more time to explain things. But then we must go. There's much danger here.

You now understand that there are four dimensions of earth, each connected but existing in their own separate universe. They were all constructed and went into use at the same time. This took millions of years. Finally, we constructed man and placed him in his completed home. Four homes to be exact. We also allowed for significant expansion. In each universe there are 148 other inhabitable planets. No need to get into that now, but those are the facts. As it stands right now you have a quad dimensional earth, or a continuing to expand two-by-two matrix multiverse. All the dimensions are expandable through increased energy which happens with growth in populations. But these dimensions can also collapse through energy fluctuations which is what is occurring now. These dimensions are stacked like blocks one on top of another, side by side, a two-by-two matrix square. Your universe is above Loam's, and directly next to the other dimensions. The discrepancy in energy between the two sides is enormous. This is of course due to the differences in populations. Man still doesn't understand the huge amount of energy emitted by one single person. The energy is the bond that connects the four dimensions. The discrepancy in this energy is causing a gradual separating, also a warp that has each universe bowing at its ends. If the bowing continues it will eventually wrap around and touch, much like a sphere. It's already close to happening. If it does, time as you know it will change. This will create portals connecting time periods. History 50-years apart will be happening at the same time."

He looks again at the Union coat. "I think it might be starting. Travel between dimensions will be even more tricky. Within a few weeks of all this, the multiverse will collapse. The odds of a complete collapse are so high that discussions have already taken place on whether to rebuild the matrix after its destruction. The early discussions are not favorable. Two of the earths including your own have become widely militarized, fighting and killing constantly. The two others remain at peace, their number of inhabitants now over doubling your own. We calculate total destruction in one month's time. Corresponding with Solomon and Daniela's mass execution of earths population."

"Sounds like you're telling us we don't have a chance! And I'm not so sure you even care!"

"I'm telling you we can't interfere or impede with the results. We didn't create you to control you like puppets. You four are the best chance the multiverse has of surviving. Find a way to make use of the information you've just been given. If you win out over Solomon and Daniela, then you can use your enormous power to bring peace to this dimension of earth. It would be enough to stop the imploding of the multiverse. Maybe then, by your inter-dimensional travels, you could help Loam toward the goal of peace. In some ways, technologically speaking, they are years behind your earth, but they are far more destructive. If peace doesn't come here, we calculate 50-60 years before they implode the multiverse."

"You seem to know a lot about our people, so I got a question for you."

"We've not much time. What's your name, sir?"

"Timothy. While we're at it, you never really mentioned yours."

"I didn't?"

"Well no. You just came in flashing light everywhere,

blinding us and telling us what a mess we've made of everything."

"Timothy, if it's all the same to you, I think I'll keep that out of my report. My name's Curtis, but I go by Curt. I've been told more than a few times I can be blunt. So, I get what you're saying. What's you're question?"

"This war with Germany. How does it end? I only ask because you seem to know everything else."

"You won't like the answer, but we calculate a 98-percent chance Germany wins. Everywhere they're fighting they're driving the other side back. They have an engineer named Porsche that's light years ahead of the rest of the world. I'm sure you've noticed he's come up with some pretty sick weapons."

"I thought about staying here since it looks so bad on the other side. But 80-percent sounds a lot better than 98. So as long as they'll have me I'm still going. Maybe I can even help the cause."

"If you stay here you'll most likely be killed. If you go with these four, chances are not much better, especially since you're not regenerated. But if things go their way you could be living a very long time. Speaking of time, we don't have much. Warplanes are being sent back to this part of the city. By the time they are done, there won't be much left.

Harlan, any time you're ready. With both of us concentrating, it'll be a snap. We'll land right square in the middle of that Museum Hotel room. When we get there, remember to use the information I've given you. At all costs do not allow the situation to plunge into a physical battle. If it does try to contain it, to end it quickly. You still have some time to work with, and about a month before it reaches the critical point.

Timothy, since you're not a regenerated one you're going to feel a tingling of the skin, maybe even a little pain with it. You're also going to lose your hearing for the first couple minutes. Don't worry, it's normal.

Harlan, once we get there I'll be of no help. I can only observe.

Angela, don't lose sight of your brain research. Aging is not how man was constructed. Regeneration is only a band-aid. Keep searching, keep studying. I can't tell you more, it's not allowed. Your fate is in your own hands.

Harlan, it's time we go."

Chapter 19

(Vietnam, 1963)

Bobby Prescott was a known storyteller who came from a fanatical religious family. So, when he shouted across the sweltering hot, rice paddy, that the president had been shot dead, Harlan wasn't sure if he believed him or not. Turning, he looks behind him trying to see through the thick, blurry texture of humidity. He wipes at the heavy moisture clinging to his face, then blinks hard trying to make out the unclear, woolly looking soldier. He hesitates a moment thinking about how Bobby, who was a Sergeant in rank, was always spouting off about this war, which had been raging now for eight years. He wonders how President Kennedy could have been shot while thousands of miles away from Vietnam. He throws his rifle up horizontally over his iron pot helmet, then down the back of his neck across his shoulders. His hands are hanging from both ends of it as it comes to rest on his camouflaged fatigues. Sweat dripping from his face, he turns and starts walking, splashing his way through the rice paddies.

"Sir, they're saying it might be part of a larger attack on the U.S. mainland!"

When Harlan returned to his platoon he sees eight or more soldiers huddled around a radio. Confusion was obvious in the camp as news of the horrific event had already shocked the world. Walking up to the men he notices several weeping openly.

"Lieutenant!" One of them shouts while giving a quick salute. "It's a bad day, Sir. The president's been murdered." The others follow suit standing at attention and saluting. "It's just been within the hour, Sir."

Without responding, Harlan reaches into his fatigue shirt pocket and pulls out a small high school photograph of his wife, then salutes. "We were blindsided by this one, men. No question. Take time to feel the pain. Let it get deep down inside you and resonate. But don't let it overwhelm you. Remember why we're here. We've still got a job to do. Use this day for motivation."

Truth be told, none of them, including Harlan, really knew why they were here. This thought suddenly hits him. He salutes again, waving the men off. Peering into the picture, he smiles because he misses her. Also, because he's remembering their honeymoon night. His wife is a blonde-haired, green-eyed, bonafide beauty. Rumors had been sifting around camp for weeks about a possible withdrawal. President Kennedy was the one said to be behind it. He lifts his eyes up from the photograph toward the sun and pans his face around a hazy white-blue sky. He does this wondering when he will see her again, *if* he will see her again. It's as if he's hoping the answers will somehow miraculously come to him from out of the distant sun. Finally, he takes off his steel-pot helmet, pulls at his boonie hat that has slid up inside it, places the cloth hat back on his head and sits down atop the helmet. Hot dust rises from the commotion into his nostrils, coating an already filthy face, and giving him the feeling of permanence. He kisses the picture and places it back in his shirt pocket, buttoning it tight.

Lieutenant Harlan Landcaster was an original. There were few officers respected as much by their men. He had the natural gift of oversight, directing his deep reconnaissance platoon with firmness while at the same time fitting in as one of them. This was a feat rarely attempted, and less rarely accomplished, but Harlan felt comfortable leading *and* being one of the guys. His platoon was divided into two squads, with one Sergeant for each squad, altogether a total of 30 men. Sergeant Bobby Prescott was a squad leader along with Sergeant Harry Deal, nicknamed by his squad *The Real Deal*.

The chaos caused by the tragic event in Dallas, Texas continued throughout the afternoon. Eventually, the whole platoon of thirty sat around the radio, listening with a quiet eagerness for any words that might give a rational end to the reasons of such treachery. They were not to come, and neither was the understanding of exact details of responsibility.

That night Harlan lay on his aluminum frame cot, still thinking of his wife, and still suffocating in the sultry, sticky airlessness. By this time, he already understood that any hope of withdrawal had died with the President. "Two more years," he whispers. "Two more years before I can see her." He reaches next to his cot, picks up a warm bottle of vodka, leans his head forward and downs two ounces of the sleeping potion. A moment later he is being talked to out of the shadows by a voice he doesn't recognize.

"Tomorrow, go right and take your men with you."

"Sergeant Prescott? Bobby? Is that you?"

"Tomorrow, go right and take your men with you."

Jumping up Harlan inadvertently drops the bottle of vodka in the sandy dirt. Before it can spill too much, he snatches it back up, then looks around his tent. "Bobby, what the heck!"

"We need you. Dimensions are separating."

"What! Where the blazes are you?" When he doesn't get an answer, he takes another swig from the bottle. He is still scanning the tent when the voice starts back up.

"Dimensions are separating."

"Bobby, if you're pulling a fast one I'll... Come out where I can see you!" His eyes had reached every inch of the tent by the time he noticed that the voice had stopped. He stood there quiet, hoping it would start back up, but this time it did not.

The voice stopping had irritated him more than it did speaking because to him it seemed to have stopped in the middle of a page. What was it trying to tell him? Was it important? *It must be,* he thought. He laid the bottle aside, slid passed his cot, pushed back the tent door canopy and looked outside. He wasn't expecting to see anything. In his heart of hearts, he knew the voice had come from another realm. He didn't want to admit it, but now looking out around his tent he

236

knew it for sure. The voice wasn't human. He had heard stories growing up about the spirit realm, about how sometimes they would talk to humans. His mother and father both believed in angels. *Was this voice one of them?* He wondered. At such a moment as this, he gets the idea to write his wife a letter. He allows the canopy door to fall, its heavy weight closing the tent back tight.

Back inside he sits at a small table and reaches into his backpack pulling out a metal container. Inside it are his stationery and pen. He takes one more look around the tent, still wondering, only now with a sense of awe. Pen in hand, he looks down at the golden swirls edging the stationery, touching them in deep thought as if they have some parallel connection to his life. He is in the midst of sinking downward, twirling like a corkscrew into thoughts about his wife and the events of the day. Deeply moved by the experience with the voice, he begins to write.

My dear Katharine,

Let me start this letter by saying how much I miss you, and how much I wish we were together. Today we got the terrible news that the world continues spinning out of control. The unprovoked murder of our President, who was beloved by many, is proof enough. It was a day I wanted desperately to be holding you in my arms, quieting any tremble you may have gotten from the shocking news. I hope my darling, that your sleep, though being hindered by the landmark day, will not completely allude you. I am softened by the thought that your prayers, which you are in a habit of doing every night, will bring you a degree of comfort.

For awhile we were excited about rumors floating around about a complete withdrawal of troops. Today, I am disappointed to tell you, those hopes were assassinated along with President Kennedy, God rest his soul. It was he, rumor tells it, that was behind the withdrawal. Still, after eight years of such a senseless war, maybe our home country will end the misery sooner than later. By now it should be clear that there will be no winners, only survivors, the numbers of which go down daily. If unexpectedly the higher-ups do indeed end this puzzle of a war, then get the confetti ready. I will be fuzzy-headed from the exhaustion of traipsing over 9000 miles back to the bluegrass of Kentucky. But never will I stop running until I kiss your milky white face again. More than anything else you are the thing that keeps me going. The other day I noticed that I was talking to myself about you. It's not that I've lost my mind, but rather, proof that you are with me, helping me. You are the thing, dear, really, that keeps me going, and you will be the thing that brings me back home.

Earlier we received orders to begin a reconnaissance mission tomorrow at 1300 hrs. We will keep our nose to the ground and do our usual sniffing around. As I've written to you before; our crew here is a good one. Hopefully our findings will do some good, maybe save some lives. I say this with the sad knowledge that our field information will be used for search and destroy missions. Hopefully I can put your mind at ease, relating to you that your husband is at the moment in an area not known for tricks or booby traps. Neither have I heard of any recent ambushes in this section. Tomorrow's patrol will be deeper into the jungle than usual, in a free-fire area. But I am not anticipating a confrontation, and certainly not a chunk of metal that can screw up any man's life. Of course, in war things can change quickly.

My mood is growing much better since I've been writing you this letter. Do you still have that long white dress, the one you wore on our honeymoon? I was thinking about it earlier, how beautiful you looked in it. Do you remember we were on the beach drinking champagne from the bottle? You were barefoot, and the waves were pushing saltwater onto the bottom of your dress. I remember your hair and the dress both blowing together in the stiff ocean breeze. It was as if they had blended and became one. When I come home would you wear it for me on our first date out? I miss you darling, and with my own eyes, I want to see you in that dress again.

In your return letter would you tell me some things about yourself. Are you still working for the elementary school? Did you decide to get a cat? I think it would do me some good to *hear about things going on in your life. Maybe you could walk me through an average day. Hearing about your normal everyday life will help keep you fresh in my mind. As you are well aware of, there is no normalcy here. So please, don't hold anything back, nothing's too boring. I need to live normalcy right through the middle of you.*

Your husband in love
Harlan Landcaster
PS, I miss you!

Harlan carefully double-folds the letter, places it inside an envelope, seals, and addresses it. He leaves it on the table while returning the stationery and pen back to the metal container. After taking a short drink of vodka, he lays back across his cot, his mind now in a much better place. He hears locust singing into the night air. Before he closes his eyes, he glances around the tent with strange thoughts of being enlightened. Like he has been given an advantage, that something, although he doesn't understand what, has been revealed to him.

When he finally closes his eyes, there is an immediate picture of his wife in his mind. They are on the beach, and she is wearing the white dress. She is walking, and the soft ends of the dress are fluttering in the wind. He is walking up behind her, reaching out, chasing, trying to touch her fingers. Wordlessly she gestures back to him. He can see her lips.

She is saying, *"I love you."* Then she says, *"Come on, handsome, let's get our feet wet."*

Early the next morning dawn light is filling the tent. After a shave, Harlan stands in front of a mirror no bigger than his hand wiping the remaining lather from his face.

The day gets started quickly with the loud, shrieking words, "Come here to me you little piss ant!"

When Harlan walks outside into the camp he notices others doing the same.

An undersized skinny soldier named Erik is chasing a small scruffy looking dog that has ventured into the camp.

"Give it back!" The soldier shouts falling face-first into the dusty soil. The tiny mutt has a boonie hat clamped between its teeth and is darting in a circular motion just inside the edges of several tents. The soldier jumps up and continues the chase. This time turning, and shooting across the camp, cutting the dog off. The dog panics, running hard into the side of a tent, the edges of its canopy covering over him. "Gotcha now, ya mangy…" Suddenly the dog reappears on the other side of the tent again running in circles around the camp. The soldier throws his arms up in disgust, then stumbles, starting the chase again.

When he comes his way, Harlan throws one arm out ordering the soldier to stop. When he does, the dog also stops. "Soldier, has the dog killed someone, possibly your grandmother?"

The soldier comes to attention, his arms straight down and tight against his thin frame. "No. Sir, Lieutenant, Sir."

"Then why are you chasing him?"

"Sir, he swiped my hat, Sir."

"Have you never trusted anybody before? And please, at ease Erik. I'm not trying to drill you."

The soldier pulls a green handkerchief from his pants and wipes at the moisture already building on his face. "I'm not sure I know what you mean."

"You don't know what trust means?"

"Well, yes, of course, I…"

Harlan bends down low to one knee looking at the dog. He reaches out his hand and gives a soft whistle. "Come here, boy. Don't be afraid, I won't hurt you."

The dog looks back at the soldier who had been chasing him, then turning he slowly walks up to Harlan, dropping the hat beside his boot.

Harlan takes the hat while at the same time petting the dog and looking back at the soldier. "Do you see that he trusts me?"

"Yes, Sir."

"Somewhere he learned that trust won't always hurt him. You have to learn when to trust, and when not to trust."

240

Harlan stands back up looking out at the other men. "Today at 1300 hrs we go on a reconnaissance mission. It's been over a month since we went into a free-fire zone. We're going hiking deep into the jungle, and there's no Beverly Hills or beaches on the trail. I want you mentally prepared. Prepare full gear, we won't be back here for two maybe three days. I don't anticipate a confrontation, but you men know by now to be ready for anything. I want this place buttoned up tight. You know the drill, so make it happen.

Sergeant Deal, you and Sergeant Prescott be at my tent for a briefing at 0900.

Oh, and men, there's plenty of time to write a letter. I encourage you to do so not because I'm worried about something happening. But because of the unknown, and because, your families, and you, deserve it." Harlan turns, stepping back into his tent.

Just as the canopy drops behind him the heckling begins.

"Hey, Erik, you couldn't catch a cold, you dimwit."

"Erik, rarities unlimited here. Your hat is worth a million dollars. Do you trust me?"

"I thought the dog must be pissing beer the way you were after it."

"Ha, ha, ha," Erik shouted back. "Everybody's a comedian. The camps full of Don Rickles today." Slapping the hat several times on his leg he knocks the dust off, turns and nearly walks right into Sergeant Deal. "Sir, Sorry, just trying to get back to my tent."

"At ease soldier." Sergeant Deal scans his eyes beyond Erik looking around the camp. Several soldiers are still snickering, shaking their heads and whispering. He focuses back on Erik, his eyes steady with a taut mix of concern and disappointment. "Don't give them a reason to laugh at you. And when they do, don't let them get to you Private. The best way to react to being laughed at is silence. Anything else just fuels it."

"Permission to speak freely, Sir?"

"I already said at ease!"

Erik takes the hat back off his head. Squeezing it in his

hands he uses it as stress relief. "I've always been laughed at, Sir. It's the reason I joined the army."

"If you want to curb it, maybe even one day stop it, you'll heed my words. A fire can't keep blazing without fuel. Don't help them make fun of you, think before you act. And don't ever respond to their laughs. Look, Private, I know you were an orphan, it's in your records. Growing up that way...it couldn't have been easy. But every man has a weakness to overcome. We call it building character. You can't get to another place without first starting the trip. I suggest you start that journey, today. Now back to your tent. I want you fully ready for the reconnaissance mission at 1300 hours."

"Sir, yes, Sir."

The briefing Harlan has with his two squad leaders is a reminder that war is a sprawling sickness. "Our mission is to locate and report the coordinates of hidden pockets of VC (Vietcong). Afterward's, well you know how it works, they'll be spraying artillery fire. We've not been to this location before, at least not our platoon."

Harlan points to a map unfolded on his table. "At this point here, you can see where two trails cross. Other platoons call it the crisscross trail for obvious reasons. We'll be following the south trail to this location. Somewhere beyond it are suspected pockets of the VC. It's a ten, maybe eleven-hour hike. We'll get seven or eight in today, camp with zero visibility (no campfire or lanterns) and finish the next day around 1000 or 1100 hours. Remind your men of VC tactics. They stay hidden in the day and like to seek and engage at night. But nothing's for sure in this area, so we'll need to keep moving. I think we'll be fine, but we've got to be on high alert. Also, remind your men of their training. If we end up in a conflict, it's the one thing that will save them. Any questions?"

"Are there armor units close by, or will they be sending in planes? I just want to know where the artillery fire will be originating from."

"Sergeant Deal, it's a good question. I don't blame you one bit for asking. Is the fire coming from over our heads or over our shoulders? Right now, my instructions are to report back to an armed unit. The friendly fire will be over our shoulders, men. Any other questions?"

"Sir, yes, Sir."

"Cut the Sir crap, Sergeant Prescott, just ask the question."

"Will there be another platoon? I mean, are they sending backup?"

"We're on a reconnaissance mission, they don't send the whole badass army for that!"

"It's just that they're always sending us into hairy situations without backup."

Harlan had anger in his eyes, but also distress. He had grown tired of these kinds of confrontations with the Sergeant. "Hairy situations are what we're here for. Unless our radio gets blown to kingdom come, don't sweat it. That's our backup. Any other questions?"

Silence from the men.

"Good. Have your squads ready to go. We head out at 1300 hours. And Sergeant Prescott, get your attitude right before we leave. I don't want you bugging out on us. If I hear of your pathetic view of things rubbing off on any of your men, it's going in my report. Are we clear?"

Bobby's face had turned an interesting blotchy shade of red. "Sir, yes, Sir."

"Then, dismissed!"

The afternoon was filled with the grueling aches and sweat of a seven-hour hike through the darkened jungle. After a dirty, hasty camp set up, four soldiers with silence orders took the overnight guard shift. In the morning the air was a little lighter, a little cooler, giving some relief. But the final hike was longer than anticipated. All told, the hiking and camping had taken a 24-hour complete rotation of the earth. Harlan ordered his men to eat, hydrate, and rest up. The next phase of the mission would take their best focus and concentration.

After the rest break, he sends out four reconnaissance teams, consisting of six soldiers each, on scouting missions. Hours later when the scout teams arrived back, they give reports of tow hidden VC camps. Harlan decides to wait in relaying the coordinates until they are exiting the area, putting more ground between the artillery fire and his men. He relays the coordinates by radio 30minutes later, not realizing all hell was about to break loose.

Guerrilla warfare consists of small-scale conflicts where stealthy combatants use the element of surprise to eliminate the opponent. Harlan was wary of this tactic and knew the VC widely used it. They would sneak up on unaware U.S. troops, attack them, and leave before risking capture. This kind of warfare had caused a lot of casualties and was the main reason Harlan's platoon was sent on this mission.

Coming to the end of a large wooded area, Harlan's platoon enters a different kind of terrain. It's largely elephant grass that varies in length from waist to shoulder. About 300-yards away the area turns back to the same wooded, jungle terrain. About fifty yards into it, Harlan can smell the enemy. He throws up his hand, ordering the troops to stop. "Keep your eyes open men!" Scanning closely, he notices patches of flat grass slowly rising. "Move back into the woods, it's an ambush! Go, and keep moving no matter what!" They hadn't gone more than ten steps when suddenly a hail of rounds zipped all around them. These were the nasty 12.7's (.51 caliber machine guns) normally used for anti-aircraft. They sounded like bullwhips snapping all around.

One of the men takes a bullet in a grenade on his belt. Suddenly there is this tremendous flash and plume of white smoke. Inside the smoke the soldier can be seen thrashing around, screaming because this thing is burning him to death. He falls out of sight and the grass around him can be seen smoldering and flopping around. The men were near mass confusion, many stopping, hiding in the grass.

"Keep moving, I said! Do you hear me? Get off your asses and move it!" Harlan, now holding an M-16 in each hand, sweeps the area where the shooting was coming from, screaming at the top of his lungs as he shoots. Finally, he turns and shouts the same command, "Keep moving!" Over and over he repeats it until his men are back in the safety net of the woods. He now orders his men to return fire, and a fierce firefight takes place. The grass can be seen moving, rolling in waves.

In the area they had just come from multiple explosions shake the ground, possibly from grenades. Due to the high grass the VC hadn't realized Harlan's men had made it back to the woods. He shouts for the rocket launcher, ordering the private with the shoulder mounted weapon to fire away. After the blast the VC start retreating, the danger level falls quickly to near zero.

The VC are not always well-trained, still, all in all, it is surprising that there is only one dead soldier. Although there are many superficial injuries, only two are serious. One soldier has metal in his leg, another in his shoulder, making the medics work quickly. After the wounded are cared for, the dead soldier is placed on a mobile stretcher, and the platoon starts advancing again, this time skirting the edges of the woods. Soon they hit a connective trail and then the main trail, where they stop at the crisscross to rest up a bit.

Harlan's teeth are clenched tight, his shoulders knotted with aches. It had been an ugly mission, and it wasn't getting any prettier. Out here you can overlook nothing, and things can still go wrong. He scans the area because there was always something oozing around the jungle.

A little later he is sitting with his eyes closed when he feels something come between his face and the hot sun. "Sir, what do you make of it?" He opens his eyes and sees the sun shining from behind a soldier, illuminating the outer edges of him.

"What do I make of what, Private?

"Of what just happened to us back there, of this war, of the danger, Sir?"

Harlan tilts his head to one side, peering deeper, softer at the young soldier. "I think it's love."

"I don't understand, Sir."

"But you do understand love. Vietnam is a gathering of love. With each step, each light year of a second, a foot soldier is *always almost dead*. In such a circumstance, you can't help but love. If you're married, you love your wife, your kids, you love your mom and dad, your football or baseball team, hamburgers on the grill, the smell of the beach. You think about these things on a different level. You love your own pulse, your future, everything that might be lost or never come to be. Intimacy with death carries with it a corresponding intimacy with life. Jokes are funnier, colors more colorful. You love the musty hot air even though it stings because it's a part of being alive. You love because you are *always almost dead.* Today we played a cat and mouse game with the enemy to try and find out their position. They're brave because they operate in places everyone else is afraid to go. In a little while, artillery fire will kill many of them. Today they tried to kill you, and you tried to kill them. Tomorrow if you saw them in a bar you might find that you like them, you might drink with them, be friends with them. They love the same as you love. They love the same things, for the same reasons. Vietnam is a gathering of love." The private nods, turns, and walks away.

Again, Harlan closes his eyes tight. As always, the balmy day hanging around him is like half congealed Jell-O. He rests until his mental alarm clock goes off, ushering him slowly to his feet. He slaps down the end of his shirt collar. One side had pushed up while he was resting. Rubbing his fingers across it, he smooths it down and wipes a handkerchief over the most recent beads of sweat covering his face. He looks down and notices that a bullet had taken off a button. *That was close,* he thinks, picking up his backpack. Directing his men to do the same, he slips his arms through the straps.

A few muffled groans could be heard as the soldiers stood up.

"It's time we move out."

"Hallelujah," one soldier standing near Harlan breathed slowly, softly.

"Check your gear. Don't leave anything behind."

In another five minutes, the platoon has gone beyond the crisscross part of the trail. "Lieutenant, Sir!" A voice shouts. "The coordinates, Sir. We go to the left, the right trail leads us back to the area of the artillery fire. Another half hour and they'll be spraying it hard."

Harlan stands frozen in place, thinking about the voice, knowing he has to go right, playing out various scenarios of how he was going to explain it. No matter how he approached it, it would still be a problem. In the end, he knew he couldn't force him with a direct order, he could only try to persuade him. Sergeant Deal was sharp and would only give in to reason. And Harlan had no reason to give. "Sergeant Deal, are you sure about that?"

"I am, Sir."

"Do you trust me?"

"Yes, Sir, but the coordinates…"

"Have I ever steered you wrong."

"No, Sir, you've gotten us out of many a pickle-jars. But like I said, the coordinates."

"I'm trying to save your head on this one, same as always. You're married, and you've two sisters I believe, not to mention your mother and father. Do you want to see them again?"

"Yes, Sir."

"Of course, you do. We all want to see our families again. I'm not going to order you to go right. If you choose to go left that's up to you, but you stand a good chance of being killed. If you're lucky you won't be spotted, but you can't count on that."

"But how, Sir? How do you know to go right?"

"The answer to that would take some time, and we've no more to waste. Besides, I'm not too sure you would like the answer."

"I think I'll stay here, Sir, with any others that feel the same way. At least until the artillery fire, then we'll know for sure which way to go."

"Suit yourself, Sergeant, but you stand a good chance of being attacked by the VC. We've stayed here too long as it is, used up our safety-net. I think you know that. We need to keep moving. In a few hours, we'll be outside the free-fire zone."

"Sir, if we don't die first."

Harlan knew if he continued the debate that more men would decide to stay. "I thought I made it clear, I've no time to explain. Stay at your own risk, you won't be written up. All those going with me, we're leaving now. So, get a move on!" Before disappearing into the jungle, he hesitates, looks back and smiles. "Try not to die before I can kill you myself, Sergeant."

"Yes, Sir, and right back at you." That was it, the two men never talked again.

Eight others decided to wait it out with Sergeant Deal. Out of the nine that stayed, two were killed, another, after being fatally wounded, died later, and still two others were seriously injured, including Sergeant Deal. A small VC squad bared down hard on them for fifteen-minutes. Had the VC not been poorly equipped they might have killed them all. As it was they disappeared after running low on ammunition. The U.S. Soldiers were later helicoptered out, but not before witnessing the artillery fire sweep the wrong coordinates. Later it was determined that the coordinates Lieutenant Landcaster had radioed in were in fact the area off the right side of the crisscross trail. The soldier relaying that made an error, resulting in friendly fire that could have taken the lives of the whole platoon had it not been for Harlan's actions.

Sergeant Deal was shipped out to a stateside hospital where he spent the next six months recuperating; he was sent home with full disability benefits. Harlan was later given the Bronze Star for Valor, along with the Medal of Honor and the Silver Star for his part in the mission. He never received the Purple Heart because, after four years of combat service as lead officer of a reconnaissance squad, he was never once injured in battle.

Chapter 20

(Lexington)

Dillon edged forward in his seat a little more because he couldn't tell if they believed what he was saying. The others weren't sure if they trusted what he was telling them. The four of them sat in the Hub coffee house waiting for ten o'clock to roll around, waiting for the meeting that would determine the world's future. Dillon had two hands raised to chest level, gesturing emphatically as he walked them through a visual of the encounter. How to respond to Old Jack was crucial, and subsequently confronting Solomon and Danny.

The plan sounded logical enough, but Carter and Jen couldn't help but wonder if they were being set up. The flight had gone smoothly from Myrtle Beach to Lexington, and nothing had happened in the time since. Carter shifts his eyes from Dillon to Jen, takes a deep audible breath, then smiles in an effort to convince her, and himself, that they had already had plenty of time to sniff out a trick. He didn't know exactly what he was expecting to go wrong as he moved his vision from Jen back to Dillon, who was still gesturing. He sat quietly, feeling strange, more afraid of the trouble he might have, than the trouble he already had, which currently was in the form of a C.I.A. operative staring back at him.

"So, what do you think?" Dillon asked, glancing at Ansel, then at Jen, and back to Carter. "Oh, and we arrive at the Museum Hotel around 10:20. We enter their room no earlier than 10:30. I want their meeting to be well underway. That way we catch them totally off guard."

He gets no response, only eyes roving, looking at each other.

"Your enthusiasm's touching. I'll ask again, what do you think?"

Carter shifts his body awkwardly in the chair, turning and twisting, but when he's finished he's left sitting in the same position. "Seems doable. How long you been working on this?"

"I'm not sure, long enough. Does it matter?"

"We're all just a little antsy that's all, but it's a good plan." He gives a fake smile, taps his fingers on the table. "Really, it's a good plan. I don't see how it could be any better." Lifting his phone, he checks the time, gives another fake smile, then slowly turns his head looking out the window. There is a streetlamp flickering in the shadows of a cloudy, light rain. Behind him several tables away, he hears faintly but clearly, waves of voices from a small gathering of tourists fresh off a church bus. They are the sound of happiness. As they converse, their voices swell and fall like the off and on rush of an ocean tide. Briefly, he grins because their enjoyment is like a contagion softly infecting him.

Approaching the coffee house from across the street, he recognizes a figure. Something about the gait, the posture, even the shape was all too familiar. He watches quietly as the person moves cleverly and determined like an animal after its prey. He leans closer to the window, touching it with his hand, breathing moisture onto the glass. Watching the person marching up the dark street, he can tell now that it's a woman. She passes under the flickering lamp, turns sharply at a street sign moving closer to the coffee house. As she nears it, her eyes raise slightly, then her head is all the way up, and she peers through the window at Carter, giving him confirmation that it's his Aunt Emma. She plants her hand on the doorknob, pushes it with purpose, and struts in without stopping until she's at his table. "You've been ditching me, and I want to know why?"

He shifts in his seat, raising up. "I... um."

"Never mind! I'm tired of your lies and excuses. Just tell me where he is."

"He's fine, really."

"I didn't ask if he was fine!"

"I know, but it's… well, it's…"

"And stop doing that thing you like to do where you act like a child, like your confused, because you're not! Like you don't half understand, because you do! Tell me where he is right now or you're going to regret I ever caught up with you!"

"He's in Myrtle Beach."

"Now we're getting somewhere. Well go on. Where in Myrtle Beach?"

"At a high-rise hotel, the Hampton Beach Resort. He's staying with an old friend by the name of Gabriel. They served in Vietnam together. Is that clear enough for you?"

'It's something, but I'm not clear what. Why have you been lying to me?"

"In a way, I wasn't lying. He asked me not to tell anyone. He's fine though, the cancer's in remission, the treatments worked. You don't have to worry about him."

"I suppose he got tired of me checking on him, but what's a daughter to do."

Carter moves his legs to one side, stands and takes her by the hand. "It's not your fault. He's been through a lot. Just give him some time. In a few weeks, he'll be back, and we'll forget any of this ever happened." He leans forward giving her a full-on hug wrapping both arms around her with force. When he leans back he is grinning, looking her square in the face. "How do you stay so pretty?"

She lightly slaps his chest, then places her hand on the side of his face. "You and me… there was always a rift between us."

"Aunt Emma, you don't have to… I mean now is probably not the time."

She glances down at the table. "These *are* your friends aren't they?"

"Well, yes."

"Good, then I need to say this. There was always a rift between us because I was the only one who didn't spoil you. Maybe I was wrong, but I don't think so. I tried to act like an underpin for you. I wanted you to feel life, not be cake-walked

252

through it. To grow up a man, a strong one like your father. You were so gentle, so tender. They were making you weak, and as much as I tried I couldn't do a thing about it. When you were in high school, and all the girls were chasing you?" She hesitates, looking at Jen. "At least this one doesn't hang all over you, and she matches you in looks. Anyway, you used to ask me my opinion a lot. Do you know why?"

"Maybe I knew I needed to hear it."

"I told you; *do what you want to do, you're going to anyway.* Do you remember?"

"Yes, you said: *but someday you're going to have to cut the cord and be a man.*"

"I didn't know you were listening. You never acted like it.

"I *was* listening... but I didn't know how to ..."

"You didn't know how to respond, even how to act around me. You were essentially selfish and spoiled, and that was very stupid of you. But they made you that way. Maybe I should have been more understanding, and not teased you so much. I thought I could toughen you up, or at least I thought I had to try. My sister's a beautiful, kind woman, but she did you no favors babying you. I heard from her two days ago. Tried to get her to pay a visit, but she said she couldn't get away right now. Canada's a long way off. You need to get past her re-marrying and call her. Do you think you can do that?"

"Soon, I promise."

"Your mother is the kind of person that needs to be married. I hope one day you'll understand that. Unless someone shares her room she's going to be lonely. I mean really lonely, the kind that causes pain. I've never been like that myself, but it's not uncommon. I always thought you could get warmth and comfort from your surroundings if you really loved them enough."

Carter puts his hand over the top of hers. "One day, if you ever fall in love, I'm going to remind you of that. I bet you were such the heartbreak growing up."

"Oh, I fended off my share of the boys if that's what you mean. Still do from time to time. They're just a little older is all. I get all the love I need from popcorn and a movie." She kisses his hand, then leans in kissing his cheek. "This is a new experience for us, talking like this. So, I'm going to leave my father's situation alone for now. I'll take your word for it that he's doing fine. You'll let me know when he's coming back home?"

"As soon as I know, you'll know."

"You won't make me come looking for you again?"

"I give my word to communicate better this time around."

"I'm not going to get into a discussion about your word, other than to say I hope it's improved substantially since we last talked. I'll leave you with your friends now. Thanks for hearing me out."

To his surprise, Carter watched her closer as she left than he did when she came. He had been brought up a very different way than his aunt had wanted, and now he found himself sort of wishing she had gotten her way. He stared at her in fascination. Her walk was still more like a march as she shoved the coffee house door open, almost forcing one leg in front of the other as she strutted over to the street corner. Underneath the flickering streetlamp she stops, waiting for the icon to flash go. When it does she fades into a misty light rain, disappearing and reappearing behind several parked cars. Then she disappears for good between two buildings. She had asked all the right questions, and he had responded with all the right answers, although they were far away from the truth.

"Someone wanna tell me what to do when she finds out I was lying. Because I gotta tell you, I'm not looking forward to facing her again."

Jen reaches up pulling at his arm. "Sit back down. You did the only thing you could do. You know as well as any of us she never would've believed the plain truth. Who would?"

"Sooner or later I'll have to come clean with her. She can get more out of a person in ten minutes than most could in a lifetime." He sits down next to Jen. "Before long she'll have me pinned in a corner again."

Jen wraps her arm around his. "You can deal with that when it happens. You didn't finish your bagel. Go on, you need to eat. We leave in fifteen minutes."

Chapter 21

The room where Danny and Solomon were had only just witnessed the spectacular departure of the four others. They had no clue that in the other dimension days had gone by. Literally, in this dimension, only three minutes had eclipsed when it all starts up again. A state of confusion still envelopes them as a slight tremor roars, quickly magnifying, vibrating the room.

"It's starting all over again!" Danny screams.

"Hold onto the freaking mini bar this time!" Solomon shouts in response.

They still didn't understand that Harlan, Angela, James, and Grace were making their return. Suddenly a misty blue illumination starts filling the room like a strange neon fog rolling in. The tremors intensify. The room is pulsating and rattling in a low audible rumbling sound. The blue illumination fills the room completely, clinging brightly to the walls, the furniture, and even their individual bodies. With the blue still magnifying, a loud ringing sensation rips through their eardrums, and they are frightened into numbness as a spherical portal opens above them. Desperately they hold on to the minibar and the furniture as they try to keep from crashing to the floor.

Through the portal they see clear evidence of another world. The sooty gray smoke hanging over a bombed-out London, and the Londoners running, yelling, groping for each other, hoping for safety. Tanks, planes and huge metal creatures ravaging the city. The multiverse travelers are transferred into the room at this second. While all of this transpires, a strong pulling sensation stretches the room into an odd tubular shape, and one of the Naibs is sucked off the couch, away into the portal. Immediately afterward the portal shrinks, giving off a sudden intense flash of bright blue light, bursting into nothingness.

When the blue illumination clears, Danny and Solomon can see six more figures standing in the room. At first Danny doesn't want to look at Harlan. Disappointed, she can't believe how much she underestimated his powers. She turns looking out over the Lexington skyline. "I want you to know something," she speaks with her back still turned. "As a last precaution I've been working on one of my abilities."

Without warning, she swings around throwing up her arms. "I think you'll be proud of me." With a jerk of her head a congealed substance shoots swiftly out of her hands forming a barrier around her. "It's a force field. Do you like it?"

Harlan takes a few steps toward her. "Why are you doing this?"

She hesitates, laughing a moment before answering. "Because it's obvious that we miscalculated your powers. You can't hurt me now though, so go ahead and try."

"I don't want to hurt you. Why do you think that?"

"You might not want to hurt me, but you still want to stop us. So, you're up to something, I can feel it."

"You're right. But it's probably not what you think. I can't kill you or I will lose my own life. I can't stop your plan, at least not completely, or so I've come to understand because there will be other ramifications. So, I've, or rather, we've decided on a compromise."

"Don't listen to him, Danny, he's lying. He's up to something!"

"Shut up, Solomon, before I mute your vocal cords or blind you! If I need your help, I'll ask for it." She walks a few steps horizontally looking over all of the multiverse travelers. "I see you brought a couple more back than you left with. Okay, so I'm listening. But this better be impressive. What could you possibly have come up with in only a few minutes?"

He takes two more steps in her direction. "In moving in and out of dimensions time doesn't work the same way. We've been gone now for nearly a week. When I go back to a dimension I've already been to, I'm limited to within a few minutes of the same time as I left."

"You got my attention. Go on."

"We're offering a compromise. I believe I can…"

"Hold on there! You mention compromise, but why would you. You've taken James' side, and he's been against our arrangement from the outset."

"Because I have to. Because I don't have a choice. Because the other realm has made it clear to me that all of us have to work this out together. I admit I don't like it, but I simply don't have a choice."

Danny lets her arms down, and the congealed force field fades to nothing. She hesitates, laughing again. "Sounds like poetic justice is on my side. So, what's the compromise?"

"You don't like my time frame of being able to regenerate the earth's population. And I get it, it would take so long that you would lose support from most of the continents. If you lose support the plan is dead, at least for now, and that's not acceptable to you. I, on the other hand, don't want anyone to lose their life. However, as was already mentioned, the plan James and I came up with is too time-consuming to be approved, and the other realm won't allow me to wreak any havoc without serious consequences. So, I propose we meet in the middle. We can regenerate half the population of the earth in just over six-months. James and I have looked it over and we're sure of it. We save billions of lives while at the same time pleasing the leaders of the seven continents, the powers to be."

"You really think they'll go for that?"

"I do. Three months turns into six, but that's still a far cry from twelve or more."

"These are considerable numbers. Do you have the documentation to back up this new plan of yours?"

"There's a folder in his shoulder bag," Angela says pointing at it. She reaches in and pulls it out. "Here, take it. Take the next 24-hours to look it over. After that, we meet back here, and you give us your decision. Sound fair enough?"

"You time travelers just bought yourself 24-hours. Now tell me about this other dimension." She asks as she pours herself a drink from the minibar. After a quick sip, she walks over to Timothy and Curtis. Is that where these two are from? And why are you wearing a Civil War uniform?

Curt responds in irritation. "You *would* remind me of that wouldn't you."

"The war's been over a long time. What ever do you mean bugle boy?"

"Nothing. It's a long story. Let's just say I was in a play when I got caught up in the invasion of London. That's when these good people whisked me away to safety."

She looks at Timothy. "What about you? What's your story?"

"Almost the same, except I wasn't in a play. Just in a bombed-out building, these guys happened to seek refuge in."

"You boys look like you need a drink. In fact, I think we all need a drink."

Harlan glances over the minibar. "I hate to break up this reunion, but we need to go. I have to find my grandson, Carter. You can imagine how concerned he's been about this meeting."

"What difference does it make? Whether we agree to a compromise or not, at his age he and his girlfriend can't be regenerated. They're going to die, it can't be stopped."

"Not necessarily. I might have worked that out. With the extra time, I can dilute the formula, then give smaller doses over a period of weeks. I can do this, not with just Carter and Jen, but also, with select others. We don't have to lose everyone under fifty years of age. If they think they have a virus that will kill them, then they'll be more than happy to accept the injections."

"That's never been tried before."

"No, it hasn't, but I'm confident it will work."

After she picks up another bottle, pouring two fingers of vodka into her glass, she turns moving her lips close-up to Harlan's ear. "Remember when we were living on the beach. We had a connection. I still want you. I think you know that.

This is our chance. It may not come again. If the documentation's correct, I'll accept the compromise happily. Then we can be together again. It's what you want, too. Isn't it?"

Without even hesitating he turns his head away and walks toward the door. "Sorry for the rush, but we have to leave now."

"Fine, then go talk to your precious grandson. Just be back here in 24-hours."

Their footpath has brought them to the Museum Hotel's lobby. Dillon, who is leading the way had just spoken a few last-minute instructions. He's holding a box with numerous whiskey brand labels imprinted into it. Jen has a large leather purse on a shoulder strap hanging to the side of her hip. Ansel and Carter eye security as the four of them approach the elevator, but not one guard seems to be concerned. Everything was happening just as Dillon had said it would.

Once on the elevator Dillon punches in the code to make it stop on the fifth floor. "Now's the moment of truth guys. Remember what we've rehearsed. Stay calm, and they won't suspect a thing."

And then the door to the elevator opens. As they walk out, their surroundings appear to be moving in slow motion. The hallway is lighted, but not well. It's more like the glow of a full moon, and for Carter and Jen, this is not what they expected.

Dillon mumbles something as they exit the elevator, though inaudible, they take it for encouragement. The lighting is so poor that it's like they're walking downhill in a tunnel. At the corner of another hallway there is a dark-gray, housekeeper's cart. Dillon takes a sharp right grazing the cart and enters a much brighter area. Not far ahead is a group of men standing guard outside a door.

As they approach them, one of the men is wild-looking with a dark complexion and a backpack swung over his shoulders. He steps out in front of the others.

"Old Jack, my man," Dillon says with a smile fully across his face. "I've got a delivery for Solomon. But first get a load of this liter of scotch I brought for you." Reaching into the box, he pulls out a bottle and hands it to him. "It's the fifty-year-old, good stuff."

"Oh, you're a good one, Dillon." Old Jack doesn't seem very concerned and shows it with his usual half-grunt, half-laugh.

As soon as he starts analyzing the bottle the four of them make their move. Jen feels a weakness like she's moving much too slow, but in actuality she's moving lightning fast. Each tiny shift of her hand is perfectly executed, her aim catching her victim unaware, resulting in a quick strike to the heart. Two others were struck simultaneously, but Old Jack would not succumb so easily. He senses trouble too late but manages to deflect the dart with the bottle, ricocheting it into his shoulder just above his heart. The result of this less than perfect execution bought him two extra seconds before he passed out. He manages to twist the doorknob and falls headfirst into the room, the bottle clenched to his chest.

All of this happens just as Harlan approaches the door from the other side. He is about to walk out with Angela and the others.

Meantime, Carter, Jen, Dillon, and Ansel were all pressed against the hallway wall reloading their dart guns. Within seconds, they all four burst over the top of Old Jack into the room, dart-guns up in the firing position. Immediately, they find themselves face-to-face with Harlan, the others standing some distance behind him.

For the first half of his life, Harlan Landcaster had lived in an exciting story like setting. At only ten years old he once saved the life of a man whose leg had been cut off by a train. He calmly took his shirt off and tightly tied a tourniquet, something he had learned to do in the Cub Scouts. What the scouts nor any others could never teach him was calmness. This was a natural gift, something he had been blessed with, born with. He seemed to thrive under pressure, and in high school it made him a star athlete. He still held records in track and field, but it was his football prowess as his team's quarterback that he was best remembered for. There was never enough pressure to rattle him, and if not for his receiver dropping a pass, his team would have won the state championship two years running. After high school he had similar success in college. Then it was on to Vietnam where he garnered a drawer full of medals for his leadership and bravery. He did all of this with the calmness that which seems only possible in the quietude and serenity of nature. Harlan Landcaster was the definition of calmness under pressure.

Until the last few months, the second half of his life had been efficiently opposite. For years his life had been so extraordinarily ordinary that it was as if he had been immobilized and buried in the snow. After the death of his wife he would spend days by himself, totally uninterrupted. This period had confirmed that he had grown old and was dying because of the spreading cancer. Every now and then he would venture out of his house into town, driving his 1998 classic Chevrolet Impala. Even during these times, no amount of traffic or noise could rattle him. He was still the definition of calmness.

During the last few months, Harlan had somehow accepted the suddenness of being young again. On top of that, he had been given extraordinary and evolving powers and had been called on to use these powers in the defense of others. Through all of this, and with the recognition that he was one of two chosen ones that would somehow have to rescue all of mankind, his calmness had not yet been overwhelmed. Not since his early years had he faced such an unexpected, out of control situation. He had come full circle--his greatest test stood in front of him.

In an instant of time, Carter screamed at Harlan to duck, and four darts were sent blasting across the room.

Chapter 22

(1896, The Beginning of Progress)

Sometimes the thing we want and value the greatest in life is the thing that disappoints us the most. The inner workings of the brain were like this for Angela. She asserted that two of its intangible gifts, imagination and the ability to reason, would someday help her unlock the secret to endless life without regeneration. Her education and subsequent understanding of the brain had always played a huge roll in her thinking. Due to this, it proved difficult to impress her, even when she was given a new and improved body. Most regenerated ones considered it a miracle, but not Angela. She was disinclined to believe that way. However, she did believe it to be a remarkable feat.

After thirty-five years of working with James, she surmised it inexcusable that she hadn't discovered the reason for the formula's success. The past couple of years she had (after being sent to college) two regenerated ones working with her. Still, there were few with whom she could discuss the brain. And still fewer, if any, could discuss it on *her* level. She now felt a burden more powerful than when she had first arrived in Tallahassee amid the country's spiraling civil unrest. She had reached that all-encompassing point of throwing-in-the-towel, of waving-the-white-flag, of giving-up her suddenly dilapidated, broken down efforts. She was hoping that the immense tide surrounding Florida would flood over into the rivers of Tallahassee, bringing with it new and enlivening prospects. Or if nothing more, that it would usher into her life the sort of energy that had at one time distinguished her.

That morning James sat sipping coffee, his eyes wandering

up and down the columns of the daily newspaper. The sunshine glistened pleasantly, flooding in through the kitchen windows, showing off the glossy oak tabletop he was relaxing at. He was content to be lazy this morning, as such he was sinking almost out of sight behind the newspaper. With no conception of what was taking place outside the wooden house, he hears the loud and earthy sentiments of one Angela Rena Gall.

"I'm not convinced any longer that I withdrew to a better world when I came here!" She excitedly, and hurriedly, comes walking (if it can be called that) into the room. "I'm quite sure there's no danger of earthquakes like there are up north, but *by God,* I just heard of a man who was eaten by an alligator!"

James peeks his eyes over his newspaper. "But, Angela, you knew there would be dangers here before you came. The Indian wars were over by then, but indigenous creatures like the alligator were here in abundance. A few years ago, we even went to see a man who wrestles with them in a show. And if you recall he made out fine. No matter where you live there will always be dangers. I believe you were fleeing from war when you came here. Am I right?"

She steps closer to the table, then even closer until she's touching it with her legs. She places both hands palm down on its surface. "Yes, and I do hate it when you talk logically to me." Out of her peripheral vision she notices Grace smiling, wiping her hands on an apron, and shaking her head in amusement. "I mean sometimes I hate it."

"You mean when it doesn't suit your fancy," Grace interjects smiling again.

"Of course."

James crumples his paper in a little, then straightens it back out. "You've never been a prisoner to Tallahassee. You can leave at your own desire. It's always been that way. *Is it what you wish* after all these years?"

"No, James, it's not. And I didn't mean to sound ungrateful. What I wish is to start making progress with our research. What I wish I could do *now* is eliminate this feeling of failure. I never expected to fail."

266

"I see." He lowers the paper a little more revealing his whole face. "Angela, have you not heard technology is taking off like a soaring bird. In Chicago and New York, they are in the middle of putting buildings up as high as they please. Forty, fifty, sixty-stories high. So high they're calling them skyscrapers. And here, look at this picture." He turns the newspaper, facing it in her direction. "See this man. Can you make him out?"

"Yes, James."

"His name's George Washington Vanderbilt. A year ago, he opened the largest privately-owned house in the United States." He flips through the paper until it rests on another page. "Look, see the picture." It has nearly 180,000 square feet. And a place this large has electric lighting, and indoor plumbing with toilets and bathing rooms for all the guests and house staff."

"It's a marvel to be sure, but what are you getting at?"

"If such a grand place as this can be built in the wilderness of North Carolina, then my dear, we can be sure that technology is becoming completely unharnessed." He drops the paper into his lap. "I think we need to get up on its bandwagon."

"How do you propose we do that?"

"I think it's time we build a new research facility."

"But we already have one, and it's probably more than we need."

"It's 1200-square-feet and has absolutely nothing to spur on the imagination. It's no wonder we can't make a breakthrough. We've fallen years behind the world's developments. That stops today! We must dedicate ourselves to never letting it happen again."

"Go on, James. I'm listening."

Grace wipes her hand again on the apron, this time vigorously. She lets it fall, walks over to the table and sits next to James. "Yes, James, go on. I'm listening too."

"Well, all right then. First, we'll start with a 5000-square-foot building. We'll fill it with all the latest contraptions and gadgets there are to study."

Grace leans in touching her face to his shoulder. "But our work is secret. Who's going to man a building that large?"

"That's an excellent question, Grace. And I'm sure Angela's wondering the same thing. It will take some time, of course. But for years now we've had regenerated ones working in the government. Some of those are in the secret service, the highest branch of security. We just need to solicit their help. We bring them aboard and keep recruiting more. I'll appoint a recruiting coordinator to find the brightest minds. We can keep our research confidential because it'll be under the guise of government security. It's the perfect front. I already rent out buildings to the state and federals. So, this won't bring any unwanted attention. Angela, until we get someone to coordinate the recruiting you can get to work on a list of excellent old persons with the right kind of education and background. When the time's right, we can regenerate them and bring them onto the project.

I also want to put together a research team just for technology. I want this facility to be on the cutting edge. It has to be if we're to ever succeed."

Angela pulls out a chair and sits down on the other side of James. She's looking at James and Grace both at the same time. "I know how we can utilize that arrangement."

"Let's hear it, Angela," James replies.

"Yes, what are you thinking," Grace softly adds.

"When we hear of something, anything new of its kind, whether it be medicine, forensics, or scientific inventions, or accomplishments of any kind. We send out a travel team as far as necessary, to the ends of the earth if it takes it. Then we pay whatever it takes, or trade our own technology if need be, in order to acquire it."

"That's a wonderful idea," Grace says reaching across the table, and putting her hand over Angela's.

James picks up where Angela left off. "From now on we will have the latest the world has to offer. So, you're with us then, Angela? Please say that you are. And remember, we still have the one thing on our side that no one else has."

"What is that, James?" Angela asked.

He stands up dropping the newspaper onto the table. "We have the security of healthfulness and youthfulness. The white locks of age will never interfere with our progress like it has with so many other great men and women. We will be able to preserve and add to our achievements unlike any before us. This facility will act as a sort of memory storage where we can harvest the most phenomenal achievements of man, keeping them in a safe place while we build on them. We will warehouse all the latest, sharpest technological breakthroughs right here in Tallahassee. And we will have a team of inventors of our own. Without old age to stop us, the sky won't even be a limit. The universe will be ours. I ask again, Angela, are you with us? Say that you are."

"I didn't expect you to take me so seriously when I first walked in this morning. Still, I don't want you to get me wrong. I'm glad that you did. It's exciting to hear you talk this way. I do think you might be going a little over-board with your projections though. You can sit down now and relax. I am still unequivocally with you, James, and with you, Grace. I never was going, or even thinking about leaving. I just didn't know where to go from here."

James sits back down next to her. "And *now,* Miss Gall?"

"And now, Mr. Jenkins, you've laid out the path for me."

His face briefly subsides into its former relaxed state, appearing less intense and more cheerful. "I must admit I felt quite impulsive there for a while, but I'll be darned if I didn't mean every word."

"You always mean what you say, darling," Grace said kissing his cheek. "It's why you had our emphatic attention. It was like we were being roused by the distant blow of a trumpet."

"I concur with your wife, James. And I have another idea that I think you need to hear."

"Please, Angela, do continue. I'm in the mood for more. Grace is too, aren't you dear?"

"I'm all ears. Go on, I want to hear."

"This man Solomon is watching you, watching all of us. With good reason, since he's the inventor of the formula and left you the keys to finding it. He's given you leadership of this region of the earth. How the regeneration process develops here is largely up to you, which is a great privilege. It's time that moves forward also, and I think I know the basis for its foundation. You've so much property here in Tallahassee. Why don't you have architectural drawings made for future government expansion? I can help research the projections. You can have ten, twenty, or upwards of fifty or more years of planned expansion needs. Having office space available as the need arises you'll have a monopoly on all the future government buildings. I guarantee it will work because you own all the vacant land in this portion of the city. You already house practically all government agencies the federals have in Florida. And there's no need to stop there. We'll keep infiltrating the government with our people, especially the secret service.

And we won't stop in Florida, eventually we'll infiltrate the whole United States, and then Central and South America. In the future we won't have to worry about confidentiality with our research. With the government involved and protecting us, there will never be an organization, now or in the future, that can find out our secret. The regeneration of people will be at our discretion, and we can speed it up dramatically when we see fit. Of course, we would need adequate facilities to do so, but over time, and with forward-thinking, we will. I think Solomon would be pleased with this plan. You could encourage him to copy it, at least the government aspect of it, and use it in other regions of the world."

"By God, Angela! That's a brilliant plan. Tell her, Grace. Tell her what a brilliant plan it is!"

"It's true, Angela. Your idea has struck gold!"

That night in front of her fireplace Angela sat thinking more about the future than the present. She was living a more real-life among her thoughts than her actual surroundings. What would the evolution of her and James' grand plan be? The progress of technology would be its main support piece, and that technology was just starting to take flight. The invention of the car and plane were in the early stages. So too was steel and the building trade with huge dams, gigantic bridges, and enormous high-rise sky-scrapers. Coney Island had the first escalator as an entertainment ride. The typewriter and telephone had been invented. The phonograph, the transformer, ironclad ships, combustion engines, the light bulb, the sewing machine. Famous inventors stretched across the world. Eli Whitney, Nikola Tesla, Thomas Edison, Alexander Graham Bell, and Charles Goodyear.

She sat comfortable in a cushioned, rocking chair with the warmth from the fireplace touching her face, sending her into fantastic speculations. She thought herself to be moving outside of what had been a narrow circle. There seemed a transformation taking place inside her. She felt a strange tingling sensation ebb through her legs and arms like some kind of physical presence was trying to make itself known. She dismissed it as too much excitement for one day, and indeed, as she did this the tingling subsided. She had been nourished by an abundance of stimulating, influential fellowship and thus had been filled with a sense of poetic hope for the future.

Chapter 23

(Calmness and the Storm)

The meeting at the Museum Hotel has just been completed. It's only moments before the doors swing open with Old Jack falling unconscious and four well-meaning mortals jumping over him, their darts blasting across the room.

Harlan and Angela now have a sudden awakening. Like a memory being seen in advance, they already picture the scene taking place. It's as if time stands still, the two co-chosen ones taking a second to look at each other in recognition of what's happening. Their minds are now in complete sync, including all past recollections leading up to this monumental moment in time.

Specific memories were providing a back story for them, like reading from a book or watching a movie, the context of which enabled them to make sense of the present and know the future. They were clearly and automatically putting together the past history of a disjointed patchwork of sights, sounds, smells, thoughts, and feelings, forming long stretches of cohesive moments into a complete picture.

A key purpose of memory had become beneficial to them by way of connecting past events in the world to their internal representation of the present, giving them a sense of continuity. Only for them, it was in a highly exaggerated form compared to other people. Vivid memories differ dramatically from person to person depending on their innate abilities, and these two with their new superhuman capacities had theirs soaring off the charts: in remembering an event, what the weather was like, whom they were with, what time of day it was, how they were feeling. Were they looking out at the scene through their own eyes or looking down at it as an observer? Did they look like they did then or in more recent times? Due to these kinds of differences most people's memories range from vague to near life-like. Harlan and Angela's memories were much more realistic and intense with a direct connection to actuality. Their memories were like being virtually in the moment at any given time, like there was nothing separating memory from reality. Due to their intrinsic abilities, they were taking past events, adding them to the present, and seeing the future.

Because of their powers, memories were now like excerpts from a movie. When they had enough of them put together they had a complete extract of what the film was all about. At that point, they had the film perfectly memorized or embedded in their minds, and they could without strain see where the following sequel would take them.

During the past few months, Harlan Landcaster had gone from not remembering anything about his life to total and perfect recall. He could pull out memory excerpts from his past or the whole movie all at once, as could Angela. With this new phenomenal ability, they could at their own discretion open the pages of the coming sequel. Harlan and Angela could know the future because they knew so completely and perfectly the past. Excerpts of future happenings were coming to them in advance. Out of their perfect recall came spewing seconds of immediate future events.

Usually, when one returns in thought all the way back to their adolescent years, the memories consist only of fragments or broken moments that are separated out for no discernible reason. The older a person grows the more detached he becomes from his childhood. This is inevitable because of the very nature of memories. When a person remembers an event, whether it's happy, special in some way, or traumatic, they are not remembering the actual event from the time of its conception. They are remembering the last time they thought of that particular scene. So, the person is remembering only the events as they were the last time he or she thought about them. It's the reason memories tend to fade the further time removes the individual from them. When the person remembers an event, he might drop a detail or two. The next time he remembers it those details will not be there, and he might now drop another detail. Eventually some memories fade away altogether.

For a select few people, this process runs in reverse. The actual event not fading, but rather being added back making it more clear-cut and comprehensible. For these people determining to recall a memory is like using a well-organized library. Their brain simply goes to the row and shelf, takes down the memory and relives it. Each time the memory is more detailed, vivid and comprehensible. This ability has been dubbed *photographic memory* and in more recent years, *total recall.*

Even in these rare cases of people with total recall, there are still rarer cases of people who see the future. These people tend to see traumatic events moments before they happen such as a plane crash, an earthquake, or the death of a friend or family member.

However, with Harlan and Angela, it was different. It would simply be any or all events of their choice. In situations of great strain, like they were now faced with, as a defense mechanism, this extraordinary gift was acting like an autopilot. Whether they wanted it or not Harlan and Angela were destined to know twenty-seconds of outcome ahead of time.

Throughout history, man has failed to understand how memories connect him to the future. Yet unseen events are being continually sculpted by the past. It's the reason patterns continue to repeat themselves. Conflicts in war, trends in dress and grooming, political philosophies and forms of governments. All of these and many more fluctuate and repeat in a constant cycle.

Now for the first time in earth's history, one man and one woman have been given the ability to see and affect future events. Their minds now perfectly meshed, their intuitiveness under extreme pressure will now determine the outcome of all four dimensions.

As the door flings open, full self-awareness of the situation has already engulfed them. Their understanding of their own location in relation to each individual in the room is precise. Every movement made, every breath released, every slight sound, every threatening thought conceived, as if it were pulsating in their fingertips.

Not only did they know every detail happening in the room, but they could also physically feel them vibrating inside them like some inhuman, instinctive, animalistic quality. As the events are streaming passed them they can not only clearly visualize and make necessary adjustments with seeming ease, they can feel the moment like it has its own texture, and they can smell *everything*. The raspberry flavored tonic, the vodka, the gin, the scotch. Danny's tiny amount of citrus perfume, Solomon's $3,000 wool suit now overwhelming like the smell of a zoo. Even the huge diamond ring his wife is wearing smells like the carbon deposits it was originally made from. All of their senses are peaking, exploding through their veins with all the connective energy of the universe.

Vivid images of previous events hover in their minds like multiple scenes on the same screen. All of them connect to each other like train tracks. All of them leading to the same location, to this specific place in time.

Harlan sees images of Danny on the beach before they met. He sees her watching him closely, analyzing him for days to see where he stands with his powers before she presents herself to him. While they were getting to know each other and living together he now sees images of her extreme carefulness not to give herself away. How she would not allow him to spend more than thirty-minutes with her unless he was asleep. She would leave the room, spend time in the kitchen or bathroom, go check on a neighbor, or spend more time than is normal checking things outside. Anything to break his connection with her. When they lived with Grace, she would go back and forth between the beach house, the hot dog stand where Harlan worked, and Grace's art set-up at the beach.

Harlan sees clearly how she questioned if he believed the old man's story, and how intently she listened, trying not to be obvious as Angela taught him about controlling the subconscious. Doing these things would keep his connection to her broken, assuring his new, emerging abilities couldn't figure her out.

Angela sees images as far back as the Civil War. The young soldier falling dead at her feet had actually mumbled her name. She sees herself bending over him, thinking how strange of him, not knowing at the time who his true identity was. She sees Old Jack filled with arrogant confidence when he first mentions the name *Solomon* to her. And she can see herself describing to James and Grace her plan to infiltrate the government. A plan that had over the many years since, worked to perfection, and that had played so brilliantly into Solomon's, and now Danny's plan. She sees too an image of Major General Mead with several of his officers. They are talking with her on that dirt road near Gettysburg. "We will win this war somehow, Miss Gall. We have to if we are to save the country. If we don't, history will go on. It just might not go on with us." She sees General Mead tip his hat, then ride along into a massive field of blue soldiers, crossing a valley to the battle of Gettysburg. She realizes that had the confederates won, Tallahassee would have been part of a different country. The U.S. Federal Government would have abandoned the buildings James leased to them. The whole plan to infiltrate them would have been over.

Both Harlan and Angela had other images, memories placed like rows next to one another, all of them in some way connecting, all of them leading to this place and time. They see Danny's sudden emergence with authority over Solomon, her ultimatum, and the alternate dimension Loam ravaged with war. They see Curtis, a spirit creature materializing with the wrong clothing, giving warning of the frailty of the quad matrix universe. And they are seeing fragments of the future splitting out from these past happenings. Ahead of time they see the door bursting open, Old Jack falling, Carter, Jen, Dillon, and Ansel leaping over him, guns raised blasting away.

And they are now seeing twenty more seconds of things to come.

The other realm is watching, waiting for the final outcome, waiting to see what direction things are to go in. Will their quad matrix universe which was millions of years in the making come to an end or will this just be a new beginning?

What happens next seems to the others as a hectic, spiraling, out of control situation. It's like a dam exploding and its waters bursting loose, the danger of imminent death lurking with no way of plugging the leak. The only thing to do is run or fight your way through it. Solomon and Danny are instantly enraged at what appears a planned double-cross. But for Harlan and Angela these events happen seemingly in slow-motion, almost like they were mechanical in nature. They're seeing these future events ahead of time causing their new intuitive, innate, cognitive qualities to saturate them in a state of pure calmness.

The room appears extremely warm as if in anticipation of the imminent struggle. Extemporaneous beads of sweat appear on Danny's cheeks. Running her fingers across her face she looks at the moisture on her fingertips. Her head angles sharply toward Solomon. "Make yourself useful and check the thermostat. It's roasting in here." He motions with his head, turns in the direction of the thermostat, then flinches as he sees the door suddenly fling open. For two brief seconds pandemonium flashes in Old Jacks's eyes. He falls and instantly all hell breaks loose with Dillon, Carter, Ansel, and Jen leaping over him, guns raised, blasting darts into the room.

The swiftness with which Danny and Solomon react is striking even to Dillon, who is well aware of their incredible powers. Illuminated white rings appear to burst out of them, the force of which is so strong it instantly reverses the darts, shoving them backward's along with glass bottles and unfinished drinks sitting on the mini-bar. They fly across the room, slam into an adjacent wall, exploding and splashing alcohol and particles of glass into the Sheetrock, barely missing the four intruders and freezing them in place.

"I've nearly been killed four times... no five," Danny

shouts. She's looking straight at Dillon. "So, go ahead, make it six." She hesitates. "You want to try don't you?"

"Hell, yes!"

She waits. "You don't even have a weapon, do you? Just those pathetic darts."

He didn't do anything more than look at her, remembering how powerful she was. Then he mutters something beneath his breath.

"You fooled me, and that's not easy to do. So, you know what I think I'll do?"

"Retract your claws, Danny," Harlan interjects. "You're not killing anyone here today."

She rolls her eyes and sneers, hating having to acknowledge him. "No! You've interfered long enough. There's no way you can stop me. How silly of you to think it. You haven't had your powers long enough. It's the way of the chosen. I'll do as I please like always. She raises one hand, palm out facing Dillon. "You're not going to like this." A white ring has formed around her. It quickly swells in diameter forming an outer circle. A magnifying power is pulsating an array of intense iridescent colors. These ultra-luminous colors range from reds, blues, yellows, and greens. They are solidifying, no longer pulsating but having leveled off into a slight vibration. There is now a large double sphere. The inside ring is made up of illuminated white, while the outer ring is a fluctuation of shining luminous colors. The beaming brilliant sphere has Danny completely encapsulated. It is both acting as a defensive and offensive weapon.

"I've vaporized people before. Just like you, they turned on me. It's going to hurt like the devil, but only for a second."

While Danny continues threatening Dillon, all the other Naibs in the room, nine others, have bright rings now encircling them. The energy being produced is already starting to shake the floor. Feeling the vibration, Carter looks down at his feet, then notices Jen doing the same. "This won't last," he says. "The building can't take this."

As the insaneness of the situation unfolds, images of past events are streaming vividly from Harlan and Angela's memories. These images are connecting to the live events in the room, moving in a definite forward direction, then acting like an undercurrent to their minds and shooting out twenty-seconds of the future. Due to the unprecedented nature of what's happening to them, they have moved passed the limits of concentration or meditation. They have involuntarily plugged into the finite lines of energy, the continually expanding black matter of the universe. With this comes the odd stretching of time. While time is being stretched, it curves, causing a deceleration of velocity with all movement in the room. To Harlan and Angela, it appears everyone, and everything is going in slow-motion. Again, they look at each other in recognition of the situation. They could not be prepared better for what was truly the coming pinnacle of an unpreparable conclusion.

A beam of energy shoots out of Danny's hand, rocketing towards Dillon. Harlan and Angela have already thrust up their arms, a congealed substance spinning out of them forming a tubular-shaped protective wall, absorbing the energy like a sponge. Solomon raises his hand in support of Danny, shooting a ray of energy into the protective wall, attempting to help break it down. When all of the Naibs join in, the room starts shaking violently, rocking upwards at its corners. Ten beams are now shooting into the congealed wall. A bookshelf falls spewing books onto the shuddering floor. Pictures, end tables, and other furnishings tumble from their perch, being shoved upwards at first, then crashing down with an explosion of noise, like the sound of metal and glass smashing together.

The floor continues wavering violently when all of a sudden a support pillar gives way and a huge hole opens up taking with it one of three sofas. Several of the Naibs stumble but maintain their footing. They are still shooting rays of energy into the protective wall. However, the floor no longer has its main support and quickly starts disintegrating. Piece by piece falls into the gaping hole, and already the floors below them are also opening up. Carter and Jen are clamped against the wall as are Dillon, Ansel, and Timothy who have just made it from the center of the room. Looking down they can see all the way to the lobby as four consecutive floors have collapsed beneath them. They are all on the verge of falling fifty-feet to their deaths.

The center areas of the floor completely collapse sending a mushroom-shaped cloud of dust upwards and dispersing it across the ceiling. All Naibs, including Harlan, Angela, James, and Grace are hovering within the confines of bright rings of light. The spheres are levitating, protecting them, and still the protective wall holds against the ten rays of immense energy.

The scene is one of disbelief for people looking up from the main floor lobby. "Aliens!" Shouts a man with a small girl clamped to his side. And then panic in the lobby at the thought of extra-terrestrials attacking. Some are glued to the scene high above them. Others panic, running wildly, desperate to get away from the building. The streets outside are getting crowded with people curious to see what's going on.

And then the edges of the room give way with the sound of an explosion. Carter, Jen, Dillon, Ansel and Timothy clamped as tightly to the wall as possible, slide downward, their bodies bending outward in a free fall. They have fallen below the protection of the congealed wall.

One last time Harlan and Angela look at each other in recognition of what they are about to do. Each of them releases one arm, pointing them beneath the five who are falling. Thin lines of light blast out of their hands shooting out more of the congealed matter. This time tiny capsules of the substance press together forming a horizontal surface underneath them. Instantly all five of them are stopped in mid-air, floating like hovering drones.

With their other hands, Harlan and Angela move the other protective wall above them, then downward in front of Danny, Solomon and the others. Their rays of energy are snuffed out, smothered by the wall as it flexes around them, burying them all in the mass of congealed substance. The imprisoned Naibs are screaming in protest from inside it.

The startling scene hovering in mid-air now lowers to the lobby level as Harlan and Angela lower the five mortals to safety, releasing them on the marble floor.

Earthquake-like conditions in the building have desisted. The situation, other than the damage to the building, is safe.

"You two pulled it off," Curtis said, giving Harlan and Angela a look of exhaustion. He had been watching everything closely but from the safety of an un-materialized, invisible body. "The emergency is over. You've bought yourself some time. The multiverse is safe, at least for now, but it will take some doing to keep it that way. When the police arrive, tell them you want to talk to the President of the United States. Somehow I think they'll manage to make that happen. As far as the other world leaders go, the President will take it from there. You have an opportunity to get it right this time. I suggest you start working on that immediately. You two are the powers to be now. If you fail, you have no one to blame but yourself. I'm being called away, sorry. It's an emergency. I have to go."

"But what about these guys?" Harlan points to Danny and Solomon imprisoned in the protective wall.

Curtis looks at them, his face half-smiling, half concentrating. "Do what you want with them. They can't hurt you. They know that now. They can't hurt anybody anymore unless you let them." He shifts his attention a moment to Angela. "Remember what I told you about your father's research. He was onto something, you already know that. Regenerating people is only a band-aid. One day that band-aid won't be enough. Find out the reason people grow old. I can't believe it hasn't been researched more. Take care of yourselves. I don't mean to rush, but I'm needed on Loam. The war is about to escalate or come to a horrible, sudden end. I can't be sure which. The Germans and the allies both have the Atom bomb. You can probably guess what they're about to do. I have a feeling we're going to see each other soon. I may need your help."

It had been going on way too long and Jen couldn't ignore the steamy noise any longer. She blinks groggily trying to remember how the day played out, then turns to see who is operating the espresso machine. Just as she thought, it was the new girl. She had missed so much work at the Hub Coffee House they had hired a part-timer. A part-timer that needed training on the espresso machine. When the girl finally gets it right, Jen sees her arms raise up high. About this time, she hears the words, *"Well praise the Lord!"* It was like the words had been held back too long, then suddenly thrown out of the girl's mouth, like she thought she had done something extraordinary.

"Yes, praise the Lord," Jen whispered to herself, partly relieved the girl finally got it right and partly relieved she was sitting here alive after all. Earlier in the day there was a moment she didn't think it possible. She sighs looking down into her mocha coffee.

"Did you just say, 'praise the Lord?'"

She hadn't seen Carter walk through the doorway. He was standing at her table freshly showered and shaved. He has on blue jeans and one of his long-sleeve, pullover shirts she likes so much. "You smell good, look good, too. And, yes, I did say, 'praise the Lord.'"

"I thought so. Any particular reason?"

She nods toward the new girl. "She finally managed the espresso machine. That and…" She smiles then motions with her eyes for him to sit down. "All the usual reasons I guess."

When he sits, he pulls the chair up close and leans over the table eyeing her. "The next few weeks this thing's going to get crazy. Harlan and Angela already have a meeting arranged with the President. After that the media gets involved. The world's not ready for what's about to be presented to them. But it's wonderful news, and I'm sure they'll see that."

"I think the sooner the better, don't you?"

He nods in agreement. "Of course, it may take a year, but everyone above fifty gets regenerated."

"You have an amazing grandpa you know that."

"Speaking of Gramps, I talked to Emma."

"Really!" She didn't bother to hold back her laughter.

"I know, right. But I had to. I just got off the phone with her a few minutes ago. Harlan's going to visit her tomorrow before the news hits the airways. I'll have to be there for that. She would never believe it otherwise." Carter's hand has gradually made its way over the top of Jen's. He leans farther over the table kissing it. "What do you say about taking down that old pair of hiking boots you got stored away in a closet."

"What for?"

"In a few weeks, this thing's going to be all over with. I thought we could go to Asheville, spend the day, then get a cabin in Chimney Rock, hike the trails, and…"

"And what?"

"I just thought… Well, I'm not sure we... What I mean is…"

She squeezes his hand. "Relax Carter… and *just say it*."

"Do you want to start again?"

"Start again, as in start all over. Do you mean you're ready to get it right this time?"

"Well, I always wanted to… Yes, I'm ready."

Smiling with her whole face, she raises both arms as high as she can get them, hands completely open. *"Well, praise the Lord."*

What if the aging process that we have been groomed to accept, and doomed to live, turned out to be a previously undetected virus? A super virus so intelligent that it hides by wrapping itself with other molecules. A virus emitting its antigens so methodically, so gradually, and in such small numbers that it mimics complete silence, producing invisibility. What if what we think we know turned out to be an illusion? And what if one day the illusion started to crumble?

Made in the USA
Columbia, SC
22 December 2020